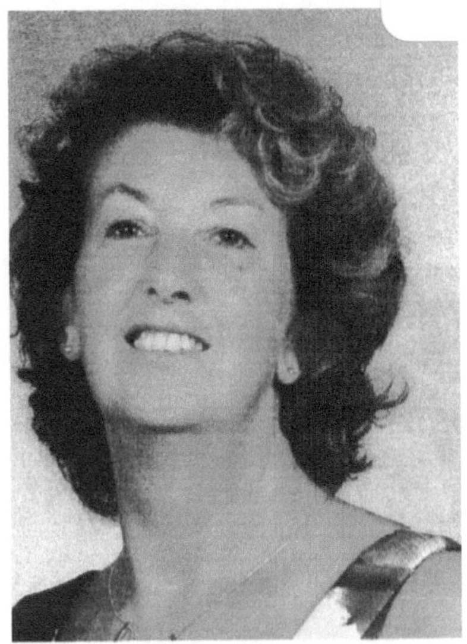

About the Author

I was born, raised and currently live in the Midlands. I have a keen interest in family history research and all the back stories it throws at you. I am also fascinated by people and the stories they can tell, and the hardships they've had. A degree in Psychology helps me try to understand the different paths we all tread through life.

Blood and Water

Pat Daniel

Blood and Water

Olympia Publishers
London

www.olympiapublishers.com
OLYMPIA PAPERBACK EDITION

A CIP catalogue record for this title is
available from the British Library.

ISBN: 978-1-78830-817-5

First Published in 2021

Olympia Publishers
Tallis House
2 Tallis Street
London
EC4Y 0AB

Printed in Great Britain

CHAPTER ONE

'There, that'll do,' Ellie murmured to herself as she glanced round the flat. It was tidier than usual, no coats draped over chair backs and shoes lurking under the sofa. The gas fire was burning brightly, giving a warm glow to the lounge. A candle stood proudly in a bottle on the small kitchen table, and some new red and white check napkins gave it a bistro feel. Ellie tried to look out of the window but all she could see was rain sheeting down, creating a halo round the streetlamp, which didn't seem to push the dark back at all. A quick glance at the clock confirmed that she had about ten minutes before he was due. He'd be soaked to the skin and probably in a tetchy mood but once he'd had some lasagne and wine then everything would be fine, at least she hoped so.

The lasagne was bubbling gently in the oven and Ellie gave it a quick glance, and felt inordinately proud. No great shakes as a cook by anyone's standards, though she could do eggs and bacon. Once she had made a cake but this had been a whole afternoon's work. She had followed the recipe to the letter and was well pleased with the result. Admittedly, the lasagne hadn't been tasted yet but if the smell was anything to go by, it was a winner. Even the kitchen was tidy and a glance told her the glasses were sparkling, ready for the wine.

OMG the wine! That's what she had forgotten to get. Ellie ran her fingers through her hair and panicked. She cursed her stupidity and abstractedly nibbled a nail, and quickly made a decision. Coke just wasn't good enough for this culinary offering, so she quickly pulled on an old ski jacket and braved the torrential rain to run down to Chandra's corner shop. This was an Aladdin's cave of all needful but forgotten things; everything from clothes pegs to wet wipes could be found on the crammed shelves. She weaved between wet weekenders and drippy umbrellas and skidded round the corner into the warm haven of the shop.

'Hi Ellie,' Ali Chandra said, his round face beaming as she shook herself like a dog.

'Sorry, sorry,' she apologized, as the droplets flicked everywhere. 'Wine?' She looked in bewilderment at him. She knew nothing about wine and was the first to admit it, and hoped he could suggest something reasonable.

'What are you eating, something special with Rory?'

'Yep, made a lasagne, all by myself,' she said proudly.

Ali slowly shook his head and replied, 'Should have been a nice biryani or vindaloo. Then I could have recommended something, but why don't you look at the Italian wines, maybe a nice Chianti would go well.'

Ellie smiled at his wisdom and wandered over to the gleaming bottles at the back of the shop. Maybe Chianti, then. She picked a bottle off the shelf that she thought had a pretty label. Ellie studied the ranks of bottles carefully and noticed another Italian one, a Valpolicella. She picked that one up as well and with one in each hand, she turned to ask the opinion of the resident wine expert.

Then time seemed to stand still and everything appeared

to move in slow motion. The shop door was thrown open with such force that the glass cracked, and Ellie stood frozen gripping the bottles. Two men carrying what seemed to be short sticks faced Ali across the counter. They were half turned away from her and tension radiated from them. They were very intimidating and Ali cowered. In their hands were guns, but Ellie had never seen guns before in real life and it didn't register what they were.

'Where's Manjeet?' the biggest guy shouted, leaning across the counter. Ali cowered back even more.

'Where's Manny?' he repeated slowly, but with more menace. 'Believe me, you and your family will wish you had answered me.' He waved the gun in Ali's face.

Ali's mouth was working but no sound was coming out. Ellie had known Manjeet since he was at school, and he seemed to be a normal Asian teenager, on track to be a doctor, dentist or some other highly paid, fast track profession. She couldn't believe he even knew who these men were.

'I don't know,' squeaked Ali, terrified. He moved to the till and opened it. 'Take it all.' He put his hand in and fetched out notes, offering them to the man. Ali's hand was roughly knocked aside and the notes fluttered to the floor. He stood rigid, as if turned to stone.

Ellie unfroze and started to move towards the men, still clutching the two bottles of wine. She didn't know what she was going to do, but was just moving instinctively. Ali's gaze moved towards her, the forgotten ally.

'No! Ellie!' he shouted and both men turned slowly to face her.

'Take her.' The big man gestured towards Ellie with his gun, while the smaller one moved towards her and stuck his gun sharply into her ribs. She smelt a citrus cologne and felt fingers digging into her arm.

Turning back to Ali the big man said, 'I'll ask you once again, where's Manny?'

'He's away with some friends,' stuttered Ali, 'they've gone on some party trip to Wales, honestly.'

'Pity you didn't tell the truth first time round, isn't it?' The big man slowly shook his head. 'Get a paper and a pen; we'll have to leave him a message, won't we?'

Ali fumbled under the counter for a pen and scrap of paper. 'What do you want me to write?' His hand shook as he gripped the pen.

'A friend says, "It's been too long since I've seen you, so I'm leaving a little reminder,"' the big man recited, and a half smile played across his lips.

Ali finished writing, looked up, and the big man pulled the trigger. Ellie didn't know if she screamed or not, but Ali disappeared in a blood red mist. The cigarettes behind him exploded and it was like red confetti spiralling down. There was a wet thump as Ali's lifeless body slumped across the counter. Ellie's fingers unclenched and the two bottles of wine fell straight to the floor and exploded. Red wine mingled with the blood dripping off the counter and Ellie felt bile rise in her throat.

'Out,' the big man gestured with his gun, 'or you will end up the same.'

Ellie was manhandled out of the door, and into a dark Range Rover waiting at the curb, with the engine running. All she could seem to think of was the damned lasagne. Ridiculous wasn't the word, as she worried about Rory and the wine, lasagne, anything to blot out the scene of Ali's last moments.

She knew it would be like a loop, endlessly replaying; the horror and the coppery smell of the blood.

Ellie was shoved roughly onto the back seat. The door was slammed shut and they sped off. The car turned right and left many times, until Ellie was totally lost in a myriad of side roads, each one looking rougher and more derelict. She sat rigidly, eyes darting right and left, trying to take in her surroundings. She was under no illusions that she was in a life or death situation. All she could see was the back of the driver's head with short cropped hair and a smudgy spider web tattoo disappearing up into his hairline. The interior of the car was hot and she could smell plastic and leather, mingling with the odour of stale cigarettes.

Big Guy turned round from the passenger seat, brandished the gun, and said, 'Knock her out.' The fingers stopped cutting off the circulation in her arm and the gun stopped bruising her ribs. It was now or never and she lurched to the side scrabbling at the door handle, but felt a sharp prick in her arm.

Falling, falling… a black cloud seemed to edge in and take her vision and a warm dark mist insidiously clogged up her brain. Her fingers wouldn't work and she slid into the pit of sleep.

A faint smell of citrus wafted into the dream and the words, 'This is for you,' filtered through the cotton wool layers of sleep. Ellie's fingers closed convulsively, and whatever she grabbed pierced the skin on her palm. The profound silence was all enveloping, heavy and oppressive. Ellie half expected to hear the ticking of the bedroom clock and the swish of the traffic outside. She wished she could just lie there another ten minutes, warm and comfortable. Instead, she was conscious of being freezing cold and cramped. Ellie struggled up through layers until she could open her eyes. She felt the need to stretch and tried to raise one arm. Then reality struck home and she found her arms were bound behind her back, and whatever it was she was bound with, chafed. Her eyes became unglued, and she found she couldn't move. A musty smell was everywhere, the shabby mattress she was lying on was damp, and she could now hear the drip of water, slow and regular, enough to drive her mad. There was enough light to see that she was facing a wall, so she wriggled over and tried to sit upright.

Ellie's ankles were bound, so it was a struggle, and she didn't manage it first time as she felt a wave of nausea overtake her. She tried again and eventually managed to sit up on the edge of the bed.

'Help.' It came out as a parched whisper. Her tongue seemed to have welded itself to the roof of her mouth and her lips didn't work properly. She tried again and it was stronger, but the sound seemed to be swallowed up.

'Help.' It now rang out loud into the emptiness. Ellie's jacket had been taken and she was chilled, but her focus shifted to what was digging into her hand. She opened her fingers and released what was in there. It was small and fell onto the musty mattress. She wriggled round and saw it was a blood-covered blade from a craft knife. If she could get it right, she could cut through the bonds and be free. Reality kicked in; free to go where? She could hardly fight her way out; basically she was sunk without trace. A tear slid down her face.

Suddenly, there was a scraping sound in the lock, and the door was kicked open by Big Guy. Ellie froze and just stared helplessly at him. Her mind ran round in a loop thinking, *this is the end, I know it's the end, but I don't want it to be the end.*

In his hand was the gun, and he gestured with it towards the door. She was meant to get up and go. She tried to stand, but her ankles wobbled and she sat down again.

'Okay, I suppose it will be quicker if I untie you but don't get clever,' he said menacingly. Ellie had no intention of getting "clever", and the thought of taking him on turned her guts to jelly; neither did she have any idea even how to fire a gun. After seeing what it did to Ali, she couldn't face that at all. Ellie nodded and dumbly sat, and held out her legs to be untied.

'This way, after you, lady.' He mock bowed and waggled the gun towards the door, and Ellie stumbled her way out into the corridor. It seemed she was in an old factory and there were corridors branching off to the right and left, painted a nauseous shade of green, peeling off in scabrous patches.

An office door was open and Ellie was shoved through the doorway, nearly falling. The room was decorated marginally better than the corridor and there was a desk and a few chairs. Ellie could smell coffee and her stomach growled. There wasn't a window, so she had no idea what time of day it was.

'Careful, careful.' A cultured voice came from the other side of the desk. 'Miss Black—yes, I do know who you are. Surprise, surprise! You may be useful to us in the future, so I haven't let Eddie have his way yet.' There was a slight pause as he let the menace and the word "yet" sink in. 'He does like some target practice, so co-operate. Pardon my manners, do take a seat.' He gestured with his hand towards an office chair facing him. 'Now, today we are going to reach an agreement.' He smiled and his eyebrows arched slightly as Ellie sat down heavily.

'I haven't got the faintest idea what you're going on

about, Mr…?' Ellie let the question hang there.

'You can call me Mr. Fox. I like that.' He leaned back amused.

'So… what do I have to do?' Ellie tried to sound confident and in control, and more than ever ready to make a deal. But in reality, it must have sounded like the terrified squeak of someone bargaining for their life.

He examined his manicured hand and flicked an imaginary speck of lint off his expensive sleeve. 'Let me see. Correct me if I'm wrong.'

He leaned forward in an almost confidential manner.

'You just happened to be in the shop when Eddie went looking for Manjeet. Any heroics there would have undoubtedly got you shot, as Eddie has a somewhat nervous disposition.' Mr. Fox glanced up at Eddie who was leaning negligently against the door, and nodded.

'We sometimes need to, how can I put this… recruit new workers and they obviously have to have an incentive to work.' He stared into her eyes. 'Are you with me so far, Miss Black?' Ellie nodded mesmerized. 'So, let's be clear, you do what I say with no silly notions of going to the police, and you will live.' He tapped his finger on the desk for emphasis. 'Any attempt to shaft us, and, do not be in any doubt we will find out, will mean that Rory's life will be forfeit.'

Ellie went rigid at the sound of Rory's name. How did they know about him? Mr. Fox leaned forward again.

'You have been here a couple of hours and I already know everything about you. You can't hide anywhere Miss Black.' He leaned back and steepled his fingers. 'Do we have a deal Miss Black?' Ellie nodded dumbly. She had been broken with a few words, and was in no doubt that he would kill as easily as swatting a fly.

'Good, good, I'm so pleased you have decided to invest in your future. There isn't any pay, but the fringe benefits are good.' He chuckled at his macabre joke.

Mr. Fox glanced up at Eddie. 'She can go now.' Eddie pushed Ellie's shoulder, leaning her forward so her hands could be untied.

Mr. Fox waved a hand expansively around the office.

'Oh, and don't bother coming back here as it will all be gone soon. The whole site will be razed to the ground as we leave, so I would get your running shoes on if I were you, chop, chop.'

Mr. Fox stood, and Ellie could see the immaculate appearance of a man well used to high finance and boardroom battles, from the top of his groomed hair, past the crisply laundered shirt, to the shine on his town shoes. 'Nice to meet you Miss Black. In some ways I hope we don't meet again, but you never know. I would shake your hand to seal the deal but you seem to have hurt yourself, and the blood… I never did like blood.' He moved past Ellie and gestured to Eddie to follow. Eddie sketched a mock salute with his gun, leered, and licked his lips suggestively before following his boss out of the door.

She couldn't believe it. They were just letting her go. She sprang to her feet and went to the door and glanced right and left, but the coast was clear, no-one in sight. Which way… She picked right because that was the way she thought she had seen Mr. Fox and Eddie turn when they left. Ellie managed a fast trot down the corridor to the next junction and saw the shadow of a footprint going right again. A set of double doors barred her path and she sidled through them. It all looked the same, until she saw something bright red. An incongruous red parcel was tied to some overhead pipes. Remembering what Mr. Fox had said about the place being razed to the ground, she knew immediately it was explosives.

The words 'running shoes' came flooding back and she sprinted like the hounds of Hell were after her. Blind panic overtook and she turned this way and that, and by sheer luck saw an external fire door. *There's an irony*, she thought as she hit the door, and shoved it with all her strength. It groaned in protest and opened enough to give her a tantalizing glance at the rain drenched wasteland outside. Ellie threw her shoulder against the door again, and it stubbornly opened another inch. This was no good and she was only hurting her shoulder. 'Think, act, don't react,' Ellie told herself again and again, like a mantra. If she lay on her back on the floor and used her leg muscles as they were much stronger than her shoulder, maybe that would work? Ellie tried but her leg muscles were stiff and sore from being tied up. Frantically, she kicked at the door. Suddenly, it opened and she scrambled out into the pouring rain.

Rain had never felt so good. She turned her face to the black sky and let it wash over her—until she remembered Mr. Fox and his dire warning. Ellie ran blindly across the site, tripping over twisted metal half buried in the long grass, dodging burned out cars in the nettle patches. She must have gone some fifty yards when she was thrown forward, and hit the ground with force. A shock wave passed over her and she clamped her hands over her ears to try to blot out some of the tremendous noise. Face down in the mud, Ellie curled into a ball as chunks of masonry rained down. Luckily, she wasn't hit directly, but a myriad of tiny needles of pain peppered all over her body as bits of red-hot brick burned her skin.

Ellie lay still as death for what seemed like hours, until the smoke cleared and the rain was soaking her clothes. She tentatively rolled onto her back and slowly wiggled her toes and fingers, checking for damage. Everything seemed to be in working order and she stared at the sky. What was happening to her? Ellie sat up and rubbed some of the grit out of her eyes. It didn't make it much better, just made her eyes sore, but it gave her a handle on life. She was alive that was the main thing; she was a living, still breathing, sentient being. The factory was gone, along with Mr. Fox, along with her coat. She shivered, both from cold and shock. She was soaked through and dirty, alone and scared, but she was still alive.

It was very dark, but the sky was lit up by the burning pyre and Ellie could see multi-coloured lights homing in on the site like bees to pollen. Help was arriving, the cavalry was coming over the hill, and she was safe and saved. No! She wasn't because Mr. Fox had said, very emphatically, that no police were to be involved. She noticed something else; she couldn't hear any sirens. Ellie picked up a brick and hit it on a piece of metal. Nothing. She was deaf from the explosion. She tried again, but there was still nothing. Then she recited out loud the first thing that came to mind, a nursery rhyme of all things. The outcome was the same, deaf. Ellie couldn't hear the sound of her own voice.

Tears began to mingle with the rain and she sat and cried, not for any one particular reason, just self-pity, fear for her own situation. It just felt right. Ellie dragged a sleeve across her eyes and wondered what to do next. Instinct must have taken over and she did what all wounded animals did—she went home. It seemed the most perfect place in the universe; warm, dry, and a haven where she could lick her wounds and curl up with Rory. That thought was like a sledgehammer in her brain. What on earth was she going to tell him? Could she really tell him? If she did, would he believe her anyway? She couldn't take that chance.

Ellie slowly stood and headed away from the blue lights to a street of identical terraced houses, where street lights gave a sullen glow to the neighbourhood. She stumbled away from the action and towards anonymity. Gradually getting her bearings, she realized she was probably about three miles from her flat and set out to walk home. Ellie realized she must have looked a wreck, so she picked up a couple of supermarket plastic bags that littered the street and filled them with bin rubbish. Staring at the floor and shuffling rather than walking, she hoped she would pass as a 'bag lady'.

Ellie turned into her street and was met by a scene of pandemonium. Blue lights were strobing everywhere and fire engines were parked haphazardly, blocking the street. Knots of people were dotted about under the sodium haze of the street lights. Everyone had a jaundiced hue, and they were transfixed by the smoke billowing out from the house near the corner shop. Ellie couldn't hear what they were saying, but from the head shakings, she surmised that it was a bad time for someone. She worked her way forward, and then her eyes widened in shock and horror as she saw it was her house, her flat, her home that had been devastated. It looked as though an explosion had ripped the front of the house out, and glass and debris lay strewn across the road. Any flames had been doused but acrid smoke still hung about, and sooty pools were gathering on the pavement.

Ellie was rooted to the spot. Her hands unclenched and the bags dropped to the floor. Then she saw the familiar shape of Rory standing, talking to a policeman. Ellie must have shouted as heads turned towards her and she ran to him. Rory looked shocked and didn't move, but she ran till she fell into his arms. Then the world went black, and the pavement rushed up to meet her.

CHAPTER TWO

Leaning back in his chair, A. T. Morgan scanned the room across the polished rare wood table. Opulent leather chairs were ranged around the table, twelve in all and the thirteenth, at the head, was his. He was the power-house, the top man and he knew it. Everyone was slightly on edge as usual and sat tensely, studying their portfolios or scratching notes with expensive Mont Blanc pens. In front of him, however, was nothing. He relied on his prodigious memory, a genetic gift from his father.

Leaning to his right-hand side, he whispered to his brother, Max, 'I trust the little problem has been dealt with?'

'Yes, of course. Karl and I had a few words with Miss Black, with all the usual provisos in place. You have seen the file. All, shall we say, weak spots have been identified and made clear to her, so she is compliant with our terms and conditions.' He smiled at Alistair, confident that he had gained his brothers approbation.

A half smile played at the corners of Alistair's mouth, and he relished the power he had over his younger brother. He had the memory that had served them so well in the past, and the ability to plan the moves of the chess pieces of his empire for months ahead. Max, meanwhile, was the 'mechanic', the man of action; he had the ability to make the plans happen. A man superb at logistics and execution. There was, however an unfortunate part to his make-up. He did rather tend to go over the top sometimes and little messes had to be cleaned up. The bodies in the bins, the staged car accidents, burnings etc… but he was very useful when 'dead wood' had to be pruned out.

Alistair didn't begrudge Max his friends and sometimes dubious pleasures. Max and Karl, his number one, worked as a team. Max never actually got his hands dirty. That was just as well, as Alistair never got his hands dirty either, and no DNA trail would ever lead back to him. Perfect deniability was his watchword, plus a very good legal team. He demanded, and received, absolute loyalty.

Today was a routine meeting, tying up loose ends, and planning the next few moves.

Addressing the table Alistair said, 'A major part of the exhibition will be removed from the site at 0800 hours on Thursday.' Murmurs of assent rumbled round the table. 'Horatio, you will be in charge of the lorries, Centro Electrics I believe?' Horatio nodded and scribbled down the time on his pristine pad.

'Arthur, the warehouse?' The question hung.

'Yes.' His eyes never left his pad and his fingers shook as he wrote.

'And now, Attila,' his gaze roamed the table and settled on a small man of Middle Eastern origin, 'is everything in place to move the items?'

Taking a gulp of the purified air, Attila met Alistair's gaze and said hurriedly, 'The larger items of 2 kilos plus should be crated as single boxes and they will be stored, but the smaller artifacts will go to the auction as soon as possible, unless there

is something you would particularly like for your collection?'
He gazed around at the walls, subtly lit, with the display
cabinets full of unimaginable treasures, glinting in the light.
'We cannot move anything larger at this time without
attracting attention, and the market forces in play at the
moment suggest that the price will be driven down if some of
the more well-known pieces are offered.'

Alistair acquiesced with a curt nod.

'Genghis, your report.'

Alistair smiled as he imagined the marauding hoards
sweeping down from the hills and laying waste to all in their
path. Genghis was an apt pseudo name for the hulk imprisoned
in his shirt and tie. The jacket strained across his massive
shoulders, but not an ounce was fat. Genghis and his band of
thugs—yes that name was apt—were his men on the ground.
He didn't know their names and he didn't want to. Alistair left
all recruitment to others, and they also cleaned up their own
mess if any of the employees had a loose mouth or sticky
fingers.

'Okay boss.' Alistair winced at what he regarded as a
common term. 'The trucks from the storage archives will go
out, and we have made a plan of the latest secret route. They
will go through some back roads and by an old industrial site,
that's where we take 'em. Our lorries with new logos will be
there and the lads will offload and disappear. The trucks will
go different directions, then meet up at the auction house.'

Genghis paused. 'Do you want to know about the museum
lorry drivers?' he asked, but already knew the answer.

'Not at all. I'll leave that to you to sort out, but no
witnesses, remember.' Genghis nodded, his part done.

'Well, gentlemen, that concludes the business of the day.'

Alistair slowly stood. 'I trust you will be staying for lunch, which will be served when we arrive in the dining room.' He gestured and the meeting dissolved with a rustling of paper and the exodus for food.

Alistair was satisfied with the way the meeting had progressed, and positively looked forward to supervising the opening of the crates. It was always a bit of a tease as to what the crates contained. The archiving system that contained the artefacts was a double-blind system. That meant that if someone made a request for an artefact, the museum assistant would check on the computer and get the location of the site where it was stored. The requisition would then be forwarded to the curator of the site. Only the curator knew where the crate was, but he wouldn't particularly have any knowledge of what was in it. Then the curator would 'pull' the box and it would be forwarded to the assistant. Theoretically neither side knew both the location and the contents of any one box.

Alistair had some tame computer geeks, who had managed to hack the system and kept track of which artefacts went where, and this seemed an ideal time to plan a big job. A new exhibition was coming up and it would be nice to add some of the larger pieces of the Staffordshire Hoard to his collection, and he knew many who would be intrigued to own a small part of Celtic heritage.

Alistair was not a greedy man and he knew that there could only possibly be one job of this nature. He never gave anyone a pattern to work to and only undertook perhaps one or two large jobs a year, or else this would draw attention to his empire. Moreover, it was fun to plan and execute such a simple but ingenious crime as this. Other men took their thrills from watching horses, or dogs run past a post, maybe watching the stylized warfare rituals of twenty-two men kicking a ball about, but Alistair liked a mental challenge.

He shot his cuffs, smoothed an imaginary misplaced hair back into place and strode down the corridor to the dining room. He treated his board of directors well, and he could hear the subdued murmurings of lunch time conversations as they partook of the best that money could buy. He made a mental note to watch Attila more closely, as there had been a subconscious 'tweak' at a subliminal level of the man's behaviour at the meeting. He had a strong enough hold on him to ensure his complete loyalty, but, there had still been something there he couldn't quite put his finger on.

Strange how fate had played into his hands, he mused. Take this wild card, Miss Black. Why she had managed to defy the odds and survive puzzled him. His brother must have had an alternative scenario lined up for her and had then became distracted, or he had used his brain and could see the future possibilities. Max and himself had discussed filling a gap in the collection with some manuscripts, and perhaps he thought Miss Black the librarian would have her uses. Perhaps a fortuitous meteoric rise up the job ladder to the British Library would be in order. He would put that into action personally.

After lunch, Alistair would be disappearing into the depths of the shires to Addingham Manor for a few days, to enjoy some countryside pursuits with a few of his fellow board members. The chosen few would be invited; those who had shown ingenuity, or had continued with their personal development according to his script. No wives or otherwise "hangers on" were ever permitted there; it was strictly a male enclave, given to the pursuit of male amusements. The shipment should arrive on Thursday night and it would be a pleasant evening, examining the treasure and planning the auction. Also, by then, he would be well away from the scene of the action and no links could, or would, be forged.

Pushing open the dining room door, a hush descended on the room as Alistair took his place at the head of the table. He waved at the assembly to carry on and the clatter of cutlery resumed. The butler hovered at his elbow and Alistair ordered just the soup. Dietary excess was against his principles, although he had been blessed with a lean physique as well as a prodigious brain.

The conversation was of an informal nature as it ebbed and flowed across the table covered with a snowy cloth. Alistair joined in and laughed at the anecdotes being traded, but kept a sharp eye on Attila. He didn't seem at ease and was unusually quiet. A nervous tic sometimes played at the corner of his eye and he once dropped his knife with a clatter, and effusive apologies were heard as it was instantly replaced by Carter the butler.

Max was again at Alistair's right hand. He leaned across and smiled as he said, 'What's the matter with Attila? He doesn't seem his usual self—is he a bit under the weather, stress maybe?

'Maybe a job for you,' whispered his brother, 'check and see if anything is causing him discomfort.'

Smiling back Max replied, 'I'll run a check and see if anything comes to light, but I agree something's not quite right. Don't want good old Attila to throw a spanner in the works, do we?' The rhetorical question went unanswered as Alistair resumed his meal.

Finishing first, Alistair rose, bid everyone farewell and

wished them Godspeed to Addingham Manor, where he would be awaiting their pleasure.

Max's gaze rested once more on Attila, and he wondered how to go about finding out the cause of the dissonance in his behaviour. As usual, tried and trusted methods sprang into his mind and he decided almost involuntarily that the direct approach would be the best. Decision made, he then had to decide if he was to involve Karl, who was a magician at extracting information but could go over the top, and Attila was too useful at the moment. Perhaps a little 'one to one' counselling session would be enough.

Rising, Max looked directly at Attila. 'A moment, if you please,' and began to walk to the door. Attila glanced right, then left at the others, almost seeking their help with his eyes, but they looked away. He scurried after Max. He caught up with him at the door and Max draped an arm across his shoulders. 'I'll only detain you a moment, my friend.' He steered Attila towards an empty anteroom. 'Do take a seat.' Max gestured to the overstuffed settee and watched as the little man sank into the depths, making him look smaller than ever. Max continued to stand, and this small act of intimidation put Attila even more on edge.

'You don't seem your usual self. Is there anything we can er… help you with?'

'No, no, you know I would never ask for your help whatever the circumstances, you have already given me so much that I would not presume to ask for more.'

Max maintained a silence, inviting more contributions.

Attila couldn't hold onto the silence and after a few moments, he began to speak rapidly.

'There is something going on within my department and I really don't want to bother you with it, but I can't take any action until I know exactly what it is. It's just a feeling that someone is working to their own agenda and if it compromises the job…' Attila didn't let his mind lead to that possibility, as the consequences to him and his family would not bear thinking about.

'I've had phone records checked and once or twice there have been calls to non-traceable disposable phones. GPS have placed them at the side of motorways when we checked locations. Sometimes I'm sure we have been followed but they were good and we couldn't pin them down. Things like that are non-provable, but I'm jittery and don't really know what to do.' He looked in askance at Max.

Max was suddenly effusive and sat down next to the little man. 'Attila, my friend, you should have come to me at the start and we would have cleared all this up in an instant. I'll see to it straight away, what are friends for. I'll ask Karl to give you a hand.'

Attila breathed a sigh of relief but realized he wasn't entirely off the hook, and that he had been watched closely by Max and the others. The nerves had given him away. He knew exactly what was going on, but was too scared to tell Max, for fear of his life. He wasn't a killer but had been 'recruited' and was rapidly sinking into a deep, dark abyss, with no way out. He was under no illusions that he would ever live a normal life again and had shipped his wife and children to Dubai pronto, for their own safety. Even this was an illusion, as his family over there didn't know what was going on, and he knew that Morgan Enterprises had tendrils everywhere and could find them, if the situation demanded it.

He swallowed the half-digested food that had risen in his throat and inwardly prayed that he hadn't signed the death warrants for his 'helpers.' He knew Karl's methods from past experience and wouldn't have wished his attentions on his worst enemies. But it was do or be done by, and he had realized his instinct for survival was stronger than his fear of being judged in the afterlife.

'I think we may have a mole that has been selling our secrets, or an infiltrator who wants to get a piece of the action, or a police informant. I don't know what it is or who it is, but something is happening.' Attila looked again at Max and watched as he stood and re-buttoned his jacket, signalling the meeting was over.

'Rest assured, we will root out your little problem but you must come to me in the future as soon as you suspect something is going wrong, or else the responsibility may end up in your lap, so to speak, and you and your family wouldn't want that, would you?'

Attila slowly shook his head at the blatant threat and walked slowly out of the room.

Max pulled out his mobile phone and put Karl on the case right away.

The 'company' was divided up into departments or cells, which were something like a honeycomb in how it meshed together.

Attila was the head of his cell and had five or six helpers to execute different tasks. These helpers were the drones, and were not known to any other department. Only Attila had the ability to communicate with other heads and any higher information was disseminated down from board level. He thought he had got to know his people well, but obviously not.

They were all subject to the most rigorous background checks and no-one had families, or any ties or affiliations with known groups. They all lived anonymously in flats owned by Morgan Holdings and were effectively 'ghosts', who didn't show up on tax or benefits registers. Sometimes their names were changed. That was the easy part and finding the records of a deceased person of the same age that were in the public domain was kids' play. Another department would come up with forged passports, driving licenses etc. Then Attila's cell was expanded.

He was the organizer of the auctions, and his work force researched the provenance of the pieces. They produced them for the secret auctions and made sure they got to their destinations. It meant they sometimes travelled, but they were well trained in counter surveillance techniques so they didn't get singled out at Customs. They were not rough and ready thugs for hire; quite a few had University degrees and they were presentable, well-spoken people who blended in. How they had been recruited for Morgan Holdings was a different story. Some had been addicts and homeless, some had personality traits that made them natural loners. The reasons were many and varied, but they were all well paid for doing what was asked with no questions. Attila couldn't put his finger on who would be the mole, no matter how he cudgelled his brain, but the signs were there.

Karl, on the other hand, had just had a short conversation with Max and snapped his phone shut. He had been given the list of names in Attila's cell and would look into it immediately. They would all be gathering at Addingham Manor for the auction, so soon they would all be under the same roof. He decided to do a bit of background checking beforehand, so he knew their movements and local haunts and would see if anything cropped up. He rang the Human Resources Department and checked out the first on the list.

This was a guy named Chris Talbot. Karl didn't know if that was his real name, but it would do. Chris was a university drop-out. Clever, but no staying power. It seemed he had taken medication for some sort of depression and had lost touch with his family. He had ended up living in a doorway and seemed far older than his twenty-four years when he was recruited. After being physically and mentally picked up and dusted off at the Morgan Private Health Facility, Chris had emerged a new man. He was a useful member of the team and appeared to enjoy his new role. There was a good balance of physical and mental stimulation to keep him happy.

Karl mentally side-lined this candidate for later attention. There wasn't any real motive for rocking the boat big time, unless he was being head hunted by rivals. But he hadn't been splashing the cash about and hadn't made any new friends for quite a while. So Karl moved on.

Next was a middle-aged man called Robert Trevis. Now Robert was a different kettle of fish. He had recently bought a new car, was seen at nice places—not "A" list but rapidly heading that way. Whilst being well paid, he could hardly have maintained that sort of lifestyle. A bit of a give-away, so Karl thought he would pay the man a quick visit before he set off for the Manor.

It was a dreary night in London, and Robert was safely ensconced in his flat. He was whistling quietly as he dressed for his night out at the Feathers Restaurant. The shirt would have to be white tonight and the tie would be one reminiscent of the Guards. Not exactly the same but enough to fool a passing glance. Life was good, and he lived for the moment. The new friends he had made were a good crowd and they were all high flyers, with all to gain and nothing, it seemed, to lose. They were always interested in him and what he did, almost hanging on his words. He carefully knotted his tie and shrugged into his jacket.

Robert heard a key turn in the lock of his door, and he turned to see Karl leaning on the door frame of his bedroom.

'Going somewhere nice tonight?' Karl gave Robert an appraising look. 'Might come along with you.' Robert blanched at the thought of this but sensibly kept his mouth shut.

He straightened his necktie and swallowed hard before saying, 'How can I help you?' Even as the words left his mouth, he realized that the evening was not going to plan and the words were ill chosen.

'Well, you might be able to help me out with a bit of information. It's like this; there is someone in the team who is not playing by the rules, and I thought you may know who it is. It may of course be you, so I will have to eliminate you from the list. Scratch you out, so to speak…'

It was the words 'eliminate' and 'scratch out' that hit home to Robert. He wasn't a coward, but neither was he a brave man, and he sank into a chair.

'Good, now I have your full attention I'm going to ask you about your new friends. They seem to like you a lot. Why is that? Are you a funny man? Are you rich enough to buy their friendship? Why are they bothering with a loser like you?' These rhetorical questions went unanswered.

'I know,' Karl said, his face lighting up as if he had a revelation, 'they want information from you, they want what you know. So you are being cultivated. Do they make you feel good about yourself, as if you are worth something? Your stint in prison probably knocked your confidence, didn't it?'

Robert sunk down lower as the words hit home. He had been drinking too much lately and he wasn't one of the tough blokes. He was quite clever when alcohol hadn't addled his brain, but it was probably true that he was being cultivated and he hadn't seen it. They knew all about him and he knew very little about them. A few drinks and his mouth got looser; sometimes he couldn't really remember the following day what he had said. He was in a very dangerous position and he finally realized it.

'So what are we going to do about this little situation then, Robbie?' Karl waited.

The flood gates opened and Robert was almost incoherent as he gushed about not going to meet them tonight and how he had been duped and he was to blame for the failing in his character. The list went on and Karl began to look bored.

He moved behind Robert and gently laid his hands on the man's shoulders. Robert quivered but didn't move. Karl began to massage the knotted muscles gently, and he felt Robert relax a little.

Karl moved his hands to either side of Robert's head, and, grasping it firmly, he twisted it sharply to the side. There was a snapping and crunching sound as the vertebrae disintegrated and Robert was a lifeless corpse. Leaving him still sitting in the chair, Karl walked to the door and pulled out his mobile.

'Put me through to housekeeping please', he said as he went to report to Max.

Alistair sat alone before setting off to his manor. He was in a pensive mood and gazed into space, musing at the huge legacy his father had left to him and Max. He had never known his mother, and he knew that Max had a different one, although there was a family resemblance. It didn't bother him one iota. He did, however, feel that a piece of him was missing. It was a totally irrational thought, but one which wouldn't go away. He couldn't imagine why he had this feeling deep down in his psyche. He fingered a small gold cross in his pocket. He carried it with him always, and Father had told him it was the key and not to lose it. He didn't know what any of it meant, but he had always stayed faithful to his father's wishes.

CHAPTER THREE

Waves of nausea washed over Ellie and memories came flooding back as she gave a convulsive twitch. Her dream was that she was still confined in the factory with her hands and feet bound. Her senses told her that this place smelled different from the cellar, more of an antiseptic smell; the light was also brighter through her closed lids. She couldn't hear anything, but then remembered the events which had robbed her of that sense. Ellie dragged herself into full consciousness and unglued her eyes. As everything swam into hazy perception, she could make out a face. It was Rory and she moved her hand to grasp his very tightly. He looked dirty and unkempt, with his hair sticking up at odd angles and smudges on his face, but he was the most wonderful sight in the world to Ellie. He also smelled of smoke.

Rory's mouth was moving but she still couldn't hear anything, and she could see other faces hovering around the bed. Their mouths started to move as well.

'I can't hear you; I can't hear anything at all!' Ellie must have shouted it as she saw everyone exchange concerned glances. A nurse scurried away and others began to check her pulse and look in her eyes with renewed activity. Ellie kept a tight hold of Rory's hand in a vice like grip. He wasn't going anywhere.

A nurse came scurrying back with a small white board and she scribbled frantically, "Can you hear anything at all? Is there any buzzing in your ears? How did this happen?"

Ellie thought quickly about what had happened and decided that she couldn't really explain anything.

'I can't really remember anything, except going to the shop for some wine. Then it's all a blank after that, except I do remember some sort of very loud bang,' she croaked hoarsely. She hoped that would suffice for the moment, as Ellie knew the police would home in on her soon. She would just have to keep feigning amnesia for the time being. She hoped she could keep it up.

The nurse wrote again. "Don't worry about anything. There was a gas blast at your home. You are okay. An ENT doctor will see you very soon." Ellie nodded.

Rory took the pad from the nurse. "I thought you were dead! I got there when the house went up and thought you were in it." His face was worried.

'It's okay.' Ellie tried to reassure him. 'You're here now and I do love you so much, and it was all terrible but I'm safe now. Don't leave me, please.'

He wrote furiously. "I'm staying right here. I love you too."

Ellie breathed a sigh of relief, relaxed slightly and a tear squeezed itself from under a lid. Rory wiped it away and kissed her gently.

A nurse came in and wrote that she was going to give Ellie a mild sedative and she should try and get some more sleep, as that would be the best medicine for now. Ellie felt a softness envelope her, and she succumbed and drifted away.

It must have been the next morning when Ellie woke up, and felt much more her normal self, she was even hungry. Rory was there, reading a newspaper, cleaned up and looking respectable. He must have gone home while she was asleep.

"Morning darlin'," he wrote with a heart at the side. He did have a soppy side and that was just what Ellie needed at that moment.

'Hiya honey-bunch', she responded. 'How's' about you get your girlfriend some breakfast? Just some cereal and toast and gallons of tea please, I'm so dry.'

He nodded and poked his head round the door. "Breakfast comin' up," he wrote. Ellie slowly sat up, and didn't know if she had ever been so stiff and sore. Every muscle creaked and her back was covered in dressings from the burns. They hurt like hell if she leaned on them. Rory pulled the table across the bed, and a man in blue scrubs came in with a tray.

Rory said something to him and he reached across and wrote on the pad, "Nice to see you're recovering, you look better than yesterday." Ellie smiled at him but the smile died as she smelt a subtle taint of citrus cologne. She just stared and nodded dumbly. Was it the guy from the cellar? She didn't know for sure, but he wore the same aftershave and it wasn't one she could identify. He smiled and left and Rory began organizing breakfast but the hunger had dissipated, leaving a nauseous void. Ellie decided to try to be as normal as possible, whatever that was.

She forced some breakfast down, and Rory ate the rest and gave her half the newspaper to read. It appeared she had made the front page. What a prize—the fifteen minutes of fame! There were pictures of the shop with crime scene tape everywhere, interviews with the grieving Chandra family, and speculation as to what had caused the supposed gas blast at the flat. Blame the lasagne, she thought.

"You don't remember anything at all?" Rory wrote.

'Nothing,' she said, and at that point resolved to keep Rory out of this as much as she was able to. He was a good guy and didn't deserve this at all.

'Ali was a good man and it's the worst thing to know he was shot like that.' Rory held her hand. 'It's like something out of a horror film.' Ellie stared at the ceiling, then squeezed her eyes shut, willing the memory away.

Rory had loosed his hand and was writing. "Well, plod is coming to see you today and also Mr. Graves (bad name), ENT will be here soon."

'I really want to hear again Rory, you can't imagine what it's like, but it's vile. A bit of a nightmare really, not being able to hear you—a pad can only go so far!'

Rory looked towards the door and the ENT consultant bustled in with an entourage of sycophantic students in tow. They filled the small side room. He said something and Ellie waved the pad at him.

'I can't hear anything at all, I don't know what happened but I don't like it one bit.' He nodded and produced an instrument and began looking in her ears. He was conversing with his students and Ellie didn't like it, as they were discussing her and she couldn't hear it. He got the pad and wrote.

'Eardrums perforated, maybe by explosion. They will heal and you will be able to hear again. Will do MRI for any further damage.'

Ellie nodded and broke into a big grin with the good news.

Rory was also smiling fit to bust.

The next few days passed, with dressings being changed, strength returning and being subjected to all manner of tests. The doc was right. Ellie did begin to hear buzzing noises and once heard a muffled sound when someone dropped a tray. She was so thankful she was going to be able to hear again.

The police had turned up on two separate occasions and Ellie had given them her version of the story and they had given her the standard comment of 'We'll be in touch'. She couldn't blame them, as she wasn't really helping at all. Ellie was just too scared.

It was getting near to the time Ellie should go home but she hadn't got a home to go to. Rory suggested that she move in with him but she didn't want him involved, and it caused a bit of a rift by her saying she wanted to have her own flat again. He couldn't understand why and went a bit huffy, but when he saw Ellie was adamant, he caved in, and said he would start looking for her.

'Could you possibly go and buy me some clothes?' Ellie asked him as her release from hospital was imminent. Reality had struck home and she hadn't got anything, not a stitch; nothing from her flat either, as everything had been destroyed in the explosion. Ellie just wanted to forget the whole business, but she knew she couldn't and wouldn't. She wanted to return to normality, go to work and spend her life in a mediocre, middle of the road fashion. She didn't crave greatness or adrenaline fixes, and didn't even particularly want to win the lottery. Her greatest wish was to be left alone.

Rory had started to bring Ellie brochures and details of flats. She immediately discarded all the basements, as the thought of being trapped again scared her silly. She was happier with second floor homes with fire escapes outside and lots of exits. Call her paranoid but… Ellie eventually settled on two that would suit her needs, and Rory said he would go and check them out. If she was honest, she wasn't really bothered what they were like as long as they had good locks on the doors and were clean.

He came back that evening and said that he had made an executive decision and picked the one nearest to her work, as it was the cleanest and the cheaper of the two. Ellie had got some money put by, but the flat insurance had come up trumps and she was going to be able to buy herself a new bed, curtains etc, as they said it was not due to her actions that she had lost everything, so they would pay up. In the first instance, she was to go to the shops and buy what she needed, then send the bills to them. Ellie quite liked that idea and started writing lists of what she needed.

Rory, by this time, had gone back to his work as tech support at the local college but came every night to see Ellie. He had managed to get loads of stuff ordered on line and delivered to the new flat so she was quite looking forward to getting out and organizing everything.

Then, the day before Ellie was due to go home, she saw Lemon man again. He came into her room, ostensibly to clear up the lunch things. Ellie was beginning to hear more every day, and had picked up some lip reading, so if someone spoke loudly, slowly and clearly, she could make out what they said.

Ellie shrank back in the bed.

'Go away, please leave me alone. I'll shout for help,' she threatened.

'Will you indeed, are you sure about that?'

Ellie shook her head.

'What do you want? I'm nobody to you, why are you watching me?'

'We are just checking you are okay, because there will be a job you can do for us later when you are better. Payment for living; I think the boss calls it a fringe benefit. You will get all the details when we are ready, but don't do anything silly now.'

Ellie shook her head again, feeling scared and intimidated, but not knowing what to do about it. At least this time she had got a good look at Lemon man (that's what she called him in her mind). He was quite tall, possibly about six feet and had light brown hair, almost blond, cut fashionably short. He actually wasn't bad looking, with his grey eyes. Pity he was an evil thug. She couldn't see any scars or marks, and in some ways, he had an Identikit face. A description would have fitted about a quarter of the male population.

Ellie just had to play along for the moment until she was one hundred per cent better. Then she would make a plan, as she was more certain than ever she wasn't going to live the rest of her life like this! Fine thoughts, but Ellie had absolutely no idea what she was going to do. A bit like a New Year's Resolution, fine for the first week, then you realize you have bitten off more than you can chew and you have set yourself an unobtainable goal. Giving herself a mental kick, she told herself there were more options. One could be to simply run away in the dead of night and change her name and appearance. So escape was possible, and even feasible. Not an option she would want to take, but it was always there.

Ellie felt pretty good as she left the hospital, and was greeted by a bright sunny day. It felt chilly, but she pulled her new coat round herself and hugged Rory's arm. She was going to stay at Rory's till she got her flat sorted, and was looking forward to a quiet evening in, healing the mental wounds. He had even managed to fill up the fridge and they were going to cook; one step on the road to normality. Today was a Thursday, and Ellie had found out that tomorrow was to be the funeral of Ali. The coroner had released the body, and the family could now continue their grieving. Ellie had decided to attend the funeral, although she was not looking forward to it at all. He had been something of a friend, and was always a cheerful soul with a good heart.

Together they strolled back towards town and just as they managed to hail a cab, Ellie saw the word 'robbery' splashed on the newspaper kiosks. She resolved to get a paper and get back in touch with the world again, but didn't in the end, as a cab rolled up.

That evening, warm, safe and secure, they cooked, then ate, and watched the news. Ellie could manage it better with the subtitles on, as the neighbours would have complained at the noise. The robbery that was being headlined was the theft of the Staffordshire Hoard. Apparently there had been a daring raid that had left two dead, and a good portion of the priceless Celtic hoard had been spirited away. The news team posted CCTV pictures of the wanted men and Ellie nearly fainted. There was the man with the spider tattoo on his neck, and also, she spotted Karl on the fringes of the blurry tape. They hadn't even worn masks. Just barrelled in and killed the unsuspecting drivers, snatched the hoard and driven away. The sheer audacity took her breath away.

Rory was looking at her intently. 'I've never said this to you before Ellie, but I actually don't believe you. You said you couldn't remember anything but that's a lie isn't it?'

Ellie looked down, with the classic guilty avoidance of not meeting the other person's eyes.

'Yes,' she said in a small voice. 'I can remember everything, but I'm scared, Rory. They said that if I wanted to live, I couldn't tell a living soul. That meant you as well and I didn't want to get you involved, and if I tell you then you will be in danger as well.'

It all came tumbling out, and once the flood gates had opened Ellie couldn't stop. She was twisting her fingers together and tears were sliding down her face as she told him everything. A thought struck her and she suddenly stopped.

'What if they have bugged this place? You know with one of those hidden microphones and they have heard everything I've just said. Then they will know I've told you! Oh God! Rory, what am I going to do?'

Rory looked at her with his mouth slightly open and a glazed look in his eyes. 'You mean all that is really true and you haven't made it up? I mean you were unconscious for a time; maybe you had a bang on the head. This isn't the movies.'

'Yes, Rory, it is true! I have lied to the police, I've been threatened with guns, I've been nearly blown up, abducted by gangsters, do you want me to go on?' Even as she said it she realized how ridiculous it must sound, but he had to believe his life might now be in danger. 'All I can do is just play along and hope for the best; I don't know what else to do.'

As Ellie said those words, she realized just how powerless and vulnerable she felt.

'I want to go to Ali's funeral tomorrow, I need to say goodbye. I mean, I saw him killed and it wasn't his fault.' Ellie looked at Rory willing him to say that he would go with her. He slowly shook his head.

'You shouldn't go Ellie, someone from this crowd may be there, and you can't risk it.'

'Rory! Don't you understand I can't hide forever and even if I do, I'm sure they will find me, so what's the point?'

'I do understand that Ellie, but you've got to go to the police on this one. I will protect you as well as I'm able, but I haven't got a gun and couldn't bear it if you got hurt.' Ellie looked at his stricken expression and knew he was right, but she couldn't risk it. For all she knew, they had a mole within the force. Money bought a lot of favours and they seemed to have plenty of that.

'I'm not going to lie to you again so…' Ellie drew a deep breath, 'I am going to the funeral. I would like it if you came with me but I'll understand if you won't or can't.'

There, she'd said it. She had been proactive and it made her feel a bit wobbly inside. Ellie looked at Rory waiting for his answer.

'Okay. You're going anyway, whether or not I go with you. I can't say that I like it much but I'll go with you.'

'Rory, you are an absolute gem and I love you to bits.' Ellie flung her arms round his neck and kissed him senseless.

For the rest of the evening Ellie felt much lighter; the large heavy cloud of her secret had been blown away and Rory would help her, she knew he would.

Friday dawned and Ellie lay listening to Rory's breathing, steady and regular. This was one of her special moments where nothing could touch or hurt her. She was warm, comfortable, and for these few minutes she revelled in the nothingness of time and space, just drifting on the edge of sleep and reason.

Rory stirred, muttered a few unintelligible words, then headed for the bathroom. Time to get going, as the funeral was quite early and Ellie didn't want to be late for anything. She wasn't even sure if Hindus wore black at a funeral or was that just a European construct? In the end she didn't go for black, just sombre. Rory went for the same and they had a quiet breakfast, then headed out into the drizzle for the crematorium. A short cab ride brought them to the crematorium and they joined a long line of vehicles waiting to get in.

Giving up, they ditched the cab and walked the last hundred yards and queued with the other mourners. Although they were fairly early, they took standing room at the back of the chapel, trying to keep a low profile, and Rory held her hand tightly.

Ali's body was carried in by some male relatives, and the coffin was gently rotated so that his feet faced south. Ellie explained to Rory that this was so that the spirit could walk in the direction of the dead. Other mourners were chanting 'Jai ram shriram' as Ali's eldest son, Manjeet, walked round his coffin three times.

Ellie stiffened when she saw Manny, as he was mixed up in this somehow and she was going to find out how. It was in trying to protect Manny that Ali had been killed. But Ellie couldn't do anything today and the official mourning period was for thirteen days after the death, so she would have to wait.

The service progressed and words of comfort and eulogies to Ali touched Ellie's soul, and she wished him well in his afterlife. Ellie and Rory left and silently walked back to town, holding hands.

As the day was still young, they decided that Rory would go back to work, and Ellie would go and visit the library to find out about going back to work. She was looking forward to it and now felt well enough to work for a full day. The lack of hearing wouldn't be a real problem, and she thought Monday would be a good day to start back. She also wanted to go and see her new flat but she had to cajole Rory to give her the keys, as he was worried and protective about her running about on her own.

The library was just as she had left it, and Ellie headed up the steps and through the doors to be greeted by Marcia, her boss.

'Come here little girl, (she was a big lady) I want to see how you are.' She enveloped Ellie in a hug that left her breathless and caused her to wince because of her back. 'I'm sorry did I hurt you?' She was apologetic and Ellie explained about the burns, which were healing nicely but still painful to pressure.

'Sit, sit.' She ushered Ellie to a chair. 'Tell me all, you must know we're all dying to know of your adventures.'

'Really Marcia, there's nothing much to tell, as I still have a big blank about what went on and am just grateful to be back. I was wondering if I could start back on Monday.' Ellie looked at her in askance. 'The doctors seem to think I'm okay now; the only thing is that I'm suffering from a loss of hearing. It's coming back really quickly now,' Ellie reassured her, 'it's just that I don't catch everything first time round, but I'm sure we can work through that.'

'Course you can come back, we've missed you something dreadful; as long as you feel all right, we'll look forward to seeing you on Monday. Come and have a coffee.' She led Ellie (as though she was made of cut glass) to the staff room, and they passed a happy half hour catching up on office gossip. Boss or no boss, Ellie loved Marcia dearly.

CHAPTER FOUR

The two lorries looked good. They were tricked out with logos and new paint jobs, denoting some spurious heating company. The phone numbers and web sites displayed were as fictitious as were the number plates. It only took two digits and one letter to be changed, and the permutations were immense, too big to be traced. The wagons had been buffered up and scratched, so they looked as if they had been in use for a good, few years. A back light smashed, a wheel arch scraped, chips in the windscreen, all pointed to a company hanging on by the skin of its teeth in recession. No-one would give them a second glance.

The gang lay in wait at the disused worksite. A derelict site with two vans in it wouldn't raise much comment from passers-by; even so, they had parked round the back, snug between the abandoned skips and rubbish.

'Okay, do we all know what we're doing?' Genghis looked round at the gang. They were decked out in overalls and carried bits of heating kit; a pipe here, a wrench there. All innocuous but deadly weapons in the wrong hands.

'No fuck ups or heroics, just a quick clean job, understand?' A few murmurs rippled through. Genghis looked at his watch. 'Five minutes to go, so van number one onto the road with the breakdown show'.

The two men raced to the van and pulled it onto the road, effectively blocking it.

Right on cue, round the corner drove a plain green Ford Transit. The driver was chatting to his mate, who was wrapping himself round a bacon sandwich, when he saw the heating wagon parked at an oblique angle across the road.

'Bloody hell!' was all he could manage as he skidded to a halt. His mate jerked forwards, restrained by the seatbelt, but began choking on the last bite as it lodged in his windpipe.

The driver turned his head to look at his mate but suddenly, out of nowhere, faces appeared at the window and a heavy wrench smashed the windscreen into a million stars. The door was opened and they were both dragged out onto the wet tarmac. The co-driver was still heaving and choking, but his problem passed from the driver's mind as rough hands dragged him onto the disused site. Both vans quickly pulled in behind them.

A big guy shouted, 'Where's the key for the back?' and gave him a swift kick behind his knees so he fell forward. His mate had gone horribly silent by this time and the driver could see two legs jutting out, lying on the floor behind a skip.

'Dunno, we don't get them, just deliver, that's all. What's happened to Dave? Dave!' he shouted, but there was no response.

'Pity. You could have been useful, but no matter.' These were the last words he heard as a sudden short blinding pain blotted out all consciousness and he met the earth for the final time.

The van was swiftly broken into and the precious crates and boxes were unloaded and stashed. The two lorries fired up and went their separate ways, leaving two bodies slowly soaking in the light drizzle.

It would be an hour before they were reported missing and nearly half a day before they would be found, livid and stiff with other discarded rubbish.

'It all went according to plan.' Genghis was reporting in, on the secure number on the disposable mobile. 'No problems that couldn't be taken care of.' He heard the appreciative murmur on the other end. 'We'll swap the cargo now and be at the Manor soon.' The line went dead and Genghis took the back off the phone and retrieved the SIM card twisting it into two pieces, then fluttered them out of the open window. The phone was taken apart and the back, cover and internal workings followed into the streaming gutter. All tidy. The lock-up came into view and the lorries pulled in, with the roller shutters quickly being pulled down behind them. Cars were ready, all 'run of the mill' family saloons but all had good boot space.

The unloading took but ten minutes, and all the boxes were transferred with bags of shopping put on top, hiding them from view. Overalls were stripped off and revealed ordinary casual clothes; just family men going about their business, collecting the mid-week shop. Engines started and the cars filtered out into mainstream life, to meet again at the Manor.

Alistair and Max arrived simultaneously at the Manor, Alistair emerging from his chauffer driven Bentley and Max alighting from the Robinson 44 helicopter. Ducking down from the rotor wash, Max hurried to meet his brother waiting on the gravel drive.

'The cars will be here soon, so let's get them unloaded

and sorted as fast as possible. Don't want anyone hanging about do we?' Alistair raised an eyebrow at Max.

'I'll get them paid as quickly as possible and off the premises, as we don't want prying eyes when we unpack. They don't know what they have just driven here, best keep it that way till it hits the news,' Max responded, and with a nod, peeled off to walk round to another entrance at the back.

Alistair continued up the front steps under the Roman pillars and through the imposing front door held open by Carter, who had managed to get here ahead of his boss. Alistair was never sure how he did that, but he was impressed nevertheless.

Carter gave a little cough which was always his preparation for speaking without permission.

'Yes.' Alistair waited.

'Everything is ready for the house party and some of the guests are already arriving. I've shown them to their rooms, and they are awaiting you in the library with drinks. Dinner will be at eight as usual, unless you wish it bought forward at all?' Alistair shook his head. 'I've approved the menu in your absence and taken into account the needs of our Middle Eastern guests. I trust that was in order?'

Alistair laid his hand on Carter's arm. 'What would I do without you? Everything will be perfect as usual, thank you.' Carter looked down at the unaccustomed praise and nodded then slipped away.

The walls of the library glowed with the patina of dark oak, reflecting the crackling fire and subdued lighting. Bright pools of light were dotted about, with up-lit paintings by Italian masters, all originals, and ostensibly hanging in major collections round the world. The proletariat of the world gawked at fakes, whilst the mastery of the long dead painters was appreciated by the few. Persian carpets that had graced a palace hushed the footfalls on the inlaid floor, and the crystal glasses winked as the richest men in the world gathered for an evening of fun.

Alistair strode in with arms outstretched to all in greeting.

'My apologies that I was held up and wasn't here to greet you all personally. I hope you can forgive me,' he told the assemblage, whilst sketching a small bow. 'Dinner will be served shortly; then we can get to more pressing business.' He took a small drink of tonic water and lemon from the footman at his elbow.

Alistair then played the crowd by swapping small talk and anecdotes with each in turn, dropping out hints of what may be in store for each of them when they viewed the Celtic hoard later. He knew each man's desires, and he also knew much about the gold and its history, that was being unpacked in the cellars.

A few of the guests came for more than just the auction. Alistair knew many had proclivities towards unusual sexual activities, and one cellar had been made over into a medieval torture chamber to accommodate this, but that was for later. Money came first, then pleasures of the flesh, a natural order.

Carter appeared and coughed deferentially.

'Dinner is served,' he announced and withdrew as the guests began filtering through to the ornate Louis Quatorze dining room.

In the cellars, the boxes and crates had been unloaded and long tables held the finds. Attila was busy at work, checking all the pieces and directing his team.

Computers were blinking away, finding the descriptions of the items from the numerous articles that had appeared since the hoard saw daylight. Speed was of the essence, as the auction would be completed tonight and the guests would depart at first light. The hoard would stay here for the smallest time possible and leave no trace. Max was overseeing this part of the job, and he would also act as auctioneer. There would be, of course, numerous telephone bids from those not lucky enough to have been invited, or who couldn't get there in time.

Dinner would be over by nine o'clock and a few items would be passed around the dinner table as a "taster" of things to come. The acquisitive appetites would be whetted and the auction would again boost the funds of Morgan Enterprises. Max duly selected a few of the pommels and helmet foils to pass round, and for theatrical value placed them on a salver with a cover to present to the buyers.

'Ah, Max, at last. We are all waiting to see what the next course will be,' said Alistair with mock jocularity when all the guests were sated. Max carried the salver at shoulder height through the double doors to the dining room. He swept the cover off and offered it to Alistair.

'Perfect, I think everyone will enjoy this course. Please, pass it round.'

Max walked slowly round the table, and Alistair watched as eager fingers reached for the gold and noted as the greed lit up the jaded faces. It would all go well, and he knew he had picked his target audience perfectly.

Ensconced in overstuffed armchairs in the drawing room with glasses at their elbows, the guests enjoyed their evening immensely. The auction was conducted with an almost hushed reverence, as piece after piece was brought out and displayed, with an encrypted camera feed for the video conferencing of the absent buyers. A few discreetly placed workers took the telephone bids, and the hoard was decimated. From the three thousand or so pieces, some two hundred went under the hammer, to be dispersed around the globe. Some buyers simply put the pieces into their pockets to gloat over later on; some were to go to Swiss bank vaults never to be seen again, while others were to be made into pieces of jewellery to be flaunted around high maintenance necks.

Alistair sat back and analysed the spectacle. He had hit the right nail with the correct hammer, and the organization had been clockwork. He was justifiably proud of his handiwork. Not that he wanted for anything; he didn't need to buy or sell another item in his lifetime, but it was the thrill of the chase. Could he do it again, he asked himself, and the answer was yes.

Max, on the other hand, was waiting patiently for the auction to be over so he could indulge his other pleasures. His goal was the gratification of the flesh, and he had seen the selection of females being brought in. They were all of eastern European origin, bought in for the sex trade, some were very young and all had no idea what was in store for them. He would have to let the buyers take their pick, but it seemed a good-looking bunch, and he would be happy with any of them. The mock dungeon had been prepared and the girls were upstairs getting into their party clothes, sipping cocktails laced with a variety of drugs to ensure their compliance.

Max had often wondered why Alistair had never joined in with the sex games, but his brother had never shown any interest in the delights on offer, and frankly Max didn't care, as long as he had his fill. "Each to their own" and "Do what you will" were his mottos.

Back in London, in a different world on the disused site, the incessant drizzle had turned into a veritable torrent, and the policemen on duty were a bedraggled bunch. The crime scene operatives had tried to rig up some tents over the bodies but the edges flapped in the wind, and rivulets of rain washed underneath.

'Not much chance of getting anything from here. They couldn't have timed it better with this rain.' Constable Jack Havers blew on his fingers and tried to stamp some life back into his feet. He was on duty at the gate, which hung forlornly, creaking on a broken hinge. Ostensibly, his job was to stop the crowds of onlookers breaching the thin blue line of crime scene tape that flapped and snapped in the wind. Today, there was no one.

'How long do you think we'll be here?' his partner asked, with a note of hope in his voice.

'As long as it takes, I suppose,' replied Jack. 'We'll probably be here till shift change, or they move the bodies and close the site. Still, can't see how they're going to get much from here, it's all been washed clean. Tomorrow will be door to door; let's just hope this bloody rain packs in by then'.

'Makes you wonder how they got away with it. There must have been millions of pounds' worth on that van, and nobody ever sees anything. What do you think they're going to do with it? They can't really sell anything like that to a fence, as it's going to turn up sooner or later. A bit cheeky if you ask me.'

'Probably going to some rich bloke's collection, same as paintings that go missing, I suppose. Though I've got to hand it to them, it was a pretty slick job,' Jack said shoving his hands into his pockets.

'Oi! You pair, Holmes and Watson, gassing by the gate.' A strident voice came from the tent. 'Have a look round the back there for any spent cartridge cases, and don't take all day about it.' Jack and his partner swapped a glance and both shouted back a smart 'Yes, sir,' as they began the task.

It was a futile exercise, as the gang had cleaned up well enough and there were no cartridge cases or anything else for that matter. Half an hour later, the morgue van drew up. The bodies were shapeless in the black body bags, and the crime scene team declared the site finished with and began packing up. The big arc lights were switched off, and the lenses fizzed and popped with the droplets of rain as they cooled.

Jack looked at his mate, a copper of many years, but who had never made it past uniform; probably now, he never would. Ron was one of the good blokes and also a friend outside of work, sharing a pint when the shifts allowed.

'Come on Ron, let's get scarce. Then we might just finish on time.' Ron nodded and they sidled out to their car.

When they were inside with the heater going full blast and the windows steaming up faster than the heater could cope, Ron turned to Jack.

'What do you make of all that then? Bit like a gang killing, but I heard someone say that there was a robbery from the van of the Staffs Hoard.'

'Dunno, but if it is, we'll be at it morning, noon and night, traipsing round, checking stories, etc. Just wait till tomorrow's briefing, bet you we'll be on door to door. Just hope the rain packs in; I'm sick of being wet. Fancy a quick pint down the Club?'

The question went unanswered. 'That one bloke looked like he'd been choked to death. Bit funny that, when the other guy was shot, point blank. Just wait till we get the report, bet I'm right. Seen too many of them.'

'I'm not betting,' said Jack, 'but I'll treat you to that pint. It might warm me up.'

As they drove back to the station, they passed the Feathers Restaurant, looking warm and inviting, but way out of the range of Jack and Ron.

Inside the restaurant was a group of four, waiting for the fifth that would never show up.

'What do you reckon, think he'll show?' Phillip addressed the others.

Claire made a moue and shrugged. 'Well, I wouldn't pass up a meal here on what Phil pays me.'

Robert just cuddled his drink.

'I suppose we'll have to give it another half an hour, but what we'll do then I'm not sure,' said Phil. 'I was sure we were getting close to some real information. You were a bit closer to him Rob by having the same name; I must say you played that one to the hilt. Good one mate!'

'Let's just recap quickly what info we have got,' said Phil. 'First, do we know where he works?' Everyone shook their heads. 'Second, we know where he lives but didn't have time to set up the surveillance.' Everyone nodded.

Claire said, 'But he did let slip the name Morgan, but then shut up like a clam.'

Nigel, the quiet one, said, 'Did anyone get his mobile? I could do some tracing and find out associates.'

'Good one Nige. Maybe we should pay his flat a visit and

check out his computer.' Phil looked at the others and they all nodded. 'Say we have a bite here then check it out in a few hours, when everyone is safely tucked up in bed.'

They all nodded and reached for the menus.

The night was still dark and cold, but the rain had eased slightly to a damp drizzle. Four figures, clad in black, walked to the block of apartments like a group of friends back from a night out. Nigel wore a black leather coat that nearly swept the floor, and Claire was in a black outfit with a black raincoat belted snug. The imposing figure of Phil was in a black suit with a black city overcoat thrown negligently round his shoulders. Robert was in his normal attire of black jeans with a leather bomber on top. Nothing to draw attention, but they walked with a purpose.

There were the usual security lights on round the building but they marched up to the front door and Claire began to look in her handbag, ostensibly for the key to the front door. She play-acted tipping the bag out, and slightly drunkenly fumbling through the contents.

Phil got exasperated and buzzed a random number.

'Hi, Claire's here but can't find her damned key... Flat 12?'

The door buzzed and Nigel quickly opened it and stuck his foot in it.

'Thanks mate, what are women like when they've had a few. See ya!'

Entry was gained and they took the lift to Robert Trevis's flat.

On the floor there was a dim energy saver burning at the end of the corridor, but they didn't press the switch for the main lights. The door to the flat was a normal hollow door, and there didn't seem to be any other security devices other than the usual Yale lock.

'Give me a minute,' said Claire and began staring into space, whilst inserting pseudo keys into the lock.

'Why do you always do that faraway look when you're fiddling a lock?' asked Phil, tapping his foot.

'Piss off. If you can do it any better or quicker, be my guest,' Claire shot back, then gave a look of triumph as the door opened.

'Okay, everyone we've got about three minutes.' Phil peeled off from the group and turned right into the kitchen.

'Nice pad.' Robert glanced around and took in the matching carpets and curtains with the big T.V bolted to the wall.

'Hey guys, look at this.' They heard Nigel from the bedroom.

They all gathered in the doorway, and stood mute at the sight of Robert's body slumped in the chair. Phil walked over and placed his fingers on his neck.

'Cold as ice, been dead a few hours now. Right, let's get gone, pronto,' he said. 'You know what we need, phones, laptop, diary etc. Move it!'

The team split up and quickly rifled through desk drawers and pockets in short order. They gathered again by the door and went into the dimly lit corridor. The sound of the lift rising got their attention. The light flashed and it dinged.

Phil quickly grabbed Claire and pulled her into an adjacent doorway and began kissing her passionately. She responded with fervour. The other two began walking towards the lift discussing gobbledygook thermodynamics. They waited as the lift door opened and then Robert jerked his thumb at the ardent pair.

'Should get a room,' he shook his head and allowed a cleaning crew to exit the lift. They were pushing a big enclosed trolley on wheels with lots of mops and brushes bristling from it. The cleaners trundled towards the room they had just vacated and sniggered, as they passed the erstwhile lovers. Claire shot them a glance then grabbed Phil's hand and they raced towards the lift.

'Hold the lift,' she shouted and they all piled in as the doors closed and they began the descent. For the camera in the lift, Claire and Phil kept up the pretence of being lovers, and Robert and Nigel talked amongst themselves whilst cold shouldering the pair. They split up outside after mouthing the meet up instructions to each other. All had got information from the flat under their coats.

There was a big white van parked nearby and amidst laughter and giggles from Claire, she apparently sweet talked the techno guys into taking her and Phil's photo on a mobile. They posed strategically so the van registration was in the picture as well.

Overnight the rain had eventually died away altogether, leaving a washed-out sky, with a few lingering tattered remnants of cloud shutting out the sun. As they had predicted, Constables Jack and Ron were on the 'door to door' enquiries. It always amazed them that anyone who lived in a close-knit terraced community will always know exactly who is doing what to whom, maybe even when and how, but asked about a stranger they immediately contracted amnesia. They eventually met at the end of a long line of houses.

'Let's walk back down to the site and get a sandwich at the corner shop,' Jack said hopefully. Rob nodded and the pair walked slowly, and swapped desultory chat about the new case that had been mentioned at the morning briefing. Apparently, the intel was that a guy had been found murdered by some undercover team, but that the scene had been clandestinely cleaned up by someone else. Interesting stuff going on, and rumour was that one of the bodies found at the robbery site had choked to death on a bacon sandwich. Speculation in the station was rife and bets were being taken if the coroner would be saying 'natural causes' for that one.

Jack stopped suddenly and looked down into the gutter. Lying there were the internal workings of a mobile phone, and a bit further on, there was the casing. He alerted Ron, and they began at the end of the street and slowly worked their way up. Eventually they had gathered all the parts, even the SIM, which had been snapped into two.

'What do you suppose this is all about, Ron?' Jack got a clear plastic bag out of his pocket. 'Could be just kids, but it could be something to do with the robbery. Let's not touch it; there may be prints.' He gently eased the bits into the bag with the end of a biro.

'You'll get a medal for this one mate, if it is', said Ron smiling. 'I'll give you the honour of giving it to the git in charge, and we'll see what the tech boys have to say'.

Well satisfied, they reached the corner shop and the meal deal of a coke and sandwiches were purchased. The proprietor of the dingy shop was only too glad of a chat. He had been waiting for the site opposite to be developed, as then hopefully, trade would pick up. It turned out he was a star witness, as he had seen it all and heard the gunshot. Best of all he had CCTV footage of it all, and had just been waiting for the cops to call.

It really was Ron and Jack's lucky day and they couldn't believe their luck at doing some real detective work and it paying off big time.

'Definitely in for that pint now, Ron, let's go murder one,' Jack said as he walked away with a spring in his step.

CHAPTER FIVE

Ellie woke and felt rejuvenated and thought that today was the first day of the rest of her life, and the best thing was just to get on with it. Today, she was going to get a few more things for her nice flat that was taking shape; she was going to move in soon. Her hearing loss was negligible now, and her world was getting back on track. Get moving soon and get back to work was the watchword of the day. Marcia was texting her every day and enquiring about her health, and Ellie had promised to start again on Monday without fail. Today, she was going to shop till she dropped.

So, coat and scarf on, she walked up the High Street and decided to get a quick cup of coffee and review her extensive "to do" list, maybe even have a latte with a dash, and sit for a moment, people watching and mentally plan her day.

The café wasn't particularly crowded and Ellie snagged an empty table, just on the left-hand side near the window. The barista had done a good job and the coffee was delicious, with its aroma wafting. She took the list and a pen from her bag, to start putting things in order. Then she smelt it. The sickening smell of lemons, would she ever be free of the visceral response to that odour?

Ellie stiffened and looked round. She hadn't seen him

come in, but there he was, nonchalantly drinking a cup of coffee and reading a newspaper. She gathered up her things in a rush so she had to get out quickly, but he beat her to it.

He stood and walked towards her table with a newspaper in his hand—and Ellie didn't know why she did it, but as he walked towards her, she stuck her foot out, rose from her chair and sent him flying into the gangway. She swept her hand and connected with the cup of steaming coffee, dousing him in the scalding liquid.

Ellie bent solicitously down to him and in between all the 'I'm so sorry,' and 'Here, let me help you,' said, 'If you ever come near me again, I'll kill you'.

Ellie added 'And I mean it!' through clenched teeth, as she mopped him up.

He was soaked in coffee; a pity really, as she had been going to enjoy that cup, but the look on her face and the fact that she was talking through gritted teeth made him back off a step.

'Sorry I was really clumsy,' he said, keeping up the pretence as he bent down to retrieve his newspaper. It was only a bit soggy round the edges and he placed it on the table. As he grabbed some more napkins from the holder on the table, he sibilantly said, 'Look at the job page and apply for it—you know it'll be the best thing for you to do. Oh, and don't shoot the messenger!'

It was Ellie's turn to step back, and she wondered if this guy was in the same position as her, just another pawn in a game she didn't know the rules of.

'Let me get you another,' he said, as he went back to the counter and with many apologies to the staff came back, with another steaming cup of the same.

The staff rallied and appeared with mops and buckets for the clean-up job and Lemon man disappeared through the door. Ellie sat back down heavily, and her buoyant mood evaporated. She thanked the staff and apologised for her ineptitude with a smile and turned the pages of the newspaper. There, marked with a big black ring, was a job at the British Library. It was recruiting a staff member for the archive and manuscript section. "No experience necessary" it said, as all training would be given to the successful applicant. Ellie hadn't got any experience in that field and was at a bit of a loss as to why she was supposed to apply.

What if she didn't do as he said? Ellie was caught by her conscience on a hook, that wouldn't let her go as much as she wriggled. She could never forgive herself if anything happened to Rory, and she was basically a coward who didn't want to end up in a ditch.

So Ellie took a swig of the rapidly cooling coffee that now tasted like mud, and pulled out her phone and called the number. A polite voice put her through to the right extension and she was informed that the vacancy would be filled very soon, and could she come along for interview today, if possible? She could fill in the application form at the same time; references would of course be followed up in due course. Ellie made an appointment for just after lunch and wondered what the hell she'd let herself in for.

Shopping was a chore in the end and her mind was only half on the job. Ellie grabbed a quick sandwich at a department store, and gradually made her way across town to the library. She looked up at the imposing frontage with the staircase of steps leading to the Roman pillars, flanking the double doors.

She mentally gave herself a shake and told herself to pull it together. Yes, she was going for a new job. One that she probably wouldn't get and the thought of what that might mean sprung into her mind. She felt that this Lemon man was the puppeteer and she was just the marionette, being jerked around according to his whim.

After a deep breath, Ellie climbed purposefully up the steps. Whilst climbing she got her brain in gear; be pleasant, be honest and smile a lot. Look capable whilst being articulate. Not a lot really! Who was she kidding! She was better off applying for a job as expedition leader up Everest, now there's a thought! She smiled and immediately felt better.

Once inside, a friendly receptionist took Ellie to the offices of the Chief Archivist, and she sat on a squeaky leather chair and filled in an interminable job application. It didn't take long, as she wrote 'none' or 'n/a' in many of the boxes. She did, however, have to think hard about her new address and post code.

Eventually Ellie was called in to see the big wig and he was just as she imagined, a sort of dried up husk of a man, very suited to the fusty, dusty archives he was in charge of. Motioning her to a chair on the other side of his expansive desk, he peered at Ellie over the top of his half-moon spectacles.

'Well, hmmm, there's not a lot in here to go on, but tell me a bit about your current job.'

So Ellie launched into a detailed job description and threw in bits of her training course at college, and how the work had touched on archives and manuscript storage. She tried to sound enthusiastic and display how this job would be a great step up for her, and what she hoped she could contribute to the department. She also smiled a lot.

'Hmmm,' was all he said, but at the end of Ellie's ramblings he offered a guided tour of the department, which she accepted, as by this time, she was getting genuinely interested.

A nodding tour of the offices was swiftly accomplished, then down in a silent lift to the rare manuscript collection. There seemed to be miles of dimly lit corridors in the basement and rooms branched off each side. There were cryptic plaques tacked onto the metal doors and in spite of his aged appearance, Ellie had to hurry to keep up.

Stopping at one door identical to all the others, he swiped a card and punched in a code, and they went into a room that was crammed with metal shelves, cabinets with pull out drawers, chart tables, all seemingly haphazard. There was also an all-pervading smell of old books and parchments.

'Here we have some great treasures,' he said pulling out a drawer.

Ellie could do nothing but gasp and stare, as nestling in some acid free paper was an illuminated manuscript with colours so rich, they looked like jewels imbedded in the page.

'Would you like to hold it?' he asked and handed Ellie a pair of gloves.

'Can I really?' She was still overcome by the privilege, and must have sounded like someone on a school trip. Handling the book was the turning point for Ellie, as she now really wanted that job more than anything in the world. Ellie peppered him with questions at that point and watched him metamorphose from a dry academic to an enthusiastic zealot. She wanted to learn from this man, to be his disciple.

After he had pried the book from her hands they wandered

back to his office, and over a cup of coffee he offered Ellie the job. She was almost gushing as she accepted, and subject to references, of course, she was to start as soon as she had worked her notice.

Ellie collected her shopping and went out into the gathering dusk; her buoyant mood had returned. Whoever he was, the puppeteer could pull her strings as much as they wanted if it meant a job like that. Ellie did experience a pang as she thought of Marcia, and how she would tell her on her return to work. Ellie would, in fact, just be working her notice, but surely Marcia wouldn't begrudge her this chance! She mentally rehearsed how she would tell Rory of the day's events, and steeled herself for the circular arguments of going to the police etc.

The evening progressed much as Ellie had forecast, and they didn't manage a smile until later on after a few beers. Rory had definitely got the hump over this latest turn of events, and Ellie couldn't seem to convince him that playing along was the best way forward. She hadn't even kept the newspaper with the circled advert to show him. He thought he was being kept out of the loop deliberately. Ellie tried to tell him that it wasn't the case, but even to her ears it sounded lame.

Back in the police station, Phil and his undercover team sat in the office and reviewed all the info they had gathered from the flat. They had got a small diary with cryptic initials written by dates, a laptop that was password protected, a phone, and various credit cards and a drivers' license pulled from a nice leather wallet.

'Okay,' said Phil, 'let's get to grips with this. We nurtured this guy for about five weeks, wined and dined him, and we've found out very little so far. We know he hasn't got family or a steady at the moment. We know his date of birth and that he has a car. Are we losing our touch?' He glanced round the table and everyone swapped glances with the others as they couldn't disagree.

Robert volunteered, 'He did keep his cards close to his chest and even when he got drunk, there was very little he told us. Maybe he just didn't know much about the workings of Morgan Enterprises, but I thought he was quite high up the ladder. Maybe the laptop will tell us a bit more.'

He reached across and began fiddling with the machine, and everyone knew that he would now disappear into his own cyber world and wouldn't reappear until the job was done.

Each had their own strengths, and Robert and Nigel were the tech geeks, who could jump firewalls and plant worms to find out any information they cared to. They liked to be in their tech lab rather than out on the streets, but sometimes what they wanted and what they got were different. It was ultimately up to Phil, and he had to admit they were both pretty good at undercover work when pushed. Nigel reached for the mobile phone and looked at it appraisingly.

'I'm going to have to do this in the lab, and I'll also have a look at the traffic cameras to see who went into the flats yesterday. Oh! And I'll check out that cleaning company we got the photo of. I mean, who just calls a cleaning company to move dead bodies. Wonder where that one will wash up?' He tapped Robert on the shoulder as he went out, and Robert gathered all the stuff up and followed him out.

'Well we won't see them for a few days now.' Claire smiled as she looked at Phil. 'Oh, and by the way, next time we are playing the "passionate pair" please keep your hands where I can see them and not inside my bra.'

Phil gave her a mock leer and smiled showing his perfect white teeth. 'Can't blame a guy for trying when he's got the most beautiful girl on the planet in his arms.'

'You're just a smooth talker. I know I'm wonderful and clever etc, you don't need to tell me. Just think on this, you know what they say, something about beauty and the beast… opposites attract!' Claire retorted, and continued, 'Do you want coffee and some carbs while we go over it again?'

'Good for me, I know you love me really.'

'In your dreams boss!' she shot back as she mock flounced out.

Phil went to the big whiteboard that covered nearly half the room, and gazed at the names and the red lines that crisscrossed, linking nearly everyone to everyone else. It didn't make any sense at the moment. He got a marker and put a big red ring round Robert Trevis's name. He was dead to them now, and had taken his secrets to the grave. There was a great deal of money washing round within the lines, but he couldn't see the direction of the flow. Common sense said it headed up the chart to the top men, the masterminds. They wouldn't be doing it for charity. Suddenly he began to see a pattern and could hardly contain his excitement until Claire came back.

She walked in carrying coffee and muffins and joined him at the board.

'Look at this,' said Phil, as he feverishly marked new lines linking names, while scrubbing out others. He added notes of other recent criminal activities that had been happening at various points.

'Yes, I can see what you're getting at now,' said Claire

chewing her bottom lip. 'This is a cell system,' and she grabbed a blue marker and began drawing big rings around groups of names.

'It's almost like different gangs are doing different parts of the same job. So if it's a murder, a group here are involved, if it's a heist, maybe it's this group,' she pointed with the pen. 'I'll get Rob or Nigel up here with their maths wizardry and see if they can run it through on a programme and make sense of it.' She clapped Phil on the shoulder.

'See I'm clever as well,' he said smugly.

'Don't push it,' she said, cocking an eyebrow, and picked up a phone to alert the tame techs.

In another part of the police station, Jack Havers and his buddy, Ron, were enjoying a cup of tea and an all-day breakfast in the canteen.

'So, Gittins lived up to his name then?' Ron asked through a mouthful of toast and beans.

'Sure did. Not a "Good work" or even a smile as I handed the stuff in,' responded Jack, looking at his rapidly congealing plate. Jack was a bit despondent, as he thought he had shown some initiative. It might amount to nothing in the end, but he didn't want to be doing "house to house" for the rest of his days on the force. He was supposed to be "fast track", and had left University with a good 2:1 and had high hopes for his future. These were fading fast, as the realities of the real world kicked in. He was going to give himself a year and if his plans didn't come to fruition, then he'd cast about for some other career. Overnight, he had given some thought to the robbery that was currently being splashed over the media.

It was strange that there had been CCTV footage but no

identifications had been made, and then there was the cold-blooded killing in the corner shop, and the girl that had been abducted. They hadn't got anything from her, but amnesia wasn't uncommon when the trauma was great enough. He had read somewhere that the mind shuts down and will block out anything too repugnant. He wondered if anything had come back to her in the meantime. No-one had interviewed her again, as everyone was tied up with the robbery of the Hoard. It was always the case that the big media stories were the ones that attracted most of their time, and other stuff got side-lined.

Maybe he would pay her another visit in his own time, just for a friendly chat and a coffee. He'd let her know that the thin blue line hadn't forgotten her. He made a mental note to give her a visit this evening, after the shift had finished.

Another job to do popped into his mind. His laptop had fried its chips, and he wondered if one of the tech guys in the basement would give it the once over before he went and bought another. There was lots of stuff he didn't want to lose stored on it, and he couldn't access it. Yes, he should go and ask first, as he did have a nodding acquaintance with a bloke called Nigel, and had shared a coffee or two with him in the canteen.

'Well if you're not going to eat that, can I?' said Ron eying up the hardly touched breakfast.

'Be my guest, though I don't know where you put it.' Jack pushed the plate across the table. 'You'll have a heart attack at this rate.'

'You know something Jack? I don't really care,' said Ron resignedly. 'I've got a few more years to do, and then what? Wife died three years ago, eldest daughter in Australia, and the youngest, God knows where. Run off with some builder when me and her mum said he wasn't her type. Just upped and left. So couldn't care less, mate.'

Jack didn't really know what to say about this revelation. Ron had never spoken about his family, but a lot of hurt and bitterness came through. He looked down and fiddled with a stray teaspoon not willing to look into Ron's eyes. He didn't know how to respond, or even if a response was appropriate.

'Come on, don't let my troubles weigh you down,' said Ron rubbing the last piece of fried bread through the baked bean sauce and popping it into his mouth. 'A nice big breakfast like that saves me having to cook in the evenings, sets me up for the day.' He patted his full stomach. 'Better go and see what Git has got for us today; least it's not raining!'

The conference room was crammed with people and the windows were beginning to mist up. Chief Gittins was there presiding over the gathering, and Jack and Ron stood quietly at the back.

Chief Gittins began his weekly spiel in his dry monotone. 'It's been a busy couple of weeks on the patch, and we have just had three stolen cars turn up on waste ground and in the canal. That's a job for uniform,' he said, glancing at the little knot by the door. 'Also, CCTV and bits of a mobile have been retrieved from the robbery site and are with forensics now.'

He said this and glanced at Jack with an almost mute apology for not giving him the credit.

Ron kicked Jack's ankle.

'Now I'd like you to welcome Claire Watson, who is going to give us a quick rundown of what we need to be looking out for. Eyes and ears on the street will crack this case,' Chief Gittins said almost jovially.

Claire took centre stage and clicked a mouse, and a big

screen lit up with a seemingly incomprehensible network of names, linked with lines of different colours.

'Now, I know it looks confusing but it seems that we have different cells doing different jobs, i.e. one group drives the cars, another kills whoever gets in their way, etc.'

She clicked again and some faces appeared. They were fuzzy and grainy, taken from CCTV. 'We haven't had time to clean these images up yet, but these are the low life that did for the corner shop guy. We don't know if it's linked yet, but it seems a bit of an overkill for something that wasn't a robbery.'

Someone sniggered and was shot a glance by Gittins; they quickly shut up.

'None of these guys seems to match any known criminal and no DNA shows up on any database, but we're tracking the movements of the car and it links to the disused factory which blew up. The car, as usual, hasn't been traced and was stolen earlier that week. Someone will probably find it burnt out on some waste ground eventually. They certainly know how to clean up after themselves. So, sorry we haven't got more to give you at the moment on this, but the medical examiner says the drivers of the van with the Staffs hoard on board both died at the scene.'

Everyone leaned forward expectantly.

'One man, now known as Richard Thomas, died instantly from a gunshot wound from point blank range, to the back of the head. Ballistics is working on that now, seeing if there's a match with the corner shop murder. The other man, now known as Keith Brown, actually died from choking. No marks on the body, except for some on the arms when he was dragged from the van. But it was a vicious attack and we are working on other links for you to follow up. Thank you.'

She stepped down and Gittins spoke from where he stood.

'Get to it, copies of the faces are at the back. Let's see if we can put some names to them.'

Ron leaned across and picked up two sheets of paper with the black and white images on. 'Not a lot to go on, but I suppose we'll be on the canal cars.'

They joined the others shuffling out.

Their day went as they had guessed. The canal cars were hauled off to forensics to see if there was any link with the robbery, but as they were full of dirty canal water no-one held their breath. Jack and Ron interviewed all three of the owners of the cars to see if they had seen anyone or anything, and they flashed the CCTV pictures for any glimmer of recognition. Nothing at all. It was a complete blank.

After the shift end Jack made his way to Ms Black's new flat, but it was silent. He also had Rory's address and made his way there. By this time, it was getting on for seven o'clock, and he began to question what he was doing.

Lights blazed out from the flat in the pre-war house, and he felt a bit more optimistic as he rang the bell.

'Rory? Rory McGovern?' Jack asked, as the door was cracked open on a safety chain.

'Yep, who wants to know?' a voice said from behind the door.

Jack found his warrant card and offered it round the door. 'I would just like to ask Ms Black a few questions. It'll just take ten minutes, if she's in?'

'O.k., I'll let you in.' The door closed, then re-opened, and Jack was allowed in.

Ellie sat drinking a cup of coffee and looked up as Jack walked in.

Rory reassured Ellie that it was all right, as Jack was a policeman and only wanted a few minutes to catch up.

'Sadly, Ms Black we are currently pursuing all lines of enquiry, but as yet haven't made any arrests with regard to the shooting at the corner shop or your injuries. I hope you are fully recovered from your ordeal?' said Jack, after formally introducing himself.

'Yes, thank you, all recovered now. Feeling much better and going back to work soon. Actually, I'm having a change and have got a new job at the British Library. So, you know how it is… New job, new flat, new life.'

Jack pulled out the papers with the photos on and offered them across to her.

'I know you suffered traumatic amnesia after the ordeal, but I wondered if you recognise any of these faces?'

Ellie blanched as she saw the blurry images of Karl and Lemon man and her hand shook.

'I… I… don't know.'

'Look carefully and see if you can remember anything at all.' Jack had noted her reaction to the photos and at this point he didn't believe Ellie anymore. 'Thank you anyway for your time,' he said formally.

He let his gaze wander round the room, and his eye settled on a computer array in the corner of the comfortable living room.

'That's impressive.' he said to Rory. 'Wish I'd got that at home.'

Rory looked at his baby and smiled. 'I do tech support at the College and it's all I've really been interested in since a kid.' He walked over and motioned Jack to join him. Jack duly obliged and pulled up a chair, as Rory began to put the machine through its paces. For the next half an hour, Rory and Jack made friends as they found common ground. Jack's degree was in Maths, and Rory's was in Computing. Jack told Rory about his computer going down and Rory offered Jack some time at the weekend to go with him to buy another, and he offered to do some "tweaking" on it to make life more interesting.

Ellie sat almost forgotten at this point and she gazed at the photos.

CHAPTER SIX

That night when Jack Havers the cop had called round had given Ellie a bit of a shock. She honestly thought they had forgotten all about her, but obviously, she was wrong. From then on, she kept to her prescribed plans and moved into her new flat. It was quite nice actually, and Rory had put extra security on the windows and doors so she felt more relaxed. It was all coming together. Ellie had gone back to work and handed in her notice, and only had a few more days to go before she left. Her workmates were planning a party for her during her last lunchtime; she wasn't supposed to know, but secrets like that can't really be kept in such a small working environment. Ellie wouldn't spoil it for them for the world.

On her way home that night, Ellie bumped into—more like fell over—Manny. He was going home walking along in a daze and so was she, till they met in a tangle of arms and legs. They extricated themselves and checked for damage.

'Oh! So sorry. It is Manny? Manny Chandra?' Ellie said, peering at him in the gloom. 'It's me, Ellie. I am so very sorry about what happened to your dad.' Ellie didn't really know how to go on, as she saw tears gathering at the corners of his eyes.

'Yes, Mum and I live with my uncle and his family now.

It's not the same; I don't suppose it ever will be.' Manjeet looked down at his shoes.

Ellie's heart went out to him.

'I liked your dad a lot Manny. He was one of the good guys. I went to the funeral and it was lovely to see so many people thought so much of him. I know that's not much of a consolation, but we all loved him. I was the one in the shop when it happened, and if it means anything to you, he never knew it was coming or even felt anything.'

Manjeet looked at Ellie as if willing her to go on.

She plunged in, 'Did you get the note?'

'What note?'

Ellie was committed now. 'The note that the—'she searched for a word, '—intruders left for you.'

He looked blank. 'The police cleared everything up and I never went into the shop. Neither did Mum, as she was out at the time.'

'You know you were away at this party in Wales with your mates at the time? Well, these blokes left you a message. It was about being too long since they had seen you, or something like that.'

Ellie would have liked to have said that Manjeet looked blank, but he didn't. She knew what must have happened. The note was on the counter and as Ali fell forward it must have been obliterated, and it had probably ended up coated in blood, along with the rest of the stuff on the counter.

'Look Manny, I'm in the same position as you. I don't know who these guys are, or what they want, but they seem to be able to control everyone they meet, usually by threats and force. What do you have to do with them?'

Wrong question, as Manny gave her a look of pure terror,

hefted his bag onto his shoulder and ran away down the street.

Ellie went home and pondered what Manny could possibly have done, or rather have to have done, to incite such retribution on his family. It was almost like a gangland, tit for tat, murder but Ellie couldn't imagine Manny as an assassin.

She would mull it over with Rory this evening, as he was coming round. He still didn't like the idea of Ellie living alone and couldn't see the point, as they lived together for weeks on end sometimes. Ellie would never get him to understand that as much as she loved him, she didn't, at this point in her life, actually want to marry him.

Any lifetime commitment for the next forty or so years just scared her. Sometimes, she needed her own company, she felt happy being alone, never lonely. Until she could get her head round that perhaps she was destined not to marry. Rory wouldn't wait forever, Ellie knew that, but right now this was what was good for her and she wasn't going to marry just to please him.

Jack had also spent time thinking about Ellie and Rory. He was convinced that they knew something more than they were letting on. It was good for him that he had become friends with Rory through their shared passion for computers, but Jack would be the first to admit that Rory's knowledge far outstripped his own. It wasn't totally self-serving that Jack nurtured Rory as a friend, but he carefully gathered and stored away tiny snippets of information that Rory sometimes let slip.

He had also made the time to go and seek out Nigel down in the basement, and what a revelation that had proved to be. Nigel had been only too happy to help, and Jack's laptop was now in bits on a workbench.

The big white board with all the lines and links had fascinated Jack, and he could see where the investigation was going and why. Nigel and Phil had explained it to him and Jack couldn't help but begin to apply mathematics to the problem.

'Nigel, have you ever wondered if you could have a stab at predicting where the next big robbery will be?' Jack asked Nigel.

Nigel looked at Jack and knitted his brows. 'Not really. What are you suggesting?'

'Well, if it could be possible to work back, say five years and look at all the major robberies. Not the small stuff like shops and supermarkets, you could even take out all the house burglaries, unless there was a work of art stolen—and then it may be possible to link all of them together.'

Jack began drawing notations on the board.

'It may be that this crew has been responsible for most of them, maybe stealing to order, as nothing has ever turned up. Or maybe something in the way they were carried out will show up. I don't really know but I can devise a programme, and we'll try to input the data and see what turns up. I'm going to need a bigger job than my laptop though.'

He glanced ruefully at the disparate components.

'So what you're saying is that if we apply "Game Theory" to the robberies, then it will certainly describe the behaviour, but maybe also explain and predict it?' said Nigel. 'A player will always play to maximize the wins, but sometimes people can be irrational. But I agree there doesn't seem to be anything irrational about what is happening here. It's worth a try, but it's going to take some time. Want to help?'

'Okay, but I can only do it after shifts, as I daren't upset Gittins. I can see that we may come up with nothing, but it could be predictive. I'll have to get my maths head on again, as it seems a long time since I've used it, but I'll think round it and see you tomorrow.'

Jack wandered out, his laptop forgotten.

Ellie's time at the library had now expired and the party for her leaving had been a success. Many promises of keeping in touch were made and tentative dates arranged, most of which would be buried without trace in the minutiae of life. Marcia had shed a tear, and she was one friend that Ellie vowed she would keep in touch with. In fact, she had promised that when she was fully ensconced in the job, she would get permission and give Marcia a guided tour of the archives. Marcia was over the moon and said she would hold Ellie to that.

Walking home, Ellie wondered what she should wear at her new job on Monday morning, and even what time she should arrive. Details like that had never really been explained to her, and she was struck again at the speed at which her life could change, and also how her path could be smoothed to suit someone else's whims. She got home without incident, but couldn't help looking for Manny as she walked.

Tonight, was to be a night out, and Rory had promised a meal and a pub disco after. It would be nice to let her hair down and have a drink and a dance. Not that either Rory or herself were any great shakes on the dance floor, but after a few drinks she let herself go and became a disco diva! It would be fun, and she had even splashed out on a new dress from French Connection; a bit pricy, but it looked really good. Maybe a bit short, but what the hell, she was going out to enjoy herself.

After a shower and a rather more liberal application of make-up than usual, Ellie awaited Rory.

'Hi, hun,' she gave Rory a kiss as she opened the door. 'Don't you look good enough to eat? I like the new jacket.' It made him look like one of those Armani male models, all chiselled with smouldering eyes.

'Hey, babe, you don't look too bad yourself,' he replied and Ellie gave him a twirl and grabbed her bag and coat.

'Where we off to then? You haven't given me much of a clue, but I know I haven't eaten since the nibbles at the office party and I'm starving'.

'I know you like Italian and I know you sometimes like the soppy stuff, so we're going to that restaurant… Luigi's. The new place with the candles in the bottles on the tables.'

Who said romance was dead? Ellie gave him a quick peck on the cheek at that point, and linked her arm through his, thinking how lucky she was.

The restaurant was perfect, with the guttering candles and, more to the point, an extensive menu. They decided to go the whole hog and have all three courses. It was after the antipasti that things started to go a bit wrong. Ellie was sipping a glass of ice-cold wine when Rory started to fumble in his pocket, and he brought out a box.

'I wanted to ask you something tonight,' he said, reaching over and holding her hand.

Oh God no! she thought to herself, as she knew what was coming next.

'I want to ask you to marry me, Ellie. I know you don't want to right away but we're so good together and I love you so much, and I want to look after you and be with you all the time,' he began to ramble.

Ellie hadn't got a clue what to say. How could she extricate herself from this without destroying him? Ellie supposed she wanted to have her cake and eat it, but she really couldn't see herself in a lifetime commitment at the moment. The wine tasted thin and sour.

He opened the box and a ring with two diamonds flanking a sapphire winked back in the candlelight. It was lovely and Ellie didn't know how he had afforded it. She gulped some more of the wine and in a split second took the line of least resistance.

'It's lovely, Rory but you shouldn't have.' Ellie saw his face fall. 'I mean, I will accept your proposal and I'll wear your ring with love, but marriage won't be just yet.' She forced a smile.

He took the ring out of the box and put it on her finger, and it weighed a ton.

Luigi bustled over at this point, effusive, in the Italian way, and cracked a bottle of champagne and they all drank to seal the deal.

What had she done? Ellie was committed now and she was destined to be Mrs. McGovern. She liked Rory a lot and couldn't imagine her life without him, but did she love him enough to be a good wife? Could she cook meals and wash socks and maybe look after some little McGovern's along the way? What did the real Ellie want? She wasn't sure.

The rest of the meal was a trial for her. She ate ashes.

They walked out into the night and began to amble to the pub, with Rory holding her hand tightly as if she would run away.

'I suppose you wouldn't consider moving in with me?' he asked.

'Oh Rory, you know what I'm going to have to say to that one—just let me get my head round this first,' and she held her hand up to the street light and saw the diamonds twinkle back at her.

In the shadows a dark figure watched the pair, and then turned away.

They did go to the pub and Ellie did have too much to drink; she also thought she probably made an ass out of herself on the dance floor, but in the end, she enjoyed it. It was great just to let her hair down and have a good time with a good companion.

The big day dawned and Ellie set off for work to arrive in good time. She had dressed very conservatively, mainly in black and white, and had taken some lunch with her just in case she couldn't get out to the shops.

The first week was something of an induction week, as Ellie began to find her way around the enormous basement. She spent time in the conservation labs, and learned much of what went into keeping old manuscripts together for the next generation. Lots of them, when they were taken apart for repair were scanned, so that deterioration over the years could be spotted. Also, a big part of her job was actually finding stuff. Luckily for Ellie, she understood the system of cataloguing used and could use the computer system in a very short space of time.

Ellie didn't meet Mr Fynch, the Chief Archivist, again until the end of the first week. He stuck his head round the door of her shared office space and asked if she was getting on okay. Ellie replied that it was a fabulous job, and just hoped she was living up to the task. He nodded, mumbled something incoherent and bumbled off.

Jeanette, the woman that sat opposite said, 'You're

honoured. I don't think I've seen him down here for years.'
She took a bite of her sandwich.

'Well, he seems to be a nice guy, maybe a bit remote, but I suppose he's got other things on his mind.'

'Yep, we're going to be working on that big exhibition soon; you know, the one in Oxford. They've asked for a pile of stuff and it's going to be a logistical nightmare getting it all there in one piece. So brace yourself. It may be that you're going to have to travel with it and all the inventories. That'll be nice, a day out in Oxford.'

Ellie's sandwich was poised halfway to her mouth.

'Me go with the collection? I couldn't possibly—you should go instead. You know lots more about it than me.'

'Don't kid yourself, that lot at the Ashmolean know more about it than you and me put together. It's only a matter of putting ticks on pieces of paper as you hand it over.' She peered at Ellie over her specs.

Ellie was practically speechless. 'Well, if you're sure?'

'It will be the biggest showing of early medieval manuscripts ever in the country, so there will be lots to find and pack up. Might be a bit of overtime, we'll just see how it goes.'

They began the next day, locating manuscripts and making inventories. The artefacts went down to the labs to be packed and stored at the correct temperature and humidity ready for transit. It was a delight to handle the books and folios and although Ellie couldn't read them, it was the colours on the pages that reached out to her. She vowed to do some more reading round the subject of medieval paints and pigments to further her knowledge. Sometimes, she wished she had perhaps paid more attention at college, but better late than never. Ellie had asked for and been given some books about conservation techniques, and had thought of going on a course as she was in the right place to get some practice. Everything about this job was interesting and she couldn't wait to get there every morning.

In the police station, the lights were beginning to hurt Jack's eyes as he gazed at the computer screen, trying to input still more data into his programme. It had taken a week to devise, and it was far from perfect. Nigel was wired on coffee, and was trawling through streams of past and present cases to pull out the relevant ones for the exercise.

'Do you think this is going to work, Nige?' Jack asked again.

'Don't know 'till we do it, right? That's what we said at the beginning, but I honestly didn't think it would be this hard. There doesn't seem to be any way of filtering them out, as we've got to go national for any really big thefts or robberies.'

'So what have we got so far?'

'I've got forty-three big cases so far, where nothing has turned up over the past five years.'

'Let's give them a go then and see where it takes us,' said Jack, rubbing his eyes. 'I can't stay too much longer, as I'm on shift again at 6 o'clock in the morning and I'm already knackered.'

Nigel looked at Jack. 'Sorry mate, I forgot all about that. Look, let me give Phil a ring, and I'll say we're near to a breakthrough and see if he can get Git to give you a week in here to crack it.

'Brilliant if you could, but I doubt he'd wear it for a second. You know how he likes us uniform out on the street being seen, community policing and all that. All I've done in the last week is fetch cars out of canals and crowd control in the freezing cold,' Jack chuckled sardonically.

Nigel had already reached for the phone and was explaining to Phil what they were doing. He nodded once or twice, then replaced the phone.

'Looks like its sorted, Jack mate. Phil thinks it's worth a punt and says to go for it, and he'll square it with Git. So away we go with the midnight oil and all that.'

They looked at each other and smiled.

'I'm still knackered though. Could we start again in the morning? I'll come in early, normal shift time at six and we'll go from there and start inputting. My brain will work a bit better with some sleep. You probably never need to.' Jack smiled as he rose.

'Too right, I'm like a vampire; I'm definitely a night owl. See you!' Nigel waved a hand at Jack's departure and turned back to the screen.

The next morning, Jack was as good as his word and arrived at six o'clock. Nigel was just as he left him, surrounded by a litter of coffee cups and sandwich wrappers. Nigel stretched to take some kinks out of his shoulders and turned to Jack,

'I did manage to get a few hours last night. I kipped down in the cells, as it was that old guy on duty and there weren't many drunks. So we all ready to go?'

Jack nodded and flexed his fingers.

'I've now got about seventy cases to look at. I haven't discarded any yet but we can now decide the parameters for filtering,' said Nigel.

The pair were hard at it when Robert, Phil and Claire

wandered in at 8.30 a.m., and Phil performed the introductions. Robert said, 'I'll try and de-bug the Trevis laptop then and finish the phone, but I don't hold out any high hopes for either. I've managed to get some numbers but they all seem to check out, and the car belongs to a leasing firm. Robbie didn't seem to be paying his own bills as the money was coming from Morgan Enterprises for the car, but that's not unusual for a perk of the job.'

Phil asked, 'Any luck with the cleaning firm; you know, "Body pick up dot com"?'

'Not had time to get onto it yet boss, sorry,' Robert replied.

'Claire and I will pay them a little visit today and have a look at their log sheets. Any luck with the computer analysis, Nigel?'

'Nothing yet, boss. Jack and I have only just trawled the crime database and got some possible cases. Jack is honing up his programme to shove this lot through; then we may, or may not, have something for you. Depends if the Gods are smiling,' said Nigel, and Jack nodded.

Everyone filtered away and Jack and Nigel began to trawl the case files and decide whether or not to input them. By lunchtime, they didn't seem to have made much headway and both seemed a bit daunted by the pile of work ahead.

'What say we give it neck for an hour and go and have a walk and a sandwich?' Nigel said to Jack. 'Just to clear the brain.' Jack reached for his coat and they walked out into the cold, clear air. As they strolled, they chatted about the merits of the latest graphic cards for gaming, and whether SSD was better than HDD drives. Jack told Nigel about his friendship with Rory, and how they had ended up gaming online as a team once a week.

'You should watch it there, as they may both have something to do with the corner shop incident, and I don't think Git is going to look kindly on that one. He doesn't seem to like you much anyway,' said Nigel.

'I know, but it was only Ellie that was involved somehow and no-one has taken much notice of that fact since she was kidnapped. Anyway, Rory had nothing to do with it,' Jack said, as they turned into the park.

It wasn't a park in the conventional sense, just a space with a few benches that some ardent conservation group had lobbied for years ago, but it was a welcome splash of green, shadowed by the grey buildings.

'Hey there's Ellie now.' Jack waved to the small figure huddled on a bench, feeding a crust to a lone pigeon.'

'Hey! Ellie, how you doing? This is Nigel; I now work with him doing some maths stuff.' They sat, flanking her for warmth.

'Hi Jack, nice to see you again. Sorry I've always been on my way out when you've called to see Rory, but those games aren't my cup of tea really,' she said apologetically.

She cocked her head at Nigel. 'I suppose you're into them in a big way as well?'

'Well, yes I suppose I am, and I was going to ask Jack if he would have a word with Rory to let me onto the team. It's more fun playing that way.'

Jack asked Ellie if she had remembered anything yet, after assuring her that Nigel was on the force like himself. She said no, and quickly changed the subject.

'I've also started a new job at the British Library and it's great. I'm really enjoying it and I've just been given a job of travelling with a large collection to Oxford. Just to deliver it, of course, but it's really exciting and I can't wait.'

Jack and Nigel exchanged glances.

'When's this Ellie?' said Jack carefully.

'I think its next Thursday, but it's really busy at the moment, trying to get it all packed up and sorted. It's absolutely priceless and it's never all been seen in the same place at the same time before,' said Ellie breathlessly, and glanced at her watch. 'God, am I really that late? Sorry guys really got to dash—may see you briefly round Rory's tonight then?'

She sketched a wave and almost trotted out of the park.

'What do you make of that then Jack?' Nigel said, as they resumed their walk. 'Could this be the next target?'

'Or maybe not,' replied Jack. 'Maybe we're just hypersensitive about this and imagining it all. We can't put the place on full alert unless we've got something concrete to offer. Just think what the reaction would be from Git if we did that. We'd be security guards before you could draw breath if we were wrong, and have big lectures about wasting police time.'

'Okay, I get your point, Jack, but let's not forget it when we run the programme,' said Nigel thoughtfully.

CHAPTER SEVEN

Nigel and Jack wandered to the café and picked up their supplies. Nothing different from what could be had in the canteen at a reduced price, but it was the walk and the fresh air that was important. They pondered the new questions as they made their way back to the enclosed bunker type basement.

Jack sat, poised at his keyboard, and began to input the details of the cases as Nigel read them out. Each one took quite a long time, as all relevant fields had to be discussed; particularly if there were any eye witness accounts with descriptions of the perpetrators. By the time they could do no more it was gathering dusk outside, and they had managed fifteen cases.

'I've had enough now, my brain's addled,' said Jack, and Nigel nodded. 'I'll give Rory a ring and see if he wants another bod on the team for tonight, if you're free, that is?'

'Good one, see if he does, I'll bring a few cans and we'll crucify the opposition,' Nigel smiled wolfishly.

Jack dug out his phone and after a few minutes' chat, he gave the thumbs up to Nigel.

'You're in mate, so see you at 7.30 ish, here's the address', he said, scribbling on a piece of paper.

They met on the steps of the flat, and Jack rang the bell

and was buzzed in. The door opened and Ellie came out, just leaving, with two bags. Ever the gentlemen, they both stood aside for her to pass, but it was a squeeze. As Jack pressed himself by the wall, he felt Ellie's body as she shuffled past. Their eyes met and Jack felt suddenly uncomfortable and Ellie flushed bright red. He bent down to help her with the bags to cover his confusion, and she muttered her thanks and looked away.

'Nice looking girl, isn't she,' said Nigel. 'Lucky bloke, hope he realizes it.'

Jack murmured something in the affirmative, and they went in and lost themselves in a game of war and mayhem on the internet. They played well as a team and moved up the rankings. Nigel had played before and knew a few shortcuts, and had a few tricks up his sleeve.

Rory was well impressed and invited them round again the following week, to play on the newly minted 'Shadow Wolf' team.

Next day, Phil called a meeting of the team and referred back the call on the Cleaning Services Company. Interestingly enough, it was owned by Morgan Enterprises but their log sheets didn't show any visit to Mr. Robert Trevis's flat the day in question. They had flashed the photo of the van parked outside and asked if the descriptions matched anyone working there, but no-one owned up to anything. There were pictures on the staff sheets, but no-one matched the men Phil and Claire had seen. So a resounding blank was drawn, but the company said it would go through the CCTV and see if any vans had been moved that night. They promised to let Phil know, but he wasn't hopeful about their co-operation.

Robert reported back that the phone had produced nothing of interest, and he had come to the conclusion that there must have been two phones and that one was missing. The laptop, however, was different. There were e-mails that showed Robbie was mixed up in something and he had alluded to the Staffs Hoard, but the server had been routed through every country under the sun and he couldn't trace who the recipient was. Robert said he was going to do a bit more digging, with Phil's permission, that would only last another half a day, as he could see that Jack and Nigel seriously needed some help with their task.

Now it was Jack and Nigel's turn, and they outlined the protocols for the search. It was the data input that was taking the time and they welcomed Robert's help. They all set to, and only surfaced when Claire announced that Gittins was going to do a press conference, with the vain hope someone would come forward with some useful information. It was a bit of a begging mission, but he had to be careful that it didn't sound as if the investigation had stalled. On top of that, there was the murder at the corner shop and the killings of the van drivers to investigate, so the force was stretched to its limits. One more big crime, and everyone knew Gittins' job would be on the line. Not that it would worry anyone unduly, as the Chief was not well liked at all.

They ended up inputting some fifty cases and Jack eventually declared the job done. He started the programme to first search for geographical locations, and the map showed the main clusters around London and its environs. There were one or two anomalies, but for the sake of speed they had to discard those and Nigel deleted those cases from the database. The next search was for similarities in eye witness accounts and possible identity matches with the names still marked up on the office white board. The programme started to churn its way through the mountain of data, and Phil suggested they call it a day and see what it had thrown up tomorrow. They left the machines doing their job and went their separate ways.

The next day, everyone came in early to see what had been processed through the night. They were all excited when they saw there was a definite pattern to the high-grade robberies. Many had eyewitness accounts that tallied, and the MO's were almost carbon copies of each other.

Nigel and Jack high fived each other, and Nigel said, 'I've got to hand it to you, mate, that's a pretty smoky programme you've got there. Look at this result, guys.'

The others crowded round and Jack explained what the analysis showed.

'It's able to crunch the data, but also to predict what possible scenarios might happen next. There's one thing showing up here, pulsing red—' he pointed with a pen, '—it looks as if the computer predicts there will be a robbery of some sort of rare books or manuscripts. It looks like someone is a collector of fine art of all sorts.'

Jack and Nigel swapped a look.

Jack spoke for them both. 'We know of a rare book collection that's being moved soon, and could be a possible target.'

'Give me the details, Jack,' said Phil, and everyone sat down. 'Let's hear it from the top.'

Jack and Nigel began the story about Ellie and how he had visited because it could be a lead, and how he didn't believe her story of amnesia. Nigel got to the part about playing the computer game, and Claire rolled her eyes skywards.

'I'm going to call you Shadow Wolves from now on; you do know that,' she laughed. 'Boys with toys. Don't you ever grow up? But seriously, I think you've got something here and it's worth doing something about it, and taking the risk of it all going pear shaped.'

Phil joined in. 'She's right. We're going to look like idiots if they do steal this shipment and we're caught with our pants down. So, any suggestions please?'

Robert chimed in, 'What about if we put Claire in there with Ellie and she wears a wire? Then we can do stealth pursuit and she can be our eyes and ears in the van. If nothing happens, then we've lost a day. If it does kick off, then we're in the middle of it, so to speak.'

'Good one, Rob. What does everyone else think?'

'What about me?' said Claire. 'I'm going to be the one in the thick of it, don't I get a say? I'll go in there as long as I've got a weapon, as these guys tend to shoot first and ask questions later.'

'Good point. I think maybe we should all be equipped with full tactical gear,' Phil said, and he looked at Jack. 'Have you done firearms training yet?'

'No, but I can shoot as it has always been a hobby of mine when I've got the cash. Mainly rifles, but I've had a pop or two with pistols.'

'You aren't cleared to carry a service issue pistol, but we'll get you a jacket anyway and you can be in the back-up car. Oh,' Phil paused, 'I don't think I have to tell you all not to breathe a word to anyone about this—particularly not Ellie or her boyfriend.' He smiled. 'I think we'll call it Operation Shadow Wolf,' and dodged a paper ball flung with deadly accuracy from Claire.

Today was Ellie's big day. She was going to travel with the collection to Oxford, and besides the driver, there was going to be someone else with her; she assumed it was some sort of rare books expert from the Ashmolean. The journey was to take about two hours, so there would time to see a bit of Oxford before starting home. Claire had been introduced as the Oxford counterpart for the movement of the shipment.

'Hi, I'm Claire, nice to meet you. Sorry I don't know your name.'

'I'm Ellie,' she said as she took the proffered hand. It was a very firm grip for a female, and Ellie sized up Claire and took in the very trim figure that screamed of work outs in the gym and long runs on a regular basis. Ellie was a little envious, not at the results but at the dedication to keep going after the initial enthusiasm had worn off.

It was a cold day outside but Ellie was a little surprised that Claire had elected to keep her heavy coat on indoors, but as they were leaving soon the thought quickly passed her by. She led Claire down through the basement, and kept up a desultory chat about the weather, and Claire seemed an attentive companion. Once in the van Claire put Ellie between herself and the driver— "for warmth", she said —and they set off. The driver's name was Philip and Ellie couldn't recall having seen him before, but it was a big place and her facial recognition wasn't the best in the world. He was a good driver and a chatty companion, so the journey went well as they made good time exiting London.

It was when they were about halfway there that Phil tensed up and said, 'We've got a tail,' and Claire leaned over Ellie to get a better view out of the offside wing mirror.

'How long?'

'About five miles now, but they keep swapping with the white van, so we may have two.'

Ellie looked at one, then the other, and said, 'What's going on?'

Phil was speeding up, but said, 'Not going to spook you, but we aren't from the Library. We're here for your protection and to look after the cargo in the back.' He jerked his head to the space at the rear, which was stuffed full of boxes tied down securely.

'Why?' said Ellie, and it was all she could manage.

Claire said, ''cos we think that an attempt is going to be made today to steal this lot before it gets to Oxford, and we're here to make sure that doesn't happen.'

Ellie's eyes flicked from one to the other, and they appeared to have shed their other personas and were now in their element, with the adrenaline flowing.

'I suppose it couldn't just be any old van and car, could it, that happens to be going the same way we are?' she said.

'Not a chance,' said Phil, 'and they're only after one thing. I hate to say this, but they may have been people you've met before.' Ellie went rigid and Claire put her hand on her arm.

'We know that you haven't told us the whole truth about what happened before Ellie, but now's the time. Any information could literally save our skins.'

Ellie took two deep breaths to calm herself and spilled the whole story out.

'Sorry to stop you, but Claire, get onto the back-up car— we've got trouble, big time,' said Phil.

She nodded and spoke into the collar of her big coat, and

as her hair swung back Ellie noticed an almost invisible ear piece hiding there.

'It's a go, affirmative,' she announced, as the tailing car suddenly accelerated and shot past them. It angled in towards their bonnet and Phil took evasive action by steering up a small side road. The tyres screeched on the slick tarmac and went into a skid. Phil corrected it and fishtailed down the road.

'We're off the main road,' Claire shouted into her mike and added, 'I don't know where we are, activating the GPS now. Affirmative,' she announced, 'they've got us.'

'Who's got us?' said Ellie tensely.

'Our backup guys who're following us, so don't worry,' Claire reassured Ellie.

'Yeah, but I am worried, worried sick in fact. I'm petrified, as I've heard that these blokes kill anything that moves,' Ellie shouted as the van sped through country lanes, whipping twigs off hedges they careered past.

Phil rounded a sharp bend and stood on the brakes. Up ahead there was a farm tractor blocking the road, and the van slid sideways and smacked the tractor hard. The jolt whacked Phil's head on the side door pillar and he went motionless, held in place by the seat belt. Claire was thrown sideways onto Ellie.

The white van that had chased them drew up, and out got two big men carrying some sort of revolvers. They yanked the van door open and motioned Claire and Ellie out. They obliged and stood on the verge.

'Which one of you is Miss Black?'

Ellie and Claire looked at each other, and Ellie knew that Claire was going to try and take her place.

'It's me,' Ellie said, stepping forwards, not looking back

at Claire.

'Okay you,' he pointed at Ellie, 'get in the van. Boss wants to see you. You,' he said pointing the gun at Claire, 'goodbye.' He pulled the trigger and Claire collapsed in a heap on the wet muddy verge.

Ellie covered her face with her hands and a strangled sob escaped her as she climbed into the van. She kept her face covered as they loaded the boxes into the back. The tractor was moved and the library van, with Phil still in it, was shoved off the road into a ditch. Claire was left at the roadside.

'Hands down Miss Black,' and as she complied, a rough black bag that smelt of engine oil was pulled over her head. Her hands were cuffed in front of her and the van rocked as it began to move off.

So where was the backup team and how come I get to be kidnapped a second time? thought Ellie. It's just not possible. Lightning just doesn't strike twice in the same place. At least I'm still alive, poor Claire, she thought and stifled a sob.

Robert and Jack had hidden their car in a field and scouted round to where they had a good view of the holdup. They crouched in a wet ditch, and Robert was surveying the scene from about a hundred yards. He held up a closed fist, and this signalled Jack to be very quiet. They watched the robbery and execution of Claire. It happened so fast that they hadn't got a plan, unless it was to go in with all guns blazing, but that seemed like a suicide mission.

'Okay, let's go,' said Robert, as the van containing Ellie drove off. He and Jack ran across the ploughed field to where Claire was lying.

They must have broken the record for the sprint and both

were totally breathless when they got there. Robert motioned Jack to have a look at Phil in the van and he crouched down over Claire, ripping away at her coat and jumper.

'Claire, talk to me, stay with me,' Robert called earnestly, and rolled her over onto her side.

'Get your hands off me,' Claire muttered and Robert rocked back on his heels.

'You all right? I can't see any blood.'

Claire slowly sat up. 'I don't think I can breathe in this bloody flak jacket, help me get it off.'

Robert gently eased Claire out of her outer clothes, and the Kevlar had a neatly drilled hole over her heart.

'God, I'm going to have a whopper of a bruise and my ribs hurt like fuck, but I'm okay. How's Phil?'

They both turned to see Jack gingerly helping Phil out of the wrecked van. He was unsteady on his feet, and blood was running down his face from a jagged gash on his hairline above his temple. Jack aided him over to the others and Phil sat down carefully on Claire's discarded coat.

'I'll go and get the car and the medi-kit', said Jack and trotted off up the road.

The back-up car soon drove into view, and Jack jumped out and began to quickly patch Phil up with a dressing and tape.

'We've got to follow them and get Ellie back', said Jack, obviously upset.

Claire responded with, 'It's okay. I know where she's going, as I slipped a tracker into her pocket when she wasn't looking. Couldn't rely on the phone GPS, as she's been made to leave her bag in the van. We can track her movements and get a lead on her; then figure out a plan to get her out. Although

I must say,' she said, gazing round, 'we're a pretty sorry bunch at the moment.'

'Got any serious pain killers in that kit, and then we'll start a plan?' said Phil woozily.

'I'll get onto Nigel in the office and get him to meet us here; then we can recce the place. I don't think you're going anywhere with that wound, Phil, so I'll do the second-in-command thing now and you have to stand down. Go back to the office when you've been patched up, and we'll keep you posted at Command Centre,' Claire said with a look that forestalled any arguments.

'I think I'll have to, as I can't walk straight, let alone run at the moment. And this headache is a blinder,' said Phil ruefully.

Claire looked at Phil and said, 'You're going to have to give Jack your gun, as we can't waste any more time. He's not firearms trained, but I'm willing to accept full responsibility if he shoots me by mistake.'

She waited for Phil to slowly work this through his battered brain.

'Okay, so why are you sitting about on your arses? Get to it and get onto Nigel, asap.' He handed his gun to Jack, who checked the magazine. 'Take the car. Nigel can pick me up as he comes past, I'll be okay. Claire, don't forget to put your flak jacket on again and Jack can have mine.' He started to unbuckle himself and Jack went to help.

Phil leaned over and whispered in Jack's ear, 'If anything happens to Claire, I'll personally string you up, got it?' Jack drew a deep breath and just said that he understood, but realized at that moment the depth of feeling Phil held for Claire.

They all piled into the car and Robert drove, with Claire at his side reading the GPS and Jack craning his neck over the passenger seat to try and get a better view. The drive was fast and furious and they drew near to a huge manor house within its own estate. This was where the GPS said Ellie had been taken.

'Lordy, how are we going to get near this place?' said Jack, as the manor was in the middle of acres of parkland and open vistas.

They parked a good way from the house and Claire took charge.

'Okay guys, what have we got? This is going to have to be a night time job, so we need camo. Jack, nice red jacket— turn it inside out as the lining's black. Who's got black socks on?' Both Jack and Robert put their hands in the air. 'Take them off and we'll use them as gloves. Get the idea?' They both nodded and set to work gathering as much equipment as possible.

As the team ransacked the car, Ellie was driven up to the main entrance of the manor. The bag was pulled from her head and she was escorted up the main steps, still handcuffed, into the huge hall. Ellie shook the restraining hands from her and gazed around.

'Wow, this place is definitely better than the last place,' she said appreciatively.

'Glad you approve, Miss Black. I am your host, Alistair Morgan. I'm glad you like the house,' said the tall imposing figure striding across the parquet floor. He held out his hand, and Ellie raised both of hers, cuffed in front of her.

'Please take the cuffs off our guest.' He looked at Karl.

'We don't want her to get the wrong impression of our hospitality.' Karl unlocked the cuffs and quickly absented himself.

'Come this way. You're just in time for tea in the library, unless you would like to freshen up first?' He looked at her muddy clothes, and hair that was a rats' nest, and she was very aware of what a state she was in.

Seizing the opportunity, Ellie replied quickly, 'Yes please, the house is wonderful, but the method of transport leaves a lot to be desired!'

'Carter will show you where to go, if you need anything just say and it'll be yours.'

'A bus ticket home, if you don't mind then', said Ellie looking him in the eye. He gazed back, and he noticed her grey eyes were flecked with violet and gold. They were a very unusual colour. Ellie gazed into his and saw the same iridescent iris, reminiscent of her own. They both stepped back a pace.

Recovering quickly Alistair said, 'Carter, show Miss Black to her room and make sure she has everything she needs. Then show her to the library for tea.'

'Yes, sir,' said the ever-present Carter. 'Come this way Miss, we've tried to put everything you need in there. There are some fresh clothes, I'll have the others cleaned for you if you wish—' he gave her a disapproving glance, '—follow me.'

He led the way up to the first floor and into a palatial suite, and opened the doors of the walk-in wardrobe, full of clothes and shoes for her, all her size. There was a bathroom the size of her flat, and fresh towels and lovely gels and shampoos to sample. It would have been great, if she wasn't a prisoner.

As Carter left, she quickly tried all the windows and looked round to see if there was any way to escape, but everything was locked down tightly. She thought she might as well get cleaned up and have some tea. She picked out some black trousers, a nice cerise top and some sling backs, and they all fitted like a glove. She had a very quick shower, and as if by magic Carter tapped on the door, to escort her down to the library and her host.

Alistair rose to greet her and she was ushered to a chair by the huge fireplace with crackling logs.

'I must admit, Miss Black, that you were not what I imagined. Not at all,' he added thoughtfully. Ellie sat mute and sipped her tea. 'I had uses for you with the rare books, but now I think there is another dimension we have to explore. Tell me a little about yourself, your former life,' he invited.

Ellie thought, *what the hell,* gathered the rest of her thoughts and began to tell him about her childhood.

'I never knew my real parents as I was adopted twenty-three years ago, but it hasn't bothered me at all. I loved my adoptive Mum and Dad, and I was an only child. We did all the usual children's stuff like holidays, and they gave me a good home and I loved them a lot.'

'You are speaking of them in the past tense,' Alistair queried.

'Yes, they both died quite suddenly, a few years apart in their 60's. It was a great shock as you never think your parents are going to leave you, but it was quite quick for both of them. So I've no brothers or sisters, and no cousins or other close relatives at all. I make my own way in the world.' Ellie placed her cup down and leaned forward, 'I also do not like death threats, being abducted, and having my friends shot and killed by thugs like you.' She stood up and put her hands on her hips. 'So you can take your tea and cakes and shove 'em. You can stick your fancy house where you like and if you're going to kill me, I suggest you do it now because I'm not going to be a model prisoner and I'm going to starve myself to death.'

'Bravo, Miss Black, I'm impressed; you really have some spirit. I thought you were a mouse.'

Ellie curled her lip in disgust and marched across to the door. It opened at that moment and in walked Max, known to Ellie as Mr. Fox. She stood, transfixed, for but a moment.

'And as for you, scum—' She drew back her right hand and gave him an open palm slap across his face with all her strength. It resounded like a whip crack, and she shoved past him and disappeared out of the door.

CHAPTER EIGHT

Dusk was falling, and Robert, Claire and Jack had relaxed for a few hours to maintain energy levels before trying to get closer to the house. Jack was now as jumpy as a cat on hot bricks and had to seriously curb his emotions, as he wanted to get going to rescue Ellie. Nigel had contacted them and had successfully picked up Phil, and deposited him at the nearest A&E, where he would get stitches in his scalp. As the gash was near his hairline, Nigel assured Claire that his good looks wouldn't be marred. She had just snorted and not deigned to answer, but her relief that he was all right was palpable.

They had been maintaining a watch on the house and had seen guards, dogs, surveillance cameras; in fact, everything possible to monitor for intruders.

'You know guys, I don't think we're going to be able to do this. We're going to need a whole bloody SAS Team to make any impression on this,' said Claire ruefully.

Jack was aghast. 'No, no you can't mean that. Ellie's in there and they could be torturing her as we speak; we've got to have a go.'

'Yep, and get yourself killed in the process. No Jack, this isn't a suicide mission. We'll wait a bit longer for Nige to turn up. Hopefully he's brought some more gear, and if he has, we'll have a go. No plans till we see what we've got—' Claire eyeballed Jack, '—okay?'

Jack subsided into the back seat and took a deep breath. 'Okay.'

Robert tried to diffuse the tension. 'I hope he's bought some food; I'm starving.' The others both nodded.

Half an hour passed and another car bumped up the rutted track, and Nigel got out with a carrier bag full of sandwiches and a paper tray of coffees. Claire practically kissed him and everyone fell on them ravenously.

'Sod the gear, I knew what you really wanted was a take-out service,' said Nigel and added a report on what had happened to Phil as he was stitched up. 'And what a palaver that was, he really was a wuss,' he commented. Phil had been shipped home and Nigel had gone to base and collected what he could.

'I didn't really know what the situation was here, but I brought a selection of stuff to play with.'

They unpacked the car and Nigel pointed out his parabolic antenna, so they might have a chance of listening to conversations in the house.

'May be worth a try if we can get near enough,' said Claire. 'The bad news is the tracker's disappeared from the screen. Her clothes may have been taken and destroyed for all we know, or they could have found it.'

'I didn't know that,' said Jack, agitated.

'That's probably because I didn't tell you,' said Claire, 'as you would have gone running in half-cocked and the whole operation would have been blown. Try and keep a lid on it Jack, or else you're going to have to stand down and we'll be a man short. I can't deal with any loose cannon right now.'

Jack nodded dumbly as the chips were down. He desperately wanted to be part of the operation, but he knew Claire would have no trouble at all in handcuffing him to the car if he messed up.

'So let's get as close as we can and see if we can hear anything.'

Everyone nodded.

They belly-crawled with the gear to a thicket they had spotted before it got dark, and Nigel tinkered about setting up the antenna. They waited and listened.

Ellie had stomped back to her suite nursing a very sore hand, and slammed the door with a resounding crash.

How very stupid, she thought, what a senseless thing to say. "I'm going to starve myself to death!" She couldn't have done if she'd tried. She sat on the bed and stared into space, and wondered what was going to happen to her next. There was a discreet tap on the door and Carter appeared.

'Mr Alastair and Mr Max would like you to join them in the drawing room for drinks before dinner.'

Ellie opened her mouth to tell him to inform the brothers that they could stick their dinner, but gave up and just nodded.

'There is a selection of evening dresses for you. It's black tie, so it doesn't need to be a floor length gown Miss. Please ring if you require anything,' he said, pointing to the push button on the wall. 'Cocktails will be served in half an hour, thank you.' He bowed his way out.

Ellie couldn't resist going to the walk-in wardrobe and fetching out a few of the dresses. They were beautiful, and just what she would have picked herself if she had the money. She sold her soul and chose a midnight blue creation, and actually felt a million dollars as she went downstairs.

The drawing room was warm and comfortable and she accepted a peach Bellini from the waiter. She sipped the amber nectar and looked at the brothers, noting the dark red mark on Max's jaw. That cheered her up, it felt good.

'Welcome, Miss Black. I hope the cocktail is to your liking; there's nothing like champagne when we're celebrating.'

Ellie furrowed her brow. 'Celebrating what? Is it your birthday?' she asked facetiously.

'A bit of a surprise for all of us, but we'll discuss it when we're seated.'

Ellie shrugged and wandered about the room examining the paintings and was surprised she could identify many of them. Bloody good fakes, she thought.

When called through to dinner, Ellie found only three places set at one end of the long dining table. The soup and the wine were served, then the footman withdrew. Ellie had given up the thought of starvation at this point and was relishing every mouthful.

'Now to our little surprise,' said Alistair. 'It came as quite a shock to both of us to find out that you are our sister.'

Ellie dropped her spoon with a clatter and coughed convulsively over a mouthful of soup. Clutching her napkin to her mouth, she could do nothing but stare wide-eyed at them both. They sat there, smiling.

'I know it must be a bit of a shock for you, but it has great implications. We are very pleased to welcome you to the family, and, whatever we have, we will share with you. Everything your heart desires can be yours for the asking.' Alistair turned to Max, who smiled back, and ostentatiously rubbed his jaw.

'I'll just look on this as a little welcome present; I do trust there will only be one. You see, Alistair has waited so long to find you that it's actually worth it.'

Ellie looked at him, amazed. 'So what was all that about in the factory, nearly getting me blown up, so that I spent nearly a week in hospital and I can only just hear properly now?'

Max explained that Karl and he had waited to see if she would make it out before the explosions had destroyed the building. They had made bets on it and happily Max had won.

'Karl said that you wouldn't do it, but I had ten thousand said you did.'

'You murdering bastard! I could have died and then you wouldn't have had a sister at all.' Ellie glared at him.

'True,' Max mused, 'but it appears all's well that ends well. You are a very resourceful young woman and I am proud to be your brother.'

Ellie sat, dumbfounded.

Alistair continued, 'It was the tea cup you sipped from in the library. I took the liberty of having the DNA analysed and it confirmed my theory. You have very distinctive eyes Miss Black; in fact, they are the same as my own. I'm sure you noticed that. You also wear a little gold ornament around your neck. Let me guess, it was a gift from your long-lost birth parents. Am I right?'

Ellie's hand strayed to the strange, cross-shaped ornament around her neck.

'Yes, it's the only thing I have.'

Alistair felt in his pocket and withdrew its twin. He placed it on the table and Ellie looked at it mesmerized. She reached up and undid the clasp and placed her own next to it. Then she looked pensive and picked both of them up and put them together. They fitted together like a key. She laid them down again and looked at Alistair.

'What does it mean?'

'I don't know as I've never seen another one like it, but well done for sorting out that bit of the puzzle. All I knew is that we share the same father and mother; Max has the same father, but a different mother. He is your younger half-brother.'

Across the table, Max smiled at her and asked, 'What do I call you? Miss Black does seem a tad formal. What does Ellie actually stand for? Eleanor, Elena? Personally, I prefer Max instead of Maximillian—such a mouthful, don't you think?'

Ellie stared at him. 'I can't believe you just said that. How can you change from a murdering gangster to a polite brother sitting at a dinner table? You must be a psycho!'

Alistair intervened. 'Don't let's squabble so soon after our reunion. Max will no doubt apologize for abducting you—' he looked meaningfully at Max, '—but you must admit it was fortuitous, otherwise we may never have met. Blood is always thicker than water and we will take very good care of our long-lost sister. You may not realize it, but we share the same birthday; we are actually twins.'

Ellie's mouth dropped open.

Concealed in the thicket that was mostly brambles, Claire and her crew were listening to this conversation and their mouths dropped open too at the same point. They looked at each other and all Nigel could manage was a sibilant 'Fuckin' 'ell!' Claire felt Jack go rigid as he lay beside her.

In the dining room, the footman had replaced the cooling soup with delicate pieces of fish enveloped in a fragrant sauce, and Ellie made an effort to eat while processing all the new information.

'So… Let's get this straight. I, Eleanor Black, am your half-sister and your twin.' She pointed at one, then the other brother, and they both nodded. 'My birth father was the same as yours. So we are now one big happy family. Well, you can forget that one 'cos I don't care and as I said before you can stick your big house, although now technically I own a third of it, and I want out!'

She reached for the gold cross key lying on the table and began to fiddle with it. 'It won't come apart,' she said, looking at Alistair.

He took it from her, and after a few moments agreed. 'It looks like we're stuck together like the crosses, because I'm not letting my twin go till I know more about her. I've waited a very long time for this and I'm damn sure I'm not giving in now, come what may.' He looked at her, and his stare met hers with equal intensity.

Max looked at the two of them and sighed, envisaging the fireworks to come.

Outside, the patrols were sweeping the mansion grounds, and the German Shepherd dogs were enjoying the scents held fast by the damp ground. The handlers were adept at reading the dogs' behaviour, and let them be the eyes and ears of the security.

On the first sweep of the grounds all was clear; then, one of the dog's 'spoke'. The body language changed and it looked towards an area of thick cover, barely discernible at the edge of the security lighting. Could have been a fox, but the training both dog and handler had endured ruled out that possibility.

In the cover, Claire noted this and signalled silently for the group to pull back, which they did with alacrity, shuffling back on elbows and knees, leaving the gear behind them. Once behind the hedge, they bent double and ran as fast as they could into a ditch half full of winter water.

The dog tugged at the harness and the handler radioed to his manager, and the others began grouping at the spot. They all moved forward, sweeping the ground as they went. Big arc lights flicked on and illuminated the area. A shout went up as the hideout was discovered, and the antenna and equipment were dragged out.

'Fan out and see where they went; I'll alert the house,' said a guard.

The dogs moved forward in unison, following the scent, and came to the hedge. Then they began casting about, as the scent had been washed away by the rank water.

Claire and her crew ran like hell and reached the cars ahead of the security.

'Quick, go now,' said Claire breathlessly, 'we'll regroup about two miles west of here. Stay on comms.'

They all got in, ignoring the mud and slime clinging to their clothes and sped away.

The meal had now nearly finished, and a footman came to Alistair's side and gave him a folded piece of paper. As he read the note, his brow furrowed.

'It seems as if we have some unwanted guests trying to crash our party. Your friends are hot on your trail, Ellie, and know you are here, so unfortunately, we will have to leave immediately instead of in the morning. I hope that won't inconvenience you too much?'

'You won't get away with this,' said Ellie triumphantly.

'We shall see,' said Alistair, 'the game is only just beginning. Please be ready to leave in fifteen minutes and I suggest you dress warmly.' He pushed back his chair signifying the end of the conversation, made a very small bow in her direction and left the room.

Max also rose and executed the same bow.

'Bastard,' hissed Ellie.

'No, that's an epithet you can direct at me, but now you know you are certainly not one.' He smiled and left.

Ellie stood and looked out onto the discreetly lit grounds, and could hear a whump, whump, noise getting closer. It sounded like a helicopter. She was going to have to go with them, like it or not, and she might as well go and get warm and comfortable, so she trotted out of the dining room to collect some more appropriate clothes.

The helicopter landed on the grass and Ellie and her two brothers ducked low from the rotor wash and climbed aboard. It took off gracefully and with winking lights, disappeared over the dark countryside.

The two cars with Claire and the rest of the team were parked in a dark farm gateway. They were despondent and they stood silently, watching the helicopter swoop away till it faded from view.

Jack spoke first. 'Now what do we do?' He addressed the question generally.

'We go back to the office, regroup, then find out where that chopper has gone. We have to assume that Ellie is still alive, and next time we go in, we'll have a better thought out plan,' said Claire emphatically.

'Yeah, I'm knackered and not thinking straight now,' said Nigel, then added, 'the adrenalines gone and I'm not up for a fight. Don't know about you lot, but I think we should meet and report to Phil tomorrow.'

Robert and Jack murmured their assent as everyone was dog tired and filthy.

'Okay, 10 o'clock meeting tomorrow, try and get a bit of rest everyone,' said Claire, as she slid wearily into the car.

Jack was drained and devoid of feeling, but sleep didn't come easily to him. Someone would have to tell Rory what had happened, and he hoped it wouldn't be him. The news that Ellie was closely related to that scum was a like a slap in the face. He tossed about on the edges of sleep, and had fantastical dreams of Ellie holding a gun and looking like her, but not being her at all. She had changed into a person with evil in her soul, that shone through those amazing eyes. He woke up sweaty and unsettled. Sleep had not restored him at all. Was this what police work at the sharp end was really all about? Chasing round the countryside at the dead of night was pure cops and robbers' stuff and was fun, but when it involved someone he knew, and wished he could get to know a little better, then that was too close to home. Maybe he should go back on the beat and do 'house to house' with Ron. That seemed a pleasant option at the moment, no hassle, and definitely no emotional involvement to cope with.

The next morning, Phil greeted them as they silently filed in. Claire must have got there early and filled him in on the previous night's events. Phil looked a bit battered, and the stitches weren't pretty and were surrounded by a livid bruise. Claire had gone stiff overnight, and winced delicately every time she moved. They were all subdued and banter was at a minimum.

'I've heard the rest of the night's story from Claire already, so no need to recap, unless anyone has anything to add,' Phil looked round at them all. Everyone shook their heads and stared at the table. 'It wasn't a total failure, although it may seem like one. We will get a trace on that chopper and see where it went. We'll assume the rare books haven't been sold yet, so they will have to hit the markets somehow—and we'll assume at this point that Ellie is still alive. Anyone any thoughts to share?'

'I'll do the chopper trace with Nigel,' said Robert, 'and get a copy of the books inventory from the Library.'

'Ellie's tracker is a dead duck, so I'll look into the family background of the Morgans and check out Addingham Manor, but I suspect a search warrant won't be any good as everything will have gone by now. I'll see what I can dig up on old man Morgan as well,' Claire said, rising painfully.

Phil looked at Jack who said, 'I suppose it's down to me to go and see Rory and keep him updated,' Jack slowly shook his head, not relishing the thought, but Phil just nodded.

Jack reluctantly collected his coat and went into the car park. The weather was doing its usual November drizzle, a fine mist that soaked everything it touched. It matched his mood, wet and despondent. It wasn't that he had to tell Rory that everything had gone pear shaped in the matter of a few hours, but his friendship with him would be called into question. Rory would feel used, and Jack couldn't explain that away easily. Jack bit the bullet and keyed in Rory's mobile number and explained he had some news, arranging to meet him at lunchtime in a nearby café.

The office was buzzing as information began to filter in.

'I've got the book list from the library, and there's some pretty heavy stuff in there,' said Robert, clutching a wad of paper. He laid it in front of Phil. 'This stuff could be worth millions even on the black market. Most of this is priceless. Nigel's working on the chopper as we speak, and it looks like it's gone out of the country. Somewhere on the Continent, but we're waiting on air traffic control from France.' He nodded at Phil before departing, anxious to get back to his work station.

'It looks as if old man Morgan did have two boys by different women, but can't find any trace of a girl online,' said Claire. 'It looks as if I'm going to have to go back to the original hospital birth records. I've found out where Alistair was born, and surprisingly enough, it was at a Maternity Unit of a local hospital. Looks like Mrs. Morgan was caught short and couldn't make it to a private facility in time. Lucky for us this time,' she smiled.

Claire set off and tracked down the hospital which was, by now, virtually derelict. There was someone in a makeshift office by the door. Claire flashed a warrant card at him, and he let her in with a few dismissive grunts. The records office was surprisingly still intact and had old ledgers piled haphazardly from floor to ceiling, awaiting transportation to an archive. Claire couldn't believe her luck. People's lives, births and deaths intermingled, an endless cycle. Fate smiled on Claire that day, as she located the ledger of the relevant year in about half an hour. She dusted off a chair and elbowed a pile of paper out of the way, and cracked the volume open. There it was the entry for Alistair Morgan, written in a perfect script. It said he was 5lbs and 2 ounces at birth, and there was a time written at the side, with a small number 1 at the side. The next entry had been obliterated, scratched out time and time again, erasing a life. Claire looked quickly over her shoulder and tore the page out, folded it and put it in her pocket. She carefully replaced the ledger and made her way back to the security man, shaking her head and shrugging her shoulders.

Jack was already seated in the café, with coffee and a baguette he didn't know he would be able to eat. His mind kept going round, rehearsing what he was going to say. Rory walked in quickly and slid into the seat opposite. 'So what's going on Jack, what the hell's going on? Where's Ellie? You must know something, is she all right?'

Jack looked Rory in the eye. 'I can't lie to you and say "we're pursuing enquiries" and things like that. The truth is that you know she went to take those books to Oxford. Well it all went wrong, and the van was hijacked and Ellie was taken captive again.'

'She's dead isn't she, that's what you're trying to tell me?' Rory put his head in his hands.

'No, we don't think so.' Jack reached across to put his hand on Rory's arm, but it was shaken off angrily.

'You don't think so… What do you lot think then? Tell me. That fucking mob has taken her again. What for? Why do they keep doing this? Where is she? You must have some clues?'

'We don't know exactly where she was taken, but we don't believe she's still in the country. We were outnumbered big time and we did try to get to her, but failed. We were with her in the van and no harm came to her while we could see her, but then they took her.'

'Well you didn't bloody well try hard enough.' Rory's voice was muffled as he sank lower in his seat. 'So what's happening now? I thought with all those policemen hanging round we'd be safe—obviously not,' Rory said sarcastically, looking back up at Jack. 'I know what your game was now. A sort of undercover thing where we were all pals together, but you were just after information really.' The accusation was there in his eyes.

'It was a bit like that—but I really do care what happens to Ellie, and I want her back with you safe and sound… but there is more.'

'More! What could be worse?' Rory's back stiffened.

'We overheard part of a conversation between Ellie, and a couple of the people that kidnapped her. It seems that she is related to them. In fact, they are siblings.'

Jack looked at Rory and saw him struggling to process the information. He had been through similar himself, and knew what a shock it had been. Disbelief was written across Rory's face.

'She's not got any parents. I know she was adopted and she hadn't got a clue where she came from. She wasn't really bothered about it, as her adoptive parents were the only ones that mattered. But now you're telling me she's got a brother.'

'Yes, a twin brother, and another half-brother, actually.'

'She's a twin?' Rory just stared.

'So now you know as much as we do. We don't think any harm will come to Ellie. In fact, we think the brothers will be looking after her very well,' said Jack ironically. 'We are tracing where their getaway helicopter has gone, and we'll be liaising with the Continental police to get her back. I'll come round later and tell you everything in greater detail, if you want?' Rory nodded. 'I've got to get back to the station now, but you've got my number if you want to call me. I'll come round at 7.30ish and see if Nigel wants to come as well, and we can then tell you how far we've got. Is that okay?' Jack took Rory's silence as a yes, and left without touching his coffee or food.

Outside, Jack turned his face up to the gently falling rain and let his shoulders sag. He felt he had let Rory down very badly. He realized that his thoughts for Ellie were more than just professional, and he felt he had failed to protect her, although he knew everyone had done their best. He hadn't lied to Rory, but inside he was aware of his betrayal and overwhelming failure.

CHAPTER NINE

Ellie climbed into the helicopter and was buckled in. She sat ramrod straight and had her hands clenched in her lap, her nails digging into her palms. Ellie hadn't been airborne before, and wasn't quite sure what it would feel like. The rotors reached a fever pitch, and as the crescendo mounted the ground fell away. Ellie managed a glance out of the window and saw the roof of the Manor, and realized it was much bigger than she had previously thought. It was actually huge, arranged around a central courtyard; there was much more to it than she had actually seen. She looked down at the backlit tree tops, then the helicopter swung round and swooped away on its course. The sudden dip of the nose and the acceleration caused a wave of nausea to reach her throat, but she choked it back and gritted her teeth. Ellie found by putting her head back a bit and closing her eyes, the nausea subsided to manageable proportions, and she felt thankful everyone was just ignoring her as she pretended to doze.

Once they were on a level course, the rotors lulled her into a state of semi-consciousness and the trip passed uneventfully. Ellie gradually managed to relax. Her muscles were exhausted, as she had been in a state of tension for many hours, and the knots gradually unravelled, as she sank lower into the leather seat. Ellie was grateful everyone had left her alone and her brain played with all the new information, by giving her half-dreams that slid seamlessly from conscious to unconscious, and back again.

The whine of the rotors changed, and Ellie jerked into full wakefulness as the helicopter descended towards what looked like an enormous chateau. It had carvings and spires that looked as if they had come from a Disney film. Windows blazed with light and the front was lit with flaming torches. The big front doors opened and liveried servants stood to attention, awaiting them.

Ellie's eyes flicked back and forth, just taking in the scene, as they landed with a small bump and the rotors began to slow.

'Where are we?' Ellie asked no-one in particular.

'Welcome to France. We are at the Chateau. It's called the Chateau of the Birds. I've never managed to get the energy to find out why, but it's a charming name, don't you think?' said Alistair turning in his seat.

'Beautiful. Very impressive, but I don't speak French,' Ellie replied.

Alistair ignored the small show of petulance and helped her out of the helicopter. As they reached the doors of the chateau, the chopper rose gracefully and disappeared from sight. The chateau inside was even more ornate than outside, and large gilded mirrors reflected the party from every angle. A marble parquet floor, inlaid with an intricate pattern was graced by occasional tables adorned with sculptures of flowers. Double doors were arranged round the edges of the room, and one of these stood open, with a footman in attendance to welcome the family.

They walked into the drawing room and Ellie tried to stifle

a yawn.

'It is a little late. I'll get someone to show you to your suite if you wish?' said Alistair, solicitously. 'A hot drink can be brought up to you.' He raised his eyebrows.

'I think I will, 'cos I don't think the conversation is going to go the way I want. So I'll leave you to it. A nice cup of tea would go down well.'

Max nodded to the footman, who beckoned Ellie to follow and he led her to a sumptuous suite of rooms on the first floor. Tea appeared almost instantly on a silver tray, which was placed gently on a side table and a butler enquired if he should pour. Ellie dismissed him with thanks and sat and savoured the brew.

Max and Alistair sat at ease in the big drawing room, each with a glass of fine cognac at their elbows.

'That was a close one,' said Max picking up his glass and swirling the contents round.

'It was never going to be easy, particularly when, by luck or fate, she had run into me before,' said Max. 'It was just bloody bad luck, but it certainly didn't make a good impression. If she'd have gone up with that factory, we'd never have found her. Maybe that's how it should have been,' he mused.

Alistair reached into his waistcoat pocket and fished out the small gold key formed by the two crosses. He twirled it in his fingers and watched the light reflect off its many facets. 'I wonder what this is. Any ideas?'

Max leaned across and took it from him, and examined it closely. 'Dad had lots of secrets and I don't suppose we'll ever find them all out, but it looks too small for a door key… maybe it's for a chest or cupboard, but there must be millions of those scattered round the houses,' Max sighed, and handed it back to his brother.

Alistair pulled himself back to the present. 'To business then, Max. The book sale didn't go ahead as planned in England, so we'll just have it over here instead. The crates should be with us in the morning, so we'll get the crew over here and get it sorted. Ellie may like to give us some hints and tips on handling this stuff as I haven't got a clue. Looks like I'm going to have to ingratiate myself to my sister to get any co-operation at all.' Alistair looked pointedly at Max's jaw, with the dark red mark still showing.

Back in London the office was a hive of activity and Jack felt better; they were actually doing something. Claire had just got back from her trip to the hospital archives. She rushed in, and without removing her coat sat down and beckoned everyone over. She pulled the piece of paper from her pocket.

'I managed to find this.' She spread it out carefully on the table, smoothing out the creases. 'It's a birth record, written by the attending midwife for a Mrs. Morgan on the right date. If you look closely, beside the birth weight, there's a time and also a very small number 1. This denotes there were twins. The next entry has been scrubbed out totally, but if Robert and Nigel want to use some of their wizardry on it, we may find out what was written.' She looked at them and they reached for the page.

Phil was standing at Claire's shoulder. 'It's probably the birth record of Ellie Black which will prove she's the true twin sister of Alistair Morgan. They said they'd DNA'd her and it had come up as a match, so it looks as if she's family all right.'

Jack rubbed a weary hand across his eyes, 'Where does that leave us then? If she's family, she's now got potential access to zillions in cash and they seem to want her on board, or else she'd have been toast by now. Are we going to rescue someone who doesn't want to be rescued?' He let the question hang in the air.

'I understand what you're saying, but we have to assume it's still a hostage situation,' said Phil, and put his hand on Jack's shoulder.

Robert said, 'well I may have some good news, or bad; depends how you look at it.' Everyone looked at him expectantly. 'The chopper made it across the Channel and landed last night, at a private address in France. It's some chateau or another, not far from Deauville.' Jack groaned.

Phil moved to the big white board and began writing. 'So now we know Ellie is a very, very close relation of an alleged crime boss. She's been abducted once and escaped. Now she's with them again in some fortress in France.' He looked round at them all. 'Anyone got anything to add to that summary?'

'So what's the plan, if there is one?' said Nigel.

'You get onto our French counterparts and explain the situation and tell them, if they agree of course, that we'll be across there tomorrow,' said Phil. Robert sketched a small salute. 'On it, Boss!'

'Nigel,' Phil looked at him directly, 'get onto the transport and get us across there pronto. Also, get some kit together.'

'Claire, sort out Jack's firearms' certs and get him up to speed with all the other accreditations, we need them fast.' Claire nodded and left the room.

'Jack, you and I need to talk, now.' Jack followed Phil to a small side office. 'Tell me everything, and I mean everything you know about what's going on.'

Phil sat and listened attentively as Jack started from the beginning, and told Phil about every contact he'd had with Ellie and Rory. Jack was aware that Phil was waiting for the details of any emotional feelings he had being experiencing towards Ellie, and how difficult it had been to talk to Rory yesterday.

'Jack, you do realize you're going to have to put all this aside, if you want to be on the inside of this operation.' Jack bit his lip. 'You could be a very important member of this team, but you're going to have to bury those feelings for a while and focus solely on the task in hand.'

Jack realised at that point that he wouldn't be going to France, unless he gave the right answers with conviction. 'Okay, I get the point. I admit I like Ellie a lot, more than just a lot, but I'm also, hopefully, still a friend of Rory's—so I'll be totally objective from now on. All the emotional stuff I'll sort out later, when the dust's settled. I'll go in with the intention of getting Ellie out of there and nailing the Morgan brothers, though what comes next is anybody's guess,' Jack tailed off.

'I know you'll do it Jack. I've got faith in you. Emotional stuff is up to you, but can you do the job at hand? Do it now to the best of your ability?'

Jack took a deep breath and nodded.

'I've taken the liberty of getting you properly seconded to the team, and I think you've realized we're not mainstream coppers. We're a team that's been put together to take on some of the biggest crime bosses in the western world, and we work undercover. There are members of the team that haven't been seen for years now, but keep feeding us intel when they can.

We think we can trust you. There won't be any medals at the end and you won't make the Honours list, but the choice at this point is still yours.' Phil looked at Jack, waiting for an answer.

'I'll do it,' said Jack.

'But only for the right reasons,' replied Phil.

'Yep, I understand.'

'Sign this,' said Phil, and slid a piece of paper across the table. He offered Jack a pen. Jack looked at the paper, which said 'Official Secrets Act' across the top. Jack took the pen, then hesitated. This was the end of his former life.

A new way of life was beginning, and Jack wasn't entirely sure, deep down, if he could do this. If he signed, he knew he would be part of a team and the sum would be greater than the parts—so he would pull his weight, without question. He wouldn't let anyone down. He signed and slid the paper back to Phil. Phil rose and offered Jack his hand.

'Welcome to the team, Jack.'

Jack rose and grasped his hand firmly.

Robert came in, and hovered expectantly at the periphery. 'I've got the transport; we're out of here in two hours from Heathrow, so better get a move on. I've got as much kit as I can muster in such a short time, and it's being shipped to the flight as we speak. It's all going across in diplomatic bags, so no Customs at the other end. Hopefully the French will come up trumps, and give us a bit of "détente" on the stuff I couldn't put together. Think Claire's okay with all Jack's stuff as well.' Rob smiled at Jack. 'Welcome aboard, it can be a bit of a rough ride at times, but it's worth it.' Jack managed a weak smile back.

'Okay, everyone, get moving and we'll meet at Heathrow Air France check in desk, hand luggage only. No ball gowns and tiaras, so keep it to a minimum. Go!' said Phil, and everyone made for the door.

The Departures hall at Heathrow was busy, but Jack managed to spot Phil, who was a tall guy standing by the Air France desk looking at his watch. He wasn't late, but he had agonized about what to pack in one small bag of hand luggage. This was all new to him, and besides his passport and toothbrush couldn't think of what else to take, besides socks and underwear. So it was a very small day sack that Jack hefted on his shoulder as he met them.

'We'll board after everyone else. Sit separately in First Class. No communication. Hopefully at the other end, there will be some cars to get us near the property—which is a chateau, by the way—and we'll do a recce and see what the score is.' Phil handed out the boarding passes and everyone went through Customs with no more than a cursory glance at their passports, as they made their way onto the plane.

It was a short, uneventful flight, and at the Charles de Gaulle terminus they disembarked and wandered through Customs, where Jack spotted his name being held up by a French agent posing as a taxi driver. Without sparing a glance round for the others, he identified himself and was taken to the drop-off point, outside where a mid-sized plain dark blue Citroen was idling. He climbed in and was whisked away through the traffic. It was the first time Jack had been to France, and he couldn't resist gazing at the magnificent architecture along the route. The car drew up outside an imposing edifice, and Jack slowly climbed the steps and entered the vast hallway. There were people busily going about their business, but Jack could still hear his shoes click on the marble floor. The receptionist said something but Jack could only shake his head, as his French language had left him in the Fifth Form. He wasn't confident enough to have a go and dredge some up. The man switched effortlessly into English, and Jack breathed a sigh of relief.

'Please would you wait in here and I'll send some coffee along. It shouldn't be long,' He stood aside as Jack entered a meeting room.

The coffee duly arrived just as the others appeared, and they all took their places round a long table, Phil serving everyone with the fragrant liquid. The French contingent came in and everyone shook hands and Phil thanked everyone for their co-operation, in English. Jack was thankful that the meeting continued in the same vein.

The first hour was taken up by Phil bringing everyone up to speed, and handing out copies of all the reports from England. They were all perused and comments scribbled in the margins.

Chief Inspector Duchamp closed his file. 'This is a very serious matter, and we will obviously help all we can. Mr. Morgan is a prominent member of society here in France, and as far as we know has not committed any crime according to French law. We will alert the provincial gendarmerie near Deauville, and they will give you every assistance, but...' he paused, '...I do not want a massive scandal and names of any politicians or leading industrialists dragged into this whatsoever. Any operation you put into practice will be, very definitely, covert. Am I making myself clear?'

'You have our word on that,' Phil replied, looking at the others. They all nodded.

'Then I will make some transport available to you—and

the diplomatic bags have arrived from the airport, so you may begin your arrangements. This room will be available to you for the next few hours. The distance to the chateau is approximately two hundred kilometres, so it should take you about two hours down the A13. It is a good road, so you can be at the coast before nightfall. Someone will meet you there.' He gathered his papers and bade them farewell, followed by the French policemen.

Phil looked at the others. 'Not as good as I hoped, but at least we will have transport. They obviously don't really want to be involved, so it looks like we're basically on our own. As usual,' he added, with a wry smile. 'So let's get the kit in here and be ready to rock and roll in a few hours.'

They gathered the diplomatic bags and began to sort it through them, stowing guns and ammo away. There seemed to be a mountain of stuff, but Robert and Nigel worked through it with practiced ease and doled out equipment.

Claire secreted away a small revolver in a holster on her thigh and patted it. 'Won't stop an elephant, but could make a bit of a mess if the going gets tough. What say we suss out their canteen and fuel up, as it could be a very long night ahead?' Everyone nodded and they all trooped out to sample French cuisine.

Ellie didn't think she would sleep but she did. She awoke to the aroma of coffee and a beautiful continental breakfast on a bed tray. A maid opened the curtains and the weak November sunlight flooded in. At least it wasn't raining over here. The maid bobbed a little curtsey and withdrew. Ellie had hoped to ask her some questions but wasn't quick enough, so she just relished the food and decided to make her own plans. As she sat up in bed, her finger strayed to her engagement ring and she absently twirled it round her finger. Looking round, Ellie saw a telephone and suddenly wondered if it would work. She reached over and picked it up, and got a tone. A voice said something in French she didn't understand, but she recited Rory's mobile number, and prayed she would be put through.

'Un moment, s'il vous plait.' Then there were crackles and a ringing tone. Ellie held her breath.

'Rory! Is that you! Oh my God, I'm so pleased to hear your voice.' A tear started from the corner of her eye.

'Where the hell are you? Are you OK?' The questions came thick and fast.

'Rory, I'm OK, but I'm in France, at some chateau, I don't know where. I don't know if they'll cut this call off, but I love you. I don't think they'll hurt me, but I can't leave this place. Phone Jack—'

The phone went dead at that point and Ellie stared at the receiver; then gently replaced it.

Over the Channel, Rory had been in a state of terror and disbelief at the way things had panned out. He was finding it all very hard to believe, and didn't know what to do next. Thoughts raced through his head and he was ready to jump on the next plane to France, but he didn't even know where she was. He would have taken the world on single handed to rescue Ellie, but instead he just stared at his mobile. He would have to phone Jack and tell him what had happened.

At the top of a small hill, concealed by scrub, Jack sat, watching the chateau through field glasses. As the day drew to a close, he was careful not to let the glasses glint from the setting sun, and give his position away. His phone vibrated in his pocket. A glance at the caller ID told him it was Rory and he took the call. Rory sounded distraught and Jack could only whisper to him that he was glad Ellie had made contact somehow. She was still in the chateau, and Jack tried to reassure Rory that the Morgan brothers wouldn't harm her. He didn't tell him where he was, because he knew that the state Rory was in he would come hot foot to France and endanger the operation. Rory wasn't pleased and vented his anger on Jack, but Jack could only sit back and take it, as he already felt he had betrayed him. He promised to text Rory when he could, and try and keep him updated. That was the best he could offer and they both felt it wasn't enough, but Jack's hands were tied.

Ellie had sat in her room for a while, then decided to explore the chateau—her chateau, and see some of its treasures. She showered and dressed and made her way down the ornate stairway to the hall. A servant pointed her towards the dining room, where she met Alistair and Max enjoying the last of their breakfasts. Max stood and showed her to a chair, but she pointedly took one on the other side of the table and ignored him.

A cup of coffee appeared at her elbow and Alistair said, 'I trust you slept well, and I hope there will be something to entertain you indoors today, as I am unable to let you roam the grounds. We have a small job for you, should you wish. The boxes of books have arrived from England and I think you have the necessary expertise to unpack them.'

'Don't you even think of touching those manuscripts without me being there. You could cause a lot of damage and they've been through enough lately. Where are they?' Ellie pushed back her chair and stood.

'Downstairs, if you want to start. There will be a house party tonight, and I want you to be there as my sister and family member.'

'I suppose I don't have any choice in the matter, do I?'

'Not really,' he replied and smiled.

A footman showed Ellie the way downstairs, and it seemed to her the walk went on for miles—until they reached the cavernous wine cellars. They were enormous vaulted rooms, carved from the rock below the chateau. There were tables set out and boxes were placed at intervals, with the lids already off.

'Stop, right now. Just don't touch anything until you have gloves on. Anything at all; even your skin contains acid, and you could damage those books forever.' Ellie's words made everyone freeze on the spot. Max had followed her down and looked at everyone.

'This is Ellie Black, or maybe Morgan—' Max raised his eyebrows, '—and she's in charge from now on. Whatever she says, goes. Okay?' Everyone nodded.

Ellie turned to Max and said, 'Gloves and table covers, acid free, now please, for everyone.' Whatever was going to happen to the books and manuscripts in the future was beyond Ellie's power, but whilst they were in her care, they would be treated correctly.

After about an hour everything was in place, and Ellie had filled everyone in on how the books and manuscripts should be handled. She was no expert but knew the basics, and impressed on everyone the fragility of the objects. They were all prepared and the first box was opened. Ellie supervised the handling of the contents, and was again amazed at the depth of colour that glowed from every page. On every single page, the work was breath-taking. Everyone crowded round. She waved them back.

'Don't even breath on them,' she admonished, and they fell back instantly. 'All right, you saw how I did that. Now go and unpack some more, but very carefully, take your time.'

Ellie turned to Max and asked, 'What's going to happen to them, you're not going to leave them here, are you?'

'That's what the house party is all about Ellie,' he explained, 'they're all going to be sold to the highest bidder.'

'No! You can't do that. It's sacrilege. This is the greatest collection of medieval manuscripts in the world, that you're going to break up and sell them in lots to the highest bidder,' she said contemptuously. 'These treasures will be lost forever! You really are despicable.'

Max took her arm and steered her out of the cellar. He shoved her roughly against a wall. 'You may be my sister, but don't think I have any finer feelings for you. If you ever show me up like that in front of others again, I promise I'll forget any fanciful familial connections.'

Ellie shook her arm loose and stared right back at him.

'Go ahead, do what you want. Do you know something— right now, I don't care. Just keep out of my way and we'll get along fine. I'll do my job here for the sake of the folios, not for you or anyone else.' She turned on her heel and strode back into the cavern. It was very quiet, as everyone had overheard the argument and when she got back, no-one would meet her eyes. It stayed that way until the job was done, and she left to go upstairs again.

CHAPTER TEN

Around the perimeter of the chateau, under what cover they could find, Phil and his team had deployed, expecting a long stake-out. Phil had to be sure that he knew the guards' rota, and what paths they took on their rounds. They all noted any comings or goings of the delivery vehicles and visitors, as well as their frequency. Hopefully, after a few days, he could identify a gap that would help them to gain entrance to the chateau. Nigel had been working on trying to get the plans of the interior layout, but that was proving to be difficult. The chateau had been in private hands since the first settlement on the land, and it seemed that all the owners had guarded their privacy closely. So they waited and watched.

On the second evening, many large chauffeured cars began to draw up to the big front doors. The flambeau down the drive had been lit and the guests were dropped off, and the cars and chauffeurs disappeared round the back of the house.

Phil's communication crackled. 'Tech 1 here, I think I've just identified someone, looks very much like the French Secretary of State.'

'Wolf 1, roger and out'.

Phil swore under his breath. 'Shit.' It looked like Duchamp's words were coming true. The Morgans were very well connected in France, and he would probably be shot at dawn if he ballsed it up. His comms crackled again. 'Wolf 1, been listening in, this is She-Wolf. What the fuck do we do now?'

Phil considered his options, not that there were many. He'd have to call the operation off tonight, and think of another way round it. He bunched his fist and hit it hard onto the wet ground. 'Shit, shit, shit.'

As the guests started to arrive Ellie went up to change for dinner, still seething at what was to happen later. She believed the threats Max had made. She was either in a no-win situation, or, to look at it another way, she had nothing whatsoever to lose. If it was the last thing she did, she was going to take that scum, who called himself her half-brother, down.

The downstairs glittered with lit candles, reflecting in the enormous mirrors, and everywhere there were footmen in full livery, offering drinks on silver salvers. The crystal glasses gave off myriads of tiny stars as the guests stood about in groups, chatting in the drawing room. As Ellie walked into the room, Alistair came to greet her, and then he led her back into the hall. He stopped at a side table and handed her a flat leather box. She looked at him and he motioned her to open it. Inside, nestling on dark blue silk, was an exquisite necklace of diamonds and sapphires. He clasped it round her neck, and she couldn't help but admire it.

'Do you like it? I believe it belonged to some empress long ago, but tonight it's yours.'

He took Ellie by the crook of her elbow and guided her round each group of guests. Ellie noticed that she was the only woman there, and was introduced to each guest as his long-lost twin. Her hand was kissed and bowed over many times with a deference normally reserved for royalty. Ellie smiled and made small talk as best as she was able, and shot the odd venomous glance at Max if he came too near. All these people were here for the auction and she couldn't really identify anyone, though quite a few of the names sounded familiar. There was a lot of money gathered in that room tonight.

Dinner was served and Ellie was thankful she was on the other side of the table, away from Max. There was extensive silverware and she was conscious of not knowing exactly which knife and fork to use, but she kept a watchful eye on the guests and copied their moves. She couldn't manage all the courses and just had a few mouthfuls of each fragrant serving.

At the end of the meal, Max excused himself and reappeared with a large silver covered dish. He swept off the lid with a flourish and made his way round the table exhibiting a book. It was opened to a page that depicted monstrous serpents entwined around wondrous griffins and other mythical creatures. The guests' greedy fingers reached out to touch it but Max wouldn't allow that, and all Ellie could do was to avert her eyes when it came past her.

The guests wandered into another large drawing room, and Ellie had thoughts of slipping away and hiding somewhere, not wanting to be a part of what was going to happen next, but Alistair appeared at her side and guided her to a comfortable chair at the back of the room. He settled her with a drink and the auction began. Ellie was pleased to see the staff had taken on board what she had said about not handling the manuscripts, and no damage seemed to have occurred so far. She sat silently as each piece went under the hammer—and bidding was fierce, with many telephone and internet bids. The millions mounted up, but as each piece was secured Ellie tasted bile as her stomach clenched into a knot. As soon as she was able, she went to her room and spent the night alternately cursing the name of Morgan and despairing of the fate of the medieval collection.

Next morning Ellie went down to breakfast, and silently took her place at the other end of the table, away from her brothers. She read an English newspaper and studiously ignored all attempts at conversation. They seemed in good spirits and it seemed the evening had been a success.

'Ellie,' Alistair addressed her, 'today is a day off, no work at all. Maybe you would like to have a tour, and explore the chateau?'

'Whatever.'

'It's really quite beautiful, and it would be a shame if you didn't see it.' His tone was wheedling, like he was talking to a six-year-old.

'Whatever, as long as he isn't there.' Ellie looked pointedly at Max.

'Just as you wish. I have come to this house for holidays as long as I can remember, but even I haven't seen all of it yet. Let us explore it together, from top to bottom.'

Ellie had to admit that her interest and curiosity were piqued. Maybe she could find something out about her parents; if nothing else, it would be better than sitting in her room, brooding. If she kicked up a fuss, she was in no doubt she would be returned to her room, but this time with the door locked.

They set off through a maze of corridors and gradually made their way up to the fourth floor and then to the attics. All the servants were on the fourth floor, but they didn't disturb them and detoured up some small twisting stairs to a locked door. Alistair fished in his pocket and brought out an old key, which fitted, but then took some jiggling about to open the door. It was a glory hole inside, with hampers of clothes, suits of armour and the trappings of decades of changes in style. It seemed each successive owner had re-done the interior design, but hadn't thrown anything away. Ellie flitted about, opening boxes and exclaiming at all the treasures that were stored haphazardly from floor to ceiling. Alistair entered into the spirit and put a cockaded hat on his head and brandished a sword, looking for the entire world like one of the Three Musketeers. Ellie couldn't help but laugh, and they spent a good hour just horsing about, relieving the tension of the past few days.

Ellie sat down on one of the hampers and her eye was drawn to a small box made of wood, that stood alone on a table by one of the tiny turret windows.

'What's that?' she asked Alistair who was examining an ancient train set.

'Don't know, let's have a look.' He joined her at the table. Ellie wiped the box with the end of a curtain and they both stared at it.

'It's locked.' He picked it up and shook it. There was something inside, as they could hear it sliding about. 'Maybe I could force it open.' He shook the box again and looked about for a tool to do the job.

Ellie suddenly had a blinding thought. 'Try the key.'

'What key?'

'The key made out of the two crosses. You remember, the pendant I wore.'

Alistair stared at her. 'Whatever made you think of that?'

'Dunno, just seemed the right sort of box for the key. Have you got it?'

Alistair put his hand in his pocket and brought out the key. 'Go on, try it,'

Alistair held the key up to the light, and as it was suddenly caught by a ray of sun, it glinted in his hand. He put it in the lock and he turned it gently, not wanting to break the key. It turned effortlessly. Ellie lifted the lid, and she realized she was holding her breath at the same time. Inside was an envelope. It was thick, stuffed with paper that crackled as she touched it with her hand. There was no name on the outside and it was sealed with a thick blob of bright red wax. Imprinted on this was an eagle or griffin, some kind of heraldic bird.

'I don't want to open this up here. Can we go down to the library or somewhere with more light. What do you think?'

Ellie held it out to him. He took the box from her. She got the feeling that it was something very important, and he also felt a mounting sense of anticipation that was exciting to him. They made their way down back from the past into the present time. They didn't speak as they went down the stairs and along corridors, each of them waiting to see what the envelope contained.

In the library, they sat by one of the big bay windows and Ellie looked at Alistair. 'Go on then, open it. What are you waiting for?'

'Ellie, for the first time in my life I feel unsure. I've never felt this way before. The key fitting the box—that was your idea, so you open it.'

He handed the envelope back to her. Ellie took it and slid

her finger under the seal and it broke into two pieces. The paper inside was yellowed, and there were four sheets folded together. Ellie gently crackled them open and smoothed them flat.

What was on the paper made no sense at all. The first sheet was a letter; at least it was set out like a letter, but no recipient was addressed. There was a signature at the bottom, but that was practically unreadable as it was all flourishes and curlicues, but Ellie thought she could make out the name 'Edward Morgan'. Ellie asked Alistair if that meant anything to him. The only Edward he could think of was his grandfather, whom he had never known. She passed the letter over to him. He studied it, then went and picked up a pad and pen and he tried to decipher what it said.

The second sheet was some sort of map. There was an arrow at the top which denoted north, and it appeared to be a plan of part of a house. Ellie passed this across to him with a shrug of her shoulders, as it meant nothing to her. The last two pages were actually one large sheet, folded once. She opened it and it appeared to be some sort of contract, with impressed seals and signatures at the bottom. The writing was very ornate again and she would have to study it carefully to decipher it. Immediately her eye was drawn to the signature of Edward Morgan, which was scribed using some sort of brown ink. There were many blots, and the signature was very scrawled, unlike the one on the letter.

Ellie handed Alistair all the papers, and he looked at them carefully.

She said, 'I don't know what any of them mean, do you? The big one seems to be some sort of contract. Your grandfather's name crops up on it again, but it isn't written the same way; it's all sort of splodgy and the ink's different. But it's not just your grandfather, is it? He's mine as well, if we're twins. Do you know anything about him at all?'

'I never knew him, as we were born late in Father's life, and he, in turn, was born late in his father's life, so Edward was probably born in the 1880's, or around that time. There is a portrait of him in the drawing room.' Alistair stood to go and show her grandfather Edward.

As they walked, he said, 'All I know is that he was some sort of self-made man, and that's where the beginnings of the family fortune originated. He rose to power very quickly and had the ear of all the statesmen of the time. He was a bit of a Midas figure, as all he touched seemed to turn to gold and the family had holdings all over the world. They imported sugar from the Caribbean, wool from Australia, minerals from everywhere and owned huge chunks of South Africa—' he turned to Ellie, '—diamonds, of course.'

'I suppose nothing much has changed then and you've just kept adding to it by stealing,' Ellie said acidly. 'Why do you keep wanting more, Alistair? You have more than you can humanly spend in a lifetime, and you're just causing so much misery to so many people. Why?'

'I can't answer that, Ellie, because I simply don't know. I just have an idea, and then I can't rest until it's born out. Other people are of no concern to me whatsoever—except you, of course. Like it or not, we are two halves of one person.'

'Rubbish,' she snorted. 'We're not identical twins, just fraternal twins.'

'I know that, but you're the only person I've ever felt any connection to at all. Even Max doesn't have that. I know I grew up with him, but I just don't feel anything.'

'Well, half-brother or not, you know I can't stand him, so don't expect me to get pally for your sake. So where's this painting of Edward?'

In a corner of the drawing room, the painting was half hidden in the shadows. It was a standard Victorian portrait, showing an overweight businessman surrounded by trappings of wealth. There were no other people in the painting, no wife or son. Edward was standing, staring at the viewer, and had a scroll in his right hand. Ellie peered more closely and pointed. 'Look that's the key hanging from his watch chain.'

'You're right. I'm going to get help to take this down and we can look at it properly.' He went to the door and signalled a footman, explaining what he wanted, and the painting was soon being transported to the library where it was propped on an easel by the window.

The cold November light threw up many details Ellie couldn't have seen in the corner of the drawing room. On the Victorian draperies there were symbols, and on a small table there were some very odd ornaments. She peered closely at the scroll.

'You know what; I think this is the same scroll we have here. Look, there's the signatures and that seal at the bottom.'

'You're right, but I've got no ideas how to take this forward—except I'll send that scroll for analysis and see what that'll tell us. Could be something or nothing. We should get the results back tomorrow.'

Alistair rang for a footman and one appeared, as if by magic. He carefully explained what he wanted and the scroll and the servant disappeared.

'I'm going to have an early night and take another look at these, if you don't mind,' Ellie said, as she gathered up the other pieces of paper. 'Instead of me killing Max tonight, I think I'll have a dinner in my room. See you tomorrow.' Alistair stood aside as she left.

CHAPTER ELEVEN

Phil and the team had regrouped at the small farmhouse where they had been billeted. The place was nearly derelict, but it was close to the chateau and well off the beaten track.

'Day one, and it's all gone pear shaped already,' said Nigel, tapping away on a laptop. 'I have identified some other bigwigs going in there, so I suppose we'll have to back off for the mo.'

Claire responded, 'Not necessarily. Jack, start on the food, will you, and we'll have a talk about our other options while we eat.'

'God, you're like a nuclear reactor with food,' said Phil, sitting down at the farmhouse table, 'but some sustenance wouldn't go amiss.'

Jack rummaged through the boxes of supplies, and decided he could make a half decent spag bol with what was in there. He wasn't a cook by any stretch of the imagination, but he had a camping gas stove and some pots and pans to work with. He almost resented being the servant who made the food, but he decided an army always marches on its stomach, and many a campaign had failed for lack of supplies. So he set to, and the kitchen was soon filled with a hot herby aroma.

Phil had been writing notes and discussing them with

Claire in hushed tones. The steaming plates were passed round the table, and as the last of the juices were being mopped up with good French bread, he laid his plans out.

'The only way we're going to get into that place is through the front door, or rather, the back door. We all noted the delivery vans going back and forth, so we're going to have to pose as delivery guys, or something like that. Once inside, we'll play it by ear and blend in with the rest of the staff. There must be hundreds of them. Chances are that no one person knows everyone else, so we get in and look busy.' He looked round and everyone nodded, except Jack.

'I've got one problem, in that I don't speak the lingo. I'd be found out in a minute.'

Robert and Nigel both made the point that their French was a bit sketchy as well.

'Looks like you and me then.' Phil looked at Claire.

'I'll do the naughty French maid, and you can be the boy who shovels the coal, then.' Claire smiled winningly at Phil. 'I do like to play rough and dirty sometimes.' Phil just sighed and rolled his eyes heavenwards.

Phil was suddenly ultra business-like, as he got them organizing their roles and kit. Phone calls were made to the local gendarmes, and some cover stories were mapped out. After a few hours, the plan was that they were to deliver fresh produce to the chateau in the morning, accompanied by an uncle of a local gendarme who would profess to have hurt his arm, and needed help to carry weights. Clothes would be supplied by the uncle, and they would arrive at the chateau about 7.00 a.m. local time. Robert, Jack and Nigel would be back on point duty round the chateau, and would be ready to move in if things went horribly wrong. They carefully mapped out ambush points and choke points if they were pursued, and a getaway plan was in place for all of them. Rendezvous locations were stored in their heads, along with passwords for when they split up. As they were to meet in the village early, they retired and tried to get some sleep on the hard camp beds. It was cold, even in their sleeping bags, and it began to rain heavily, and water dripped incessantly through the broken tiles.

No one had slept well as they crawled out of their cocoons at 5.30 the next morning, and they ate a scanty breakfast as they reviewed the plans for the day. Everyone was word perfect and Phil gave a "thumbs up", as he and Claire made their way to the car to get to the village in time. The others began piling on layers of clothes and waterproofs for the long wait.

In the chateau, Ellie had slept well and woke early to the pouring rain lashing against the window. She reached out and picked up the map again. She orientated it towards north and looked at the room plan, which was carefully drawn but without notations. Ellie noticed that fireplaces were marked and stairways depicted, but there was nothing else to help her. She resolved to pick Alistair's brain over breakfast and dozed again with the map in her hand. The next thing she knew, the maid was drawing back the curtains to let in the cold grey light. The rain had lessened to a persistent drizzle but it was an unprepossessing day, and Ellie was glad she had something to tax her brain with. She sat up and had a sudden thought, and beckoned the maid over.

'Do you speak any English?' she enquired, and the maid nodded. 'I have a map here and wondered if you thought it was anywhere in the chateau, as I don't know my way round yet.' The maid took the map, went to the window and began to turn it round and examine it closely.

'Oui, I know where this is.' She pointed at a large room. 'It is the bedchamber of Monsieur Morgan. Sorry, I mean the older Monsieur Morgan, the father of Monsieur Alistair.' She bobbed and left the room and Ellie looked again at the map.

She couldn't wait any longer and got dressed with alacrity, and clutching the papers went downstairs to the dining room. The breakfast was just being set out on the side with continental and English food on offer. Ellie requested tea, and it was placed at the right-hand side of the head of the table. She would have to wait for Alistair to appear before she could check out what she had been told, so she got a plate and helped herself to bacon and scrambled egg. Alistair came in at that point and sat beside Ellie. She had a mouthful of breakfast, but pushed the map across to him and gestured, pointing to the room.

'Bonjour Ellie, I trust you slept well,' he said, ignoring her frantic gestures. She swallowed hastily and coughed.

'I've cracked the map; well the maid did it for me, but this room is your father's old room,' she said, stabbing the map with her index finger.

'Again, bonjour Ellie, I trust you slept well.' Ellie would have to play the game if she wanted his attention.

'OK, bonjour Alistair, yes, I slept like a top. Now can you stop arsing about and look at this.'

'All in good time, I will have coffee first. Then you can explain.' Ellie turned her attention back to her breakfast and fumed.

'Stop treating me like a child,' she muttered under her

breath.

'Yes, I will—when you have learned just a little restraint,' he said, and the only restraint Ellie could muster at that moment was not to pick her plate up and dump the rest of the egg on his head. He sipped his coffee and Ellie stubbornly stared at her plate. She couldn't stand it any longer and half rose, reaching out for the map. She would go and see on her own, but his hand shot out, quicker than a snake striking, and covered hers. Ellie sat down again.

'Now, we will talk. I'm sorry that I played with you a little, but everything really does happen in its own good time. Besides, you have an enthusiasm I can't muster; I'll now share yours. Tell me all.'

He released her hand and Ellie laid the map flat between them. She explained what the maid had said about it being his father's room, and how it now all made sense with the stairways and fireplaces in position. He looked more closely and pointed at the fireplace in his father's room on the map.

'See, here, there is a stairway from that room to others. I've never seen a stairway in my father's room before. Maybe we should go and look. I'll ring for the key, as it hasn't been opened since his death twelve years ago.'

'You mean no one has been in there for that long?'

'No, we decided to close the room up when he died as neither Max nor myself wanted to use it. At the time we missed him terribly, and it seemed the best thing to do.'

The key duly arrived and they set out to view the room.

The rain outside had eased considerably when Phil and Claire met up with Jacques who was to take them to the chateau. They had been practicing their French en route, and Jacques put them right on small inconsistencies and local words. Their clothes were now reminiscent of workers in the local wholesale market; tatty jeans and trainers, with big brown aprons covering the bulges of the guns. They drove round to the rear of the chateau and began unloading the boxes of produce, whilst Jacques launched into a saga about how he had hurt his arm. He was obviously convincing and was taken away for coffee and croissants. The boxes were put into a big pantry, and everyone just went about their business, ignoring the imposters.

CHAPTER TWELVE

Claire peered round the pantry door. 'Right, coast clear. Now we go for the laundry.'

They walked purposefully down the corridors, until they could smell the clean linen of the huge laundry. They dodged inside and hid behind the big wheeled hoppers of dirty sheets and towels. There were racks of clean, pressed garments awaiting retrieval, and Claire quickly rifled through them until she found some black trousers, a white shirt and a waistcoat that looked about the right size to fit Phil. She threw them to him. For herself, she found a plain black dress and a white apron. Bent double, they changed behind the bins and Claire stashed their old clothes behind a washing machine.

'Great, why are all Frenchmen shorter than me?' said Phil, as he stood up and the trousers swung round his ankles. He stretched his arms and the cuffs strained.

Claire stood and viewed him. 'You look okay; you'll just have to sag a bit, you know, be a hunchback,' she smirked. 'The one thing we didn't think about is shoes though.' She glanced down at their trainers. 'We'll just have to swipe some as we go round. Wait, this'll do for the time being,' and she pulled a tin of shoe polish from a rack and began blacking up Phil's shoes. After she had done a passable job on them, she hefted a pile of clean sheets into his arms and took some towels as they went out.

Looking purposeful and walking quickly, they finally found their way up the servants' stairs to the second floor. Here there were other maids and houseboys cleaning, so they followed the cues and began to dole out the towels and sheets. If anyone asked them anything, they apologized profusely and said they were new, and everyone proved to be most helpful and showed them what to do.

Ellie and Alistair were outside their father's room. The door was still locked, as Alistair had left it, and he slowly put the key in the lock. He paused and looked at Ellie, as if not wanting to step back into that part of his past. A servant came down the hall and waited respectfully, and then put a piece of paper in Alistair's hand.

'It's the analysis on the scroll. Wow, wait for this,' said Alistair, 'the scrawly signature is definitely Edward's, but it is signed in his own blood!'

Ellie stood aghast. 'His own blood? You've got to be kidding.' She snatched the paper from him and scanned the page. It was there, in black and white, that the signature was definitely blood, and DNA proved without a doubt that it was Edward's. 'We've got to have another look at the scroll and see what it actually says.'

'So, what do you want to do first—look at the scroll, or go in here?' Alistair put his hand on the key and withdrew it from the lock, waving it at her.

'No; I mean, yes, we'll do this room first. I'll just try to contain my curiosity and we'll look at the scroll later.'

'You sure? We could do it next week or next year…'

Ellie snatched the key and opened the door, not happy with his teasing. The room was sumptuous, even when covered with dust sheets. It was obvious nothing had been touched from the moment of death; there was even a book left open on the bedside table. Little puffs of dust rose from the carpets as she moved about the room. Ellie lifted the odd corners of dust sheets and gently replaced them, as if not wishing to disturb the dead. Alistair had the map in his hand and was examining the fireplace.

'The map says there should be a stairway here, but there's nothing I can see.'

Ellie went to him and began banging the fireplace and trying to twist bits of the carving, but nothing happened.

'What are you doing?' Alistair enquired.

'Well, if there's a stairway on the map, and we're in the right room, then it looks as if the stairs are behind the fireplace somehow. Come on… You must have seen some of those adventure films, where they prod a carving and the fireplace moves.'

'Not really, but I'll bow to your better judgment in this matter.'

'God, you really have led a sheltered life!'

They both prodded and pulled the ornate carvings till they looked at each other, defeated.

'It's got to be here somewhere, it says so on the map,' Ellie said, perusing the map again. 'Perhaps the entrance is not in the actual fireplace but at the side, maybe in those bookshelves,' she said, looking at the shelves flanking the alcoves. 'You do that side, I'll do this.' She headed off to the right and, placing a chair strategically, began to pull the books from the shelves. She had got about halfway across, when there was an exclamation from Alistair. Ellie looked across.

'These few books are fakes, although they look like all the others.' Ellie scrambled from the chair and joined him. He held the books at the top of their spines and they dropped forward, exposing a keypad.

'Crafty old devil,' said Alistair, as he looked at the electronics. 'I can't even hazard a guess at the combination.'

'Well, you're no good in crisis then, are you,' Ellie said racking her brain. 'Try some birthdays or other significant dates.'

Alistair punched some numbers, but nothing happened. 'We could be here all day. Let's go and look at the scroll and have a think about it.' They left reluctantly, and Ellie noticed that Alistair carefully locked the door behind him.

Down in the library, the scroll had been placed under glass on the table by the window. There was a copy of the analysis and summary of what it actually said.

'Your guys seem to have surpassed themselves; they've translated it for us. It was just a bit tricky to read with all the curly bits, and the language was difficult with all the "hereintos" and "aforementioneds",' Ellie said, as she looked at the scroll, then at the translation. It seems to be some sort of contract, between Edward and another guy named S'tan. There are no other names that stand out and the ink's almost faded away on the other signatures. 'Do you know a S'tan?'

Alistair shrugged. 'Could be anyone, I don't really know anything about our grandfather. I can't even remember Father talking to me about him.'

'Hey, I've just had a thought. I saw in a film where someone was breaking into a bank vault, and they sprayed some stuff on a key pad and the numbers that were used the most were highlighted. Do you think your tech men could have some of that stuff and try it?'

'It's probably only something you would ever see in a film, Ellie. Perhaps it does really exist,' Alistair mused. 'It could be worth a go, I'll ask.' He picked up the phone and had a rapid conversation in French and replaced the receiver with a smile. 'Looks like they know what you're on about, and we can give it a try. It will only perhaps be four numbers, so the permutations will be narrowed down a lot. We could be here past Christmas otherwise.'

'Alistair,' Ellie said quietly, 'are you going to let me go home soon? You mentioned Christmas and I would really like to spend it with Rory. We are engaged to be married.' Ellie held her hand up indicating the ring.

'No, Ellie. I'm sorry, but now I've found you, I can't let you go. You are my other half; I feel more complete than I've ever felt before. I've had relationships in the past, but I've not felt anything deep down at all, just gone through the motions. I feel that our destiny is together.'

'You're wrong, you know that. I don't feel anything like that at all. I must admit, I have revised my opinion of you slightly, but I'm still a prisoner. Also, that brother of yours, Max, if he ever comes anywhere near me, I swear I'll kill him. Be warned!'

'Warning duly noted, Ellie, but I have to keep you near me for the time being. I promise Max won't bother you again.'

They turned back to the scroll and after about an hour, they thought they had made some sense of it. There appeared to be an agreement between Edward and S'tan, and great riches and power would be all his, if Edward gave the future unborn "one of two" to him for eternity. It made no sense at all.

After drawing a blank, they decided to go back up to the bedchamber and have another look at the key pad. Alistair put through a call and a tech man would be there to meet them. He was standing outside the door when they got there, and when they had revealed the pad, he sprayed some stuff on it and left. After a few minutes, two numbers had a faint glow.

Ellie was amazed and said, 'I suppose that stuff picks up the grease from fingers, and people only use the numbers they need to.'

The numbers that glowed were 6 and 1. 'I assume it's a four digit key pad,' said Alistair and he began to push the numbers. Suddenly there was a hiss, and part of the bookcase swung open. Cool air wafted up with a faint musty smell; there was even a pull cord light switch, that gave some illumination from overhead bulkheads. A stairway made of stone spiralled downwards.

'Oh my God, it's like something out of an Indiana Jones film,' Ellie exclaimed.

'Who's that?' said Alistair looking puzzled.

'I give up with you; don't you ever even put the television on?'

'No, not really. Popular culture doesn't really interest me at all.'

'Try it sometime, you could be surprised. Are we going down this hole or not?'

Ellie let him lead the way and they spiralled down the stone staircase. The hewn stone eventually gave way to rock. The lights gradually got dimmer and dimmer, until they were lit only by a sulphurous glow. They were below the chateau, and there were rivulets of water running down the walls. The stairs became slick and they had to go very carefully. The stairway ended with a door—not just any old door, but a massive edifice, with studs and iron bands. There was a latch, but no lock. Alistair grasped it firmly, and the door protested and creaked as it opened. They both just stood and stared at the sight that met them.

It was a huge natural cavern, and everywhere there were blood red draperies fixed to the walls. Signs and symbols decorated every available space, and rich carpets covered the floor. It was warm and didn't smell musty at all. Overstuffed chairs and sofas were ranged around the sides, and there were tables set with chalices and other relics of a disturbing nature, daggers and knives. It looked like the set from a Hammer film.

Ellie was drawn to the bookshelves and pulled down volume after volume. She called Alistair over to look. There were some massive tomes bound in leather, some with ornate clasps and inlaid covers. She reached for one and placed it carefully on a table. She opened it, and it was hand scribed in old English. It was a Grimoire. Ellie explained it was a book that depicted how to cast magical spells and invoke supernatural entities, such as spirits or demons. Some of these types of books were considered to have magical powers of their own. Alistair's face was a picture of disbelief.

'I can't imagine Father having anything to do with this stuff. This must have belonged to someone else.'

'Alistair, I don't think so. The keypad was well used, and it was in his bedroom. My bet was that he was into this mumbo jumbo, but you didn't know.'

They gazed about the room and it all became clear; the signs and symbols included pentacles and other esoteric markings. Ellie knew nothing about these things, except for visiting the shop on her London high street that had sold charms and crystals that supposedly made you feel good. After a short while and some more exploring, she began to feel uneasy about being in the room, and asked Alistair if they could leave. He was still pulling books from the shelves and flicking over the pages.

'Can we go now? I really don't like this room,' Ellie said, as the hairs at the back of her neck began to stand up.

'Okay, but I'll take a couple of these to have a look at later; maybe it'll help me understand all this a bit more.' Alistair tucked a couple of the smaller volumes, along with the grimoire, underneath his arm.

'Please don't Alistair; I don't like them at all. I don't think they should be moved from here. Leave them,' Ellie said, suddenly afraid.

'No, it'll be fine. Let's go now, but I don't think we should tell anyone about this.' Ellie agreed wholeheartedly.

They climbed back up the stairs to the bedroom in silence, and carefully closed the bookcase door. They headed off back down to the library and Ellie trailed behind, lost in her own thoughts. She told Alistair that she was going to her room for a while and would meet him for a late lunch. He nodded and strode off, eager to see what secrets were in the books.

Ellie had begun to feel a headache coming on, and thought a quiet moment alone might make it feel better, so she rang for some tea and settled down with a magazine. A tap on the door heralded the tea, and a new maid brought it in. Ellie didn't pay her much attention as she laid things out on the side table. The maid leaned over as if to pour, but whispered in Ellie's ear.

'I'm Claire. I'm with the English police and we're here to rescue you.' She put her finger on her lips, signalling Ellie not to speak. Then louder, she said, with a French accent, 'Maybe you would like that I run a bath for you?'

Ellie played along and said that would be a good idea, as she did have a headache. Claire went to the bathroom and turned the taps on full force and the steam billowed, filling the bathroom.

Ellie followed her in, and Claire began to talk fast, in a very low voice. 'I haven't got much time, but we're here to help you. Now we've made contact, we'll get a plan together very quickly and get you home. You must wait for the instructions that will be written on the bathroom mirror. Just breathe on it and they'll show up. It may be tonight or tomorrow night, but it'll be soon, I promise. I have to go now.' She raised to a voice and asked Ellie if there was anything else she wanted. Ellie thanked her and she left.

As Ellie lay in the bath with the cup of tea at her elbow, she wondered how they were going to execute the rescue. There must be a whole force of them hidden in the chateau, just waiting to spring into action. The question was, if they did rescue her, what might happen? Alistair and Max weren't just going to let her go, and there was the threat made against Rory. It looked as if she and Rory would have to be spirited away, and go on some sort of protection plan and disappear to the other end of the country.

Knowing Alistair as she did now, Ellie and Rory could disappear to Timbuktu and he'd still find them. Ellie's mind raced round like a rat in a trap and she was getting more wound up, not being relaxed by the bath at all. She decided to dress and go and see what Alistair had found out, then get something to eat, although her stomach had clenched with nerves and fear.

Alistair was sitting in the library and looked up as Ellie entered.

'Have a look again at the painting of Edward.' He joined Ellie as they stared at it. 'Notice anything?'

He ran his index finger over the painting. Ellie suddenly recognised the curtains and the side table with the chalices on it, from the cave.

'It's the same stuff as in the room—and look, there's that big book with the leather binding.' Ellie looked at him. 'So Edward was into this stuff as well. Were your whole family warlocks and witches?'

'Sorry, but it's your family as well. Have you got hidden powers you've not told me about?'

'You should know, as you're the one who's always sounding off about this "connection" we're supposed to have.'

'That's just something I've never felt before with anyone. I can't explain it well, or put it into words, but it's a new experience. You'll just have to learn to like it.'

'Yeah, sure I will,' Ellie answered, her voice laced with sarcasm.

Changing the subject, Alistair said, 'But the scroll has to fit into this somehow. It's right there in the picture, so it's probably very important.'

'There are still a couple of things that don't make sense. What is the "one of two", and who on earth is S'tan?'

'I think all will become clear soon enough, and as I've told you before, try to practice some restraint and let things take their course.' Ellie turned away as she thought of her impending escape; she didn't want to display her anxiety.

At lunch, Alistair informed Ellie that Max would be back and joining them for dinner, and it was a three-line whip to attend. She blanched at the thought, but Alistair wouldn't hear any excuses—and she was not only to attend, but also be civil. Not on your life, Ellie thought, and mused how she could shove poison in his food and how the world would be a better place without him.

Ellie left Alistair looking at his spell books and went again to her room. Aimlessly she went through the wardrobe, looking at all the clothes for something better to wear. She tried a few pieces and walked into the bathroom, to get a better view in the long mirror. She was viewing herself from all angles, when she noticed some smudges on the mirror. Ellie breathed on it and words began to appear as her breath condensed.

"Tonight @ 6.30"

That would be when she was changing for dinner, so she would be here in her room anyway. She made a plan to keep out of Alistair's way till then, and just slip away with the police. Ellie's mind didn't want to go to the scenario of what might happen when Alistair found out. It was just too horrible to contemplate. She couldn't settle to do anything, and eventually ended up just pacing up and down her suite. She requested some more tea, but it was a different maid again that brought it to the room, and Ellie ended up very frustrated.

Hidden from view in a linen closet, Claire and Phil were quietly reviewing their plan.

Claire ticked the items off on her fingers. 'One, we know that Max Morgan is coming back tonight and he should be arriving by helicopter. Two, I've let Ellie know that we're ready to move at 6.30 tonight. Have you had comms with the others, to let them know what's going down and when?'

'No luck on that front, as there seems to be a radio communication blackout within the chateau. We'll just have to trust to luck that they're where they're supposed to be, and not down the pub.' Phil smiled and put his hand on Claire's arm. 'Don't worry; it'll be all right on the night.'

Claire put on a mock reassuring voice. 'Usually what can go wrong, does go wrong, you know that. I'll make for the chopper with Ellie and take out the pilot, then you'll give chase, then do your usual disappearing act into the bushes in the chaos.'

'Roger that. Synchronise watches at 5.45 p.m. local time, good luck. Break a leg.'

Claire opened the linen closet door a crack and slid out when the coast was clear. She walked purposefully to Ellie's room and tapped the door. Ellie put her head round the door and let Claire in.

'So get something warm on 'cos we're hopefully going for a helicopter ride; also, put some decent shoes on as you're going to have to run.'

Ellie fetched some shoes and sat on the edge of the bed to put them on. 'So what's the plan? Are you going to nick a helicopter?' she whispered.

'Yes and no. Max is arriving by chopper at 6.30ish and we're just going to borrow it for a time to get away.'

Ellie looked at Claire. 'You make that sound very easy, but I know nothing's ever that simple.'

Claire glanced at her watch. 'We're going to have to move soon. Give me your coat and I'll carry it for you and follow you down the stairs like I'm taking it for cleaning. When we get to the hall, turn and have a conversation with me, perhaps point out a spot on the coat. As we talk, keep moving towards the door and as soon as the chopper touches down, we'll make a dash for it.'

'What about Max? He'll be in the helicopter, he won't let me get away,' Ellie said nervously.

'No worries about that—just concentrate on getting to the chopper and we'll look after the rest,' said Claire reassuringly. Through the window they could hear the distant whump of a chopper as it got nearer, and hovered prior to landing. 'Get going Ellie, just focus on what you have to do,' said Claire, and took the coat.

Ellie's hand rattled the door knob and her knees wobbled as she walked down the stairs. She nearly forgot and walked straight out the front door but a discreet cough from Claire reminded her of her bit of play acting. Ellie turned and beckoned Claire closer. 'Oh, and make sure that this mark is removed, perhaps come closer to the light and you'll see what I mean.'

They moved towards the door. A footman appeared and began opening the large doors to welcome Max back home. Ellie felt a shove in the middle of her back, and elbowed the footman aside. She began to run towards the helicopter idling on the lawn.

Claire reached down and got the gun that was in the holster on her thigh. She draped the coat over her arm to hide the gun and began to run after Ellie. Max was getting out of the helicopter and, ducking low, began to walk towards the house. Ellie hesitated and Claire caught up with her giving her another shove. Behind her, Ellie could hear voices shouting, and suddenly Max clutched his leg and crumpled to the floor.

Claire had overtaken Ellie by this time and pulled open the helicopter door. She grabbed the pilot by the scruff of his neck and yanked him onto the grass. Before he could work out what to do next Claire shot him, at point blank range, in the kneecap.

Ellie had caught up by this point and fell across into the rear seats, with her legs dangling out of the open door. She felt the helicopter rise, but it yawed suddenly to the side. She grabbed a seat belt to stop herself falling out, and the helicopter stabilized as they rose to treetop level.

Suddenly Ellie felt a hand grab at her and fasten round her ankle, and she kicked frantically with her other leg. She must have screamed, as Claire looked over her shoulder but had both hands full with controlling the roll. Ellie realized that someone was hanging from the skid of the chopper with one hand, and had another hand firmly round her leg. She kicked and struggled but the grip only got tighter, and it felt as though her leg was breaking.

Suddenly the world was bathed in a blinding light, as big search lights strobed the trees and turned night into day. Ellie managed to wind her arm round the seat belt for a better grip and twisted slightly, so she could see who was hanging on. It was Max and his face was demonic, with his lips drawn back into a snarl.

He screamed at her, 'You're mine Ellie Black! Do you think you can take my place, hell bitch!'

Ellie loosened her grip on the belt a fraction and they both jerked forwards into the night; with her other foot, she began to kick at his head and eventually made contact with his face, as it was turned upwards, shouting obscenities at her. She wanted him dead, that was all she could think of, and she began kicking with renewed vigour, feeling a crunch as her foot met his nose. Instantly his grip loosened and Ellie pulled her foot back in, leaning out to watch his body, picked out in the searchlight, spiral down. They were high up at that point and no one could have survived that fall.

Ellie went limp. All her energy drained away and it was all she could do to buckle herself in, then curl into a ball, as the icy wind chilled her.

CHAPTER THIRTEEN

Phil had followed Ellie and Claire out of the house, running fast and ostensibly giving chase as they saw Max begin his walk across the lawn. Phil had drawn his gun and taken a wild shot, and luckily hit Max in the lower leg. He had gone down, as if pole axed. Phil pointed round the side of the chateau and shouted something intelligible, as if he'd seen someone run that way, then hared off as fast as he could go. He peeled off at the last moment and crashed through some bushes, the twigs whipping his face and tearing at his clothes, but he didn't lessen his pace.

Around the edges of the chateau perimeter Robert, Jack and Nigel were lying in their fox holes, alternatively glancing through their field glasses, and doing isometric exercises to stop seizing up from the cold. Jack's comms crackled.

'It's on, I've just seen Ellie and Claire, they're going for the helicopter,' shouted Nigel excitedly. Jack jammed his glasses to his face and clipped his nose in the process, making his eyes water.

'Dammit,' he swore under his breath, and wiped his eyes. He saw someone who had the stature of Phil running very fast round the side of the chateau, and plunge into some bushes.

'Think I've got Phil, he's heading this way, prepare for

extraction,' Jack shouted into his mike.

'Got him,' called Robert, 'pull back to recce point 1.'

Jack saw a torch flash once and that was the signal to Phil. It was also the signal to pull back with whatever kit they could bring in 30 seconds or less. Abandoning most of it, Jack put his small day sac on his shoulder and began to run to a thickly forested slope about half a mile away. Jack ran blind, as it was very dark, tripping over ruts and powering through muddy puddles as he made his way up the slope, heaving for breath when he was still only half way up. A shadow appeared at his side and grabbed his elbow, making him jump a mile.

'Only me mate,' said Nigel, and dragged Jack the last four hundred or so yards. As soon as they were in the forest cover, they fell into a thicket and looked back to the chateau. The helicopter was picked out in the searchlights and there was a figure dangling from a skid. They both watched silently as the figure fell, almost in slow motion, tumbling down to a certain death. Jack gasped and breathed the word, 'Ellie.'

'No mate, it wasn't her. It was definitely a bloke, got 20/20 vision see, and that was definitely a fella.' Jack breathed a sigh and relaxed, sending up a quick prayer that Ellie and Claire were safe in the helicopter. Then two more figures came running up the hill. Jack could hear them before he could see them, as Phil and Robert hit the recce point dead on.

'All accounted for?' asked Phil, who seemed hardly out of breath.

'Yes,' everyone murmured.

'Doesn't seem to be any pursuit just yet but they'll find the hideouts soon and we can expect the dogs, so let's split,' said Phil, and everyone set off at a jog. They reached the farmhouse and piled into two cars. Nigel went with Robert and set off back to Paris, while Phil and Jack piled into the other vehicle and began to drive to the coast. Their escape route was by sea, and they had to try and find the helicopter before Alistair's men got there.

The chopper had headed northwest and would hit the coast within a few minutes. The plan was to land on a deserted beach or a field nearby and make contact with Phil, if he had got away unscathed. Claire looked back over her shoulder and saw that Ellie was safe, but very shaky. It was icy cold in the cockpit and Claire handed her the coat, and signalled to put on a headset. Ellie's hands shook, but she managed to tuck her coat round herself and put the headset on. Claire's voice came over, loud and clear.

'You did well Ellie and we're safe now. You did great, don't forget that,' said Claire trying to reassure her.

'I didn't! I killed Max. I was the one who killed him,' Ellie shouted at her. 'I kicked him and he fell. He's dead.'

Claire couldn't answer that, and started to tell her the plan to deflect her self-recriminations. 'We're going to land soon and there will be a boat for us, so we escape by sea. Jack will meet us and we'll all be home in no time.' It just sounded to Ellie that Claire was trying to keep her calm and tell her everything would be all right in the end. Every fairy story had a happy ending–or did it?

The chopper began to descend and Claire flicked a landing light on then off briefly. It illuminated the French countryside, and there was a strip of sand at the side of a choppy sea. The tide was nearly in and Claire decided to head for the dunes a bit further back.

'Get ready to land Ellie; could be a bit bumpy as it's not

very flat.'

Ellie curled up into a ball even tighter and felt the helicopter going down, and the rotors whine reached a fever pitch as they hovered.

Ellie heard the word 'shit' as they landed and the chopper tilted to one side. The rotors bit into the soft sand and sprayed it up into the air before they got torn off. They cart-wheeled away into the darkness and the cockpit began to tumble. Ellie and Claire were thrown about, as if in a giant washing machine. Ellie banged her head a few times on the fuselage and saw stars. She was conscious of a hand pulling her out, and she managed to scramble up through the wreckage to get to relative safety.

'Come on, move, it might go up any second,' shouted Claire. Ellie was dragged down to the beach, slipping and sliding on the loose sand, eventually falling and rolling, coming to rest in a tangle with Claire. Ellie spat out some sand and sat up. It was freezing cold, and she could hear the waves as they broke on the narrow strip of beach.

'You OK?' asked Claire as she extricated herself and sat beside her. Ellie felt a reassuring hand on her arm and heard the concern in Claire's voice.

'I think so, but I haven't stood up yet. That was one hell of a ride. You OK?' Ellie looked at her and could just make out her shadowy figure. 'It's really dark here.'

'Yep, well, there's no ambient light from houses or street lights, and no moon, so it really is as black as pitch. We've got to get to a road, as I can't see a boat light. Someone can pick us up from there. You ready?' She hauled Ellie to her feet and they began to walk along the beach, then climbed up the dunes. 'I reckon we're on the Cote Fleurie somewhere, we didn't fly that far. We'll just head inland and see if we can make contact. The original plan was that we got away by boat, but that's gone pear shaped now as I'm not a hundred per cent sure where we are. So it's Plan B.'

Ellie just trudged along behind her. She ached everywhere, and didn't want to think about the myriad of bruises and scrapes she would have tomorrow. Thankfully nothing seemed to be broken, but she was so tired she could have just curled up on the sand. Claire was a dynamo and appeared to have endless energy, and Ellie struggled to keep up. They topped the dunes and saw lights winking in the distance.

'Lights mean people, people mean roads, so that's where we're going,' said Claire, and set off across a field. Sand turned to mud under Ellie's feet, and kept sucking at her shoes. The icy water soon seeped in and numbed her feet, and she couldn't feel her hands at all. There was a small tumbledown barn at the edge of the field by a country lane. Ellie called out to Claire.

'Stop, wait for me. I don't think I can walk another step, I'm just so cold. Stop, please,' Ellie begged her.

Claire came to her and grasped her hands, and felt her face, which was like ice. 'Yep, you're going to go hypothermic if you don't get under cover soon. Do you feel sleepy?'

'I'm totally knackered, to be honest. I'm sorry, I really can't go on.' Ellie's legs collapsed and she sat down on the freezing earth; it had never felt so good.

'OK, into this barn and we'll see what we can find to make you warmer.' Claire unceremoniously dragged Ellie upright and led her through a broken-down wall into the barn. There were some piles of musty hay in a corner, and some animal feed bags scattered about. She pushed Ellie into the hay and began to pile it on top of her, after wrapping her feet in the feed bags. It stank to high heaven but Ellie didn't care; she just curled up and felt her eyelids grow heavy. Claire said something to her that Ellie didn't quite hear, and then she disappeared.

Claire set off at a steady jog, which ate up the miles, till she found a phone box. Punching in a code, she got straight through to Nigel, and he immediately set up a trace on the phone box to see where she was. That information was relayed quickly through to Jack and Phil, who were scouring the countryside at breakneck speed. They did an illegal U turn and raced to where Claire was. It took about ten minutes, and they dimmed the lights as they drew up. Claire jumped in the back and directed them to where Ellie lay. She gave them a précis of the events as they raced back to the barn, and Phil filled her in with the rest of the team's escape.

'Helicopter?' he asked.

'Trashed,' she said.

'That makes four now, what have you got against whirlybirds?'

'Dunno, can't seem to find the places to land them these days.' Claire shrugged her shoulders.

They arrived at the barn and pulled the car just off the road. Ellie was where Claire had left her and appeared to be comatose, as she didn't respond to their shakes.

'Clothes, please—Jack, get the car going and get the heater up to full blast, we'll put her in the front seat,' said Phil, stripping off his coat and jumper. They unceremoniously took off Ellie's clothes and manhandled her into the outsize menswear, so she was warmer and dry. They carried her into the car and propped her in the front seat, as the warm air began to do its job. A few moans began to escape Ellie's lips and her eyelids flickered.

Phil leaned over from the back seat and said, 'I don't know if you can hear me, but you're safe now. You'll get warmer, but you're going to have quite a lot of pain as the feeling comes back into your hands and feet. Try and move them if you can, and the blood will flow back quickly.' He leaned back, frustrated, as that was all he could do for her at the moment.

Jack put his foot on the accelerator and revved off into the darkness.

'Head north Jack, it looks like the boat plan is defunct so it's now Plan C,' said Phil.

'So, we've done A and B, what's C then?' said Jack, puzzled that he'd missed something at the planning briefing. He'd always thought that all eventualities were covered and teams like this didn't fly by the seat of their pants, though they seemed to be doing that at the moment, and it felt uncomfortable.

'We get to Caen and get a ferry, what could be simpler than that?' Phil looked at the others and they couldn't think of anything to say. 'We'll dump the car, tell Duchamp where it is, and go on as foot passengers. Back to jolly old Blighty as tourists. Rob and Nige are probably nearly back in Paris now, and they'll take Euro star or the plane, doesn't really matter, as they aren't known. Once we hit British soil, then we'll contact our department heads and get a safe house somewhere up north for Ellie and Rory.'

Jack nodded, 'I think Rory and Ellie will like Plan C better than the others. It's obvious they can't go back to London, as they'll be sitting targets for Morgan. I wonder what really happened in that chateau. I don't think he would have hurt her, but she's killed his brother. That's a very sticky situation.'

'Yep, you're right! I don't think he's going to like that one bit,' said Claire, 'better that they're well out of it, but we're going to have to hit an all-night mall and get some clothes, as they probably won't even let us on the ferry in the first place looking like this. Perhaps we could get a disposable phone as well and try and set things up, so that the ball's rolling when we get to England.'

There was an all-night mall near to the ferry port and Ellie felt a bit more with it. She was not so sleepy, but the tingling and pain in her hands and feet was awful. She tried to keep wiggling her toes, but the pain brought tears to her eyes. Jack parked up, and when she tried, she could barely walk.

'Ellie, I'm going to get you some clothes and some pain killers if I can. I'll also get some hot coffee and something to eat. Stay here and pretend to be asleep for about half an hour, but you're going to have to walk onto that ferry,' said Claire, who appeared to be totally unaffected by the crash and the freezing conditions.

Ellie felt very weak and inadequate as they split up and went to get the supplies. She'd been kidnapped and these people had risked everything to save her—and she was conscious she hadn't even thanked them.

They were soon back with bags of cheap clothes and Ellie was told to change into the jeans and jumper and put a ski jacket over the top. She was given hot chocolate to drink, with some croissants and pain au chocolat to eat. Food had never tasted so good and she wolfed the lot down ravenously. Claire had even got some pain killers from a pharmacy, and Ellie took two with the last of her food. With the hot drink and the food, she immediately felt better and warmer inside. The pain killers began to work, and the terrible aching subsided to a tingle she could cope with. Ellie wasn't aware but she had scrapes on her face from the crash and a big lump was developing on her head. Claire seemed to have thought of everything, and gave her a knitted hat to pull down over her forehead and then slapped on some heavy-duty concealer and foundation on her face. Ellie looked in the mirror of the visor and she looked hideous.

'Don't get a job with Max Factor, whatever you do,' Ellie said, making a weak attempt at humour.

Claire smiled and replied, 'That sounds a bit more like the old Ellie. Doesn't look much like the old one, but that's a good thing at the moment.'

Phil and Jack had been busy with the phone and it appeared Duchamp had come up trumps again. None of them had got passports and Duchamp basically wanted them off French soil as quickly as possible, so he was getting a motorcycle courier to deliver the necessary papers within the hour. Everyone would have diplomatic papers to get on board the ferry. He had also arranged a cabin, so no-one would be bothered on the crossing and he probably breathed a sigh of relief they would all disappear in the next few hours.

A courier duly screeched up and put a package in Phil's hand, which he signed for, and the motorcycle roared away. More cars began to turn up, and people were stocking up on wines before boarding the ferry. The team split up and began walking around, mingling in with the foot passengers, who all looked tired and cold this early in the morning. The group followed the signs and eventually boarded the ferry. Passport control wasn't a problem as Ellie just handed in her papers, smiled, and was waved through. She almost heard everyone breathe a collective sigh of relief that nothing had gone wrong so far. Ellie got to the cabin and fell on the bunk fully clothed, and eventually slept most of the trip. Besides eating again, she didn't move from the cabin till the ferry docked.

CHAPTER FOURTEEN

At the Chateau of the Birds, Alistair was in full possession of the facts of Ellie's escape and sat in icy silence as the Chief of Security outlined how he had failed in his job.

'You mean these people infiltrated the chateau and nothing was picked up by anyone at all?'

The grimoire lay on the desk by Alistair's right hand, which he placed almost reverently on the inlaid cover. 'So appraise me again of what your job entails? May I refresh your memory; I think it means you keep the chateau secure, that you vet all the staff, that you don't have people with guns wandering about, that you don't let my sister get kidnapped—and my brother doesn't get killed. Have I missed something?'

The Chief stared at the floor and mumbled something incoherent.

'Pardon,' Alistair enquired, 'you wish to say something in mitigation of your shortcomings?'

'I'm sorry and it won't happen again,' the Chief said inadequately.

Alistair stood and leaned over the desk. 'It's hardly likely my brother is going to get killed twice, is it?' he said sarcastically. 'I suggest you get out of my sight immediately… Make that forever, or I may do something I certainly won't regret.'

The ex-Chief vanished with alacrity.

Alistair sat down and composed himself with a few deep breaths and opened the grimoire. It fell open at a page that was heavily decorated, headed in an archaic script that appeared to be some sort of incantation. It began "invenire et perdere" and Alistair began to mouth the words. As he did so, his mind focused on the hapless Chief of Security and before he knew it an hour had passed. He shut the book and laid his hand again on the cover. He could have sworn he felt a tingle run through his fingers.

The ex-Chief had gone quickly to his room, gathered up as many of his belongings as he could carry and left the chateau without speaking to anyone. He jumped in his car and drove to Deauville, where he booked himself into a room at a hotel under a false name. He knew he was in danger and would lie low for tonight, then formulate a plan. The room was a small single, situated at the rear of the hotel; he sank onto the hard bed, and breathed a sigh. So far, so good, he had managed to get away. He was under no illusions about his life hanging by a thread, and he would be dead meat in an instant should Mr. Morgan wish it.

The room began to get chilly and he got up and felt the radiator; it was still pumping out warmth. Small fingers of rime began to crystallize on the window, which was soon iced up. He scratched at it with his fingernails. It scraped off, but soon reformed into ice flowers. He was getting deathly cold now and decided to go and complain to the concierge, but the door wouldn't open and his fingers stuck frozen to the brass knob. He cried out as he pulled them away, and left slivers of his skin behind. His breath was coming in small cloudy puffs, and each inhalation in seared his lungs. It grew darker and darker in the room, and the shade carried an icy menace with it, making his skin crawl. There was an eddy forming and the air swirled faster, until it made a vortex and a shape coalesced. It was a huge griffin with scales and an enormous hooked beak. He fell to his knees in terror as the creature lunged forward, tearing at him with its claws and beak. He felt chunks of flesh rip away and tried to fight it off with his hands. He began to pray out loud and the beast just laughed and continued the carnage. His dying thought was that death would be a blessing but his soul had already been captured and bound, then carried off to Hell.

The next day the maid opened the door and was confronted by a bloodbath in the room. It looked as if the poor man had been through a mincer, as blood was sprayed everywhere and chunks of him were scattered about. She crossed herself and began to scream and scream, not stopping till the doctor gave her a sedative. What the police could not fathom in this particularly brutal murder was that the door was locked on the inside. Enquiries were made at the Chateau, as it was the deceased's last place of work, but everyone had seen him leave in a hurry and could throw no light on the horrific occurrence.

Ellie got off the ferry feeling much better for the sleep and food, and had finally thawed out. The pain had subsided to mild pins and needles, which was bearable. She had managed a shower but her body was covered in wheals and huge bruises, which were very tender from the crash. Claire must have been the same, but was stoic. Ellie's face was a bit battered but she used some more of the concealer, and it was a passable job when she looked in the mirror. A car was waiting and they drove northwards.

'We're not going to London then?' Ellie asked.

'No, there's a safe house for you and Rory up North, and he's already on his way. Jack will stay with you both, as we've got to get back to the smoke,' said Phil. 'We're going to catch a train at Basingstoke and begin to sort this mess out.'

The car ate up the miles and stopped to let Phil and Claire out at the station, and Ellie gave Claire a gentle hug, as she knew she was probably as sore as she was.

It was a very long drive, and late that night when Ellie and Jack finally bumped their way up a track to a farmhouse. Jack seemed very tired, and Ellie had soon given up trying to make conversation. She was looking forward to seeing Rory again. It had seemed like months and Jack hadn't let her talk to him on the phone, so she wondered what sort of reception she was going to get. You think you know someone well, but now she wasn't sure at all. There were some lights showing through chinks in the curtains, and smoke from the chimney was wafting up to the winter sky when they drew up. Ellie eased herself stiffly out of the car and went to the front door. It was flung open before she could get there, and Rory bounded out of the house and swept her up in the biggest hug she could have wished for. He was practically crying and they stood there for five long minutes, before he released her and held her hand to take her inside. Ellie was back in heaven and suddenly felt safe again. She hadn't realized how much she wanted him, and Ellie was also crying by the time they got to the hall.

There was a guy whom Ellie assumed was another policeman in the kitchen, and he was stirring something on the

Aga. Rory took her coat and they all sat down at the kitchen table.

Rory was still holding Ellie's hand. 'What happened to your face, Ellie?' He gently touched the scrapes and bruises.

'That's nothing, wait till you see the rest of me, every colour of the rainbow,' Ellie said, with a big grin.

'So who did this to you? It was that bastard wasn't it, the one who reckons he's your twin brother?'

'No, he didn't lay a finger on me at all, it was a helicopter crash.'

'A helicopter crash,' said Rory incredulously.

'Yep, it all happened when I was rescued by Jack here and his buddies. Claire and I got away in one of Alistair's helicopters and we tried to land on a beach, but we crashed.'

The culinary policeman began to dole out food, which appeared to be some sort of stew, onto plates and everyone helped themselves to a baked potato each and began eating. He gave Ellie her plate.

'Smells wonderful and tastes even better.' Ellie smiled at him. 'How long have you and Rory been here?'

'I'm John,' as he introduced himself, 'and I'm here with Jack to do shifts and provide protection. Sorry I'm not much of a cook, but I hope it fills a gap. We got here yesterday and have made ourselves at home. We've got plenty of supplies and enough firepower to stop an army.'

'I hope we don't need it.' Ellie glanced at Rory, who looked horrified at the thought.

CHAPTER FIFTEEN

The evening progressed, sometimes better, sometimes worse than expected. Ellie and Rory had taken themselves off to the small sitting room, whilst John and Jack had stayed in the kitchen discussing shifts and defensive strategies. Ellie had started at the beginning, and given Rory a no holds barred account of the kidnapping and the ensuing debacle. He had listened to her exploits with an air of disbelief, particularly at the point where she had killed Max.

'You have actually killed someone, Ellie—you do realize you could be done for murder,' he said earnestly.

'I don't think so, as he was trying to kill me at the time. Anyway, it's a bit of a moot point and I don't think the French police are going to do much about it. It's a question if they know at all, as I doubt Alistair will be running to them shouting about it. He did kidnap me, remember?'

'You've changed Ellie,' he said, holding her hand. 'A few weeks ago, you were in hospital totally shocked about Ali's murder; now you seem so matter of fact about it all, even the murder of your own half-brother.'

'Rory,' Ellie said, tightening the grip on his hand, 'he was trying to kill me. I was hanging out of a helicopter, and I would have died if I hadn't have kicked him off. Let's just leave it at that, but I never thought of him as any relative of mine. He was evil and would have killed me the first chance he got, as he thought I was going to take his place at Alistair's side.'

'And were you?' said Rory picking up that point.

'I never said that, Rory, please don't twist what I say. A lot's happened to me over the past week or so, and I'm still trying to get my head round it all. We're going to be stuck here for quite a while, so let's not fight about it now. I'm really sorry you're involved and I did try to keep you out of it, but I failed and the threats against you are real. They will use you to get at me.' Ellie tried to lighten the mood at that point and held up her hand with the engagement ring. 'For better or worse?'

Rory was only partially mollified and was a bit quiet for the rest of the evening, but he didn't lose her hand at all. Everyone went to bed early and Rory was again horrified at the state of her body, with all the bruises now showing in full Technicolor. Ellie thought that it had bought it home to him what a rough time she'd had, and he was the old gentle, caring Rory for the rest of the night.

Next morning everyone gathered in the kitchen, and Ellie was full of questions as her brain had been processing information all night.

'So how long are we going to be here?' Ellie asked Jack.

'Don't know yet, as we've got to have word from London on what to do next. All we'll do is keep you safe and let them sort all the legal stuff down there.'

'So we could be here for Christmas then… but that's three weeks away. Anyway, where are we? I came here in the dark and haven't got a clue. Where's the nearest town, as I would like some supplies. You've done a pretty good job, but there's some other stuff I want to get.' The questions welled up thick and fast.

'Yes, you're both probably going to be here for Christmas. Give me a list and I'll make sure you get what's important, and you're up North somewhere in a remote farmhouse, and that's all I can tell you. Also forget the phones, they don't work up here anyway, but we've got a satellite link for emergencies. So… sit back and enjoy your Christmas break, compliments of Her Majesty's government.' Jack gave Ellie a slice of toast at that point.

Rory began to bluster, 'You can't keep me here and I certainly won't stay that long. I'll lose my job and what about my flat?'

John tried to placate him by saying, 'Don't worry about that, it's all taken care of. As to staying here, we obviously can't make you stay but for your own safety we strongly recommend that you do. It's your choice in the end, but they'll use you to get to Ellie.' Faced with that option, Rory subsided into silence.

The days melded into each other and the first snows fell as the threats seemed to retreat, as nothing happened out of the ordinary. Boredom insidiously crept in, as everyone exhausted the supply of books, and even the turns at cooking were a highlight of the day. John and Jack were still vigilant and constantly reviewed the plans if they came under attack from Morgan's men, but even that became a routine after the first few weeks. Ellie had become a good poker player and could always out bluff Rory, as he had quite a few unconscious tells that she'd never noticed before. Basically, he couldn't lie at all well, and he gave himself away on an unconscious level. She didn't have the heart to tell him, and he was always greatly in her debt on the washing up rotas. She had devised a keep fit programme that was endorsed by Jack and John, as Ellie had seen how Claire had coped with the terrain after the crash, and she wasn't going to be the team wimp again. She found she could run faster and longer than before and began to become more toned, her clothes becoming looser. She didn't think for a moment that Alistair would give up. This was just the calm before a huge storm.

In the chateau, Alistair had appointed a new Security Chief, and they had reviewed every angle of the CCTV footage again and again. He had remembered every nuance of the stance and facial characteristics of the infiltrators.

He had ordered Karl and his men in England to scour every avenue to find Ellie. They had reported that she had been seen leaving a ferry and had gone to Basingstoke, where two of the group had left for London. As far as they knew they were still there. Ellie had been taken northwards by car, and there the trail had gone cold. There were many men positioned in towns up North, but no sightings could be positively verified. It was a manhunt of massive proportions. All Alistair could do was sit and wait, and that didn't agree with him at all. He toyed with the idea of going back to England, but realized he was probably safer in France for the time being.

Alistair had spent many hours looking at the books from the hidden room and had tried to delve deeper into their arcane mysteries. They all dealt with black magic, and he realized that the family wealth had been built with other forces governing their dealings. It was hard to believe that both his grandfather and his father had been initiates into some sort of secret society, and it was harder to comprehend that his father had set such store by this. He remembered his father as the hard-headed business man, with a gift for spotting trends in markets and knowing the perfect moment for making a deal. He'd been handed the reins and had tried to follow in his father's footsteps. He believed he hadn't done too bad a job but the question was—would he do better with some help?

He looked again at the grimoire and touched his hand on the cover. He felt again that slight tingle through his fingers. He sat back and cleared his mind, and thought only of Ellie. He pictured her wearing the family jewels, a perfect picture, formed in his mind. Suddenly a gust of wind blew the book cover open and riffled the pages. They stopped turning of their own volition, and he looked at the incantation, written with a flourished hand. The top of the page was headed "circumspicio". He began to say the words under his breath, and in his mind, he began to fly over the English countryside, now speckled with snow.

In the farmhouse, it had been a day like any other, and the strain was beginning to tell on Rory. He had begun to find fault with everything and was now pacing up and down the kitchen, hampering Ellie's attempts at cooking the evening meal on the Aga. It was a temperamental beast at the best of times, and now was rapidly cooling for lack of wood.

'Just go and get some more wood will you, make yourself busy or just go and find Jack or John to play with.'

'Yeah, but it's snowing and I'll have to get all dressed up,' he whined.

'So, I'll do it as well as cooking. You'll just have to wait for your dinner, then won't you?'

'Oh, all right, I suppose so.' He went with bad grace and pulled on wellies and an overcoat. He opened the back door, letting in an icy blast. Ellie was sure it wasn't just the arctic wind that made her shiver—and she then suddenly got the feeling someone or something was watching her. Immediately she heard a shout from outside and she yelled 'Jack!' at the top of her voice. She heard footsteps pounding down the hallway, and the kitchen door crashed back as John and Jack stormed into the kitchen. Ellie pointed outside with her finger.

'Rory went for wood and I've just heard him shout.' Ellie picked up a carving knife and everyone rushed outside. Torches flicked on and reflected off the falling snow. Rory was standing by the woodpile, and logs were scattered round his feet. He was pointing at the side of the shed and his hand was shaking. The torch beams followed where he indicated, and, crouched in the shadow, was an enormous bird; far bigger than the buzzards they had watched wheeling above the hills. It slowly turned its head, and its eye reflected golden in the light. It rose up onto scaly legs, which were finished with huge claws, and took one pace forward. That was too much for Jack and John and they opened fire on the creature. The bullets just seemed to pass through it, with no effect.

The great curved beak opened and the creature hissed; it almost sounded like the words 'Found you'. Ellie swore, and it laughed. It stretched its wings and knocked Rory over in the process, then rose up and flapped lazily away into the swirling snow. Everyone stood transfixed until Rory groaned and Jack and John rushed over, and carried him into the kitchen.

'What in God's name was that?' Jack said, as he examined Rory for broken bones. 'I've shot things before and they've twitched a bit, but never flown off.' Turning his attention back to Rory, he helped him sit up and said, 'Nothing broken as far as I can see, but you'll have a bruise on your head tomorrow.

Take it easy, and I'll get you a painkiller for the headache you're going to have.'

'I've got one already thanks, I'll just sit here for a bit.' Rory sank into a kitchen chair, with his head in his hands. 'What the hell hit me? I could have sworn it was a bird but I've never seen one of those before. It landed me a right crack on the head and I woke up in here.'

John came in with some wood and stoked up the Aga. The ensuing warmth quickly dissipated the chill in the kitchen. He carefully locked the back door and drew the kitchen curtains. 'There's nothing in the snow at all, no prints, blood, not even a feather. No sign of it at all. I know I hit it at least twice, should've been some blood, or something. I'll use the sat phone and call in. See if they can shed some light on it.'

Ellie hadn't said a word, but she knew it was something to do with Alistair and those damned books. She didn't believe in the occult and had called it "mumbo jumbo", but she'd seen something none of them could explain.

Ellie also knew without a doubt that it had come looking for her. She had seen it turn its head and look straight at her, eyeing its prey. She also could have sworn on a stack of bibles that it spoke the words "Found you" to her alone. She busied herself and made a cup of tea for Rory. Some colour had returned to his face and he perked up a bit, so she returned to making dinner and salvaging what she could. It was a subdued crew that finally sat down and picked at the meal.

Ellie said, 'So what are we going to do now? Do we stay here, or move somewhere else? I think that Alistair sent that thing to find me. He couldn't do it by normal means, so he sent that.'

Jack looked at her in a peculiar way. 'What do you mean,

he sent it?'

So Ellie told the whole story of finding the hidden chamber in Alistair's father's bedroom, and the way he had taken some of the books to read. 'It was all to do with the occult and they seemed to have some sort of esoteric group going. Don't underestimate Alistair; if he wants something, he'll get it, by fair means or foul. The chateau was called the "Chateau of the Birds" and I didn't see any bird carvings or pictures while I was there, but that was definitely a big bird I saw outside.'

'That's a pretty tenuous link, Ellie,' said Jack. 'What if it was just some sort of unknown species that's been lurking on the moors that no-one's ever seen it before?'

'Well, it should have been a dead and extinct species by now, as I definitely shot it twice,' said John taking a gulp of cola.

Speculation was rife for the rest of the evening, and the farmhouse that had become their home suddenly seemed insecure and unwelcoming. Every creak of the boards and rumble of the wind in the chimneys took on a sinister meaning, and Ellie lay wakeful for most of the night, listening for odd sounds.

The dawn broke to a white world, with a weak wintry sun dazzling off mounds of snow. It had fallen with a vengeance overnight and they wouldn't have been able to get the car out, even if they'd wanted to. John and Jack were already in the kitchen when Ellie went down the creaky stairs with Rory in tow, now sporting a large bruise across his face. She was tired and only managed a slice of toast and a mug of tea sitting up in the corner, huddled in the warmth of the Aga.

Jack put the sat phone down on the table. 'I've been onto

London quite a few times last night and our big bird has certainly ruffled a few feathers.' A quiet 'ha ha' came from John.

'This is quite a turn up for the book from their point of view. No-one seems to have any answers at the moment, but they're all agreed that we should stay put here. Not that we can go anywhere fast, as there's more snow forecast today; then we're officially cut off. One good point is that if we can't get out, no-one can get in.'

'Don't be too sure about that,' Ellie muttered darkly from her corner.

Alistair was still murmuring "circumspicio" as pictures began flashing through his mind. Countryside scrolled by at an amazing speed and hills appeared in the distance, white with snow. The ground rose up to meet him at an alarming rate and he mentally winced as he anticipated the shock of landing on the frozen earth. Instead he landed gently and saw someone pointing at him. Other figures came out of the darkness and he was lit up in torch glare. Ellie stood there, magnificently defiant with a large carving knife in her hand, surrounded by men who pointed guns and shot at him. He felt nothing except exhilaration. He breathed the words 'Found you', and he knew that she had heard and understood. He felt a sudden surge of anger against the figure pointing at him and raising his arm caught him a blow that laid him on the floor in the snow. By just willing it, he then rose into the air to fly away, laughing as he did so.

Reality slammed back into Alistair as he sat on his library chair. He had his hand on the grimoire, and now felt he understood the power of the book. He could go, at will, wherever he wanted, and he felt jubilant that he had found Ellie where others had failed miserably. All power was his and he could control it whenever he wished, just by holding the book and letting it show him the right words to use. He was very tempted to try again, but underlying the joy at finding Ellie was the fact that he was tired to his very core. This flying around the countryside was exhausting, and he felt physically and mentally drained. Better now the foot soldiers should take over and complete the job. He picked up the telephone.

Karl answered at the first ring and took the details directly from Alistair. He was surprised at first that Alistair had managed to locate Ellie, whilst still being in France, but he knew there were many operatives on the ground searching for her. Alistair gave him the notable landmarks, descriptions of the countryside and roads, almost as if he had seen them himself. Karl informed him that Google Earth would find the location in an instant. Although the weather was closing in fast, a helicopter could get there as long as it wasn't actually snowing. Alistair seemed well pleased with the answer and said he would await further developments, with anticipation of a successful outcome.

In the farmhouse, the survival drill suddenly became more intense, and they all worked on their physical fitness till they were dropping with exhaustion. Jack and John had put together a kit, each to be picked up quickly if they were forced out into the open on the moors. It was well below freezing now and still snowing sporadically, but they were prepared if circumstances made them abandon the farmhouse suddenly. In the back of her mind Ellie had been preparing herself for the inevitable day when she would be captured again. No-one could keep on running forever, and she knew Alistair would never give up. She even had a half-formed plan of what she would do if it happened, but decided not to share it with anyone just yet. The bird thing was very unsettling, and Ellie wondered what Alistair had managed to uncover in the secret room. She could hazard a guess and that made her even more uneasy.

Rory had stopped whining about being there, and the realization that it was a life or death situation for him had finally struck home. He saw now how he could be used as a pawn by Alistair and that he was in it up to his neck, like it or not.

The day before Christmas dawned cold and clear. There wasn't a cloud in the sky, and a watery sun highlighted every ice crystal. It was a beautiful day and everyone decided that it was too good to miss, and they all revelled in outdoor pursuits, racing round like children, playing snowballs and making a misshapen snow person. It was John that insisted on the political correctness and it was named Sam, which could be male or female. It was a great morning, and everyone had trooped back into the kitchen to thaw out when they heard a whump, whump noise, and Ellie knew immediately it was a helicopter. She went to the window and over the crest of the hill came a big black chopper, capable of carrying six men. It hovered by the farmhouse looking for a place to land. The snow whipped up from the rotors making a whirlwind of ice, and it settled within twenty yards of the house.

Ellie felt a hand grab her arm and she was roughly pushed out of the kitchen and her mind clicked into the survival drill immediately. She ran for the cellar door and scurried down the steps, with Rory hot on her heels. Ellie knew Jack and John had taken up covert positions, where they could rain maximum fire down onto the helicopter. She sat down on the mattress on the floor and pulled her knees up to her chest, hugging herself tightly.

Rory was tinkering about in the corner with some sort of smoke grenades, that could be used if the cellar was breached. It was a last ditch if everything else failed, but Ellie didn't fancy the odds of six against two at all.

'Rory, what would you say if I told you I could end this now?'

'What do you mean, "end it now"? You're not thinking of suicide, are you?'

'No, don't be silly. I mean, stop all this running and hiding. We'll be doing it for the rest of our lives and I just want to go back to being normal, you know, like we were before.'

Rory was silent for a moment. 'I know what you mean. You don't miss something till it's not there anymore, but the guys down in London are trying to go through the legal channels to get him put away.'

'But how long's that going to take? It could be years, as he is insanely rich and probably has the best legal team on earth. It's never going to happen; besides he's probably still in France, and he'll stay there till the heat's off.'

'What are you saying, Ellie?' He came and sat by her putting his arm round her shoulders.

'I'm saying I should go out there and go with them back to France, and see if I can reason with him.'

'You're mad. You can't Ellie, he might kill you!'

'No, he won't. I'm much too precious to him for him to hurt me in any way. I know him a little bit, and when he wants something, he'll move heaven and earth to get it. Rory, he won't ever give up till he gets what he wants.'

Ellie stood up and walked to the door.

CHAPTER SIXTEEN

Rory was beside himself and physically restrained Ellie when the first gunshot rang out and they both jumped a mile.

'You're definitely not going out there now they've started shooting.' He had her arm in a vice-like grip. 'You'll be killed. If you, go I'm going with you.'

Ellie gently loosened his grip, and facing him, said, 'No Rory, you're not going anywhere. They'll kill you straight away; it's me they want not you. Only I can sort this mess out, and I'm going to do it now.'

Ellie opened the cellar door and stepped into the hall. The rate of gunfire had accelerated and a real battle was beginning. She didn't want anyone to be killed on her account, as there had been enough bloodshed already to last her a lifetime. Rory was right behind her and she pushed him back to the cellar. 'Stay there, be safe for me, please.'

Ellie bent double and went up the stairs to Jack's position in the back bedroom. There was an icy blast as the window had been shot out, and Jack was at the side of the window, looking at a mirror that had been strategically angled down onto the yard. He motioned for her to get down onto the floor.

'What in God's name are you doing here, you'll get yourself killed. Get back downstairs, that's an order. Do it now!'

'No, Jack. I'm going to stop this now, once and for all. No more killing or death. It's finished, I'm going out there to be taken back to France and confront Alistair. He won't kill me, but he will kill all of you, that is a certain fact. So find something white and wave it out the window.'

A bullet zinged off the window frame and Jack drew his head back further. Ellie glanced in the mirror and saw a black clad figure run across the yard, towards the back door. 'Do it now Jack, please.'

Jack lowered his gun and told Ellie that he would do it, but only if he could come with her. She told him he was insane, but he was adamant. They argued for another 30 seconds; then bullets started to whizz past Ellie's head and bury themselves in the opposite wall.

'Ok, Ellie, you win, but I'm coming with you.' He tied a pillowcase to a coat hanger and began waving it out of the window, shouting 'Ceasefire,' at the same time. The bullets gradually stopped, and John came bounding into the bedroom to find out what was going on. Jack quickly explained and John didn't like it at all, but Ellie had already gone downstairs and was nearly at the back door. She grabbed a tea towel and began to open the door. She heard running feet as Jack appeared and pushed her to one side, then stood in front of her as the door opened.

'Ellie is coming out! Ceasefire, now!' Jack shouted twice. 'It's not a trick; she's here and wants to talk.' Everyone moved slowly and grouped together by the back door. A figure came round the side of the barn with his gun held high in the air. Jack raised his gun to match the marksman. 'You get everyone out where we can see them, and then we'll all come out,' shouted Jack.

A voice from round the corner of the house shouted, 'How many in the house?'

'Four,' shouted Jack, 'how many are you?'

'Six,' came back the voice.

'Okay, here's the deal. I've got a gun to Ellie's head. I know how much your boss wants her back, so let's not get silly and we'll talk in the middle of the yard.'

'OK, we're coming out now,' and six men began to sidle out from various points on the yard and round the house. Jack had moved Ellie in front of him, and she felt the gun barrel pressed to her temple. Behind them, John and Rory were moving forward.

Jack said, 'We all know Morgan will kill each and every one of you if anything happens to her, so if you put your guns down, I'll put mine down.'

The six men were armed to the teeth and they bent and put their guns down, black against the snow. Ellie sensed John do the same.

'Ellie has decided to go back to France voluntarily and I'll be going with her. You lot can be our armed escort, but John and Rory must go from here unharmed. I may have put my gun down but I have a knife by her spine, and believe me she'll meet Morgan in a wheelchair if you don't play ball.' There was such menace in Jack's voice that Ellie almost believed him.

There were a few mutterings but the spokesman for the assault team said, 'Okay, it's a deal. You come with us and they'll go free; they are of no importance anyway.'

Jack said, under his breath, 'Give me your handcuffs, John.' John stealthily passed them to his hand that was hidden behind Ellie's back.

'Ellie, put your hand behind your back.' She did so and felt the plastic cuff snap shut round her wrist. Jack then raised his hand and hers with it for all to see. They were cuffed together. 'Just so there's no funny business on the way,' he said, and they walked forward slowly.

The helicopter fired up and the rotors began to turn lazily, slowly picking up speed as they neared the machine. Ellie looked back at Rory and John. Rory was holding his head with his hands, watching them go, and John was already on the sat phone, updating London on the latest turn of events.

Ploughing through the snow to get to the helicopter wasn't easy cuffed together, and their eyes were stung with the swirling ice. Ellie was also freezing cold as she hadn't got a coat, and it was welcome relief just to climb aboard and get out of the rotor wind. They were strapped in, side by side, and took off into the clear blue sky. Ellie saw just how isolated the farmhouse really was. There weren't any houses for miles and all the roads had disappeared under the blanket of snow. The assault team had retrieved their weapons from the snow and sat in an impassive silence, with the rifles resting across their knees, just staring at them.

Ellie was scared, but felt more in control of the situation than she had ever done before, and decided to test the water. She looked at the "soldier" sitting by her and said, 'I'm cold, take your coat off.' He looked at her surprised. 'I said, take your coat off, I'm cold.'

He looked at his boss who shrugged and nodded, and with bad grace the coat came off. She slid her free arm into the warmth and draped the coat round her shoulders. 'He's cold as well.' Ellie addressed the next one and fixed him with a stare. Jack was also passed a coat to ward off the chill. Ellie looked at the boss and thanked him politely, adding that his courtesy had been noted. She decided to push it further and requested a hot drink.

'We'll be landing soon to swap to the jet and there will be food and drinks then. All I can offer now is the dregs from the thermos,' he said almost deferentially.

'Thank you but no, I'll wait.' Ellie was happy and felt that she had scored a victory. She wouldn't get pushed and shoved about, and generally treated badly anymore. Ellie was Alistair's twin—and with that came power, and from now on, she was going to use it to her advantage.

The helicopter soon landed at an airport and a wagon was de-icing the wings of the jet, for the short hop across the channel. They disembarked the chopper and Ellie gave the soldier back his coat. They walked across to the open door of the jet. The steps down and an attendant waiting to greet them. Ellie and Jack had to crab up the steps still cuffed together, and Ellie informed the attendant that they would require hot drinks immediately, before take-off, and a jumper or coats for both of them as they were cold. The drinks appeared as if by magic within a few moments, and also, she got a blanket for her knees. They sipped the steaming drinks and she waved the cabin staff away, as she wanted to talk to Jack. Ellie was told by the staff that it would delay the take-off but she just shrugged.

'So be it, I don't care.' Ellie informed them. 'Just sort it out with the air traffic controllers; I'll be finished in 10 minutes.' They disappeared and she looked at Jack.

'I hope you know what you've got yourself into here. This is only the beginning, and I don't know where it will end up. This is your last chance to get out now. Unlock the cuffs, and you can walk off this plane and be safe. It's your choice.'

'No, Ellie, I'm going with you. I couldn't face Rory again knowing I'd let you down, and he would probably kill me if he thought I'd left you to go alone. So you're stuck with me, sorry.' He raised the cuffed hands and smiled.

'I think those can come off once we're in the air, as they were only to stop those thugs getting any big ideas. Life will get very interesting very quickly if you have to go everywhere with me,' Ellie put emphasis on the word "everywhere", and Jack nodded.

'Yes, it could, but I'm going to be your shadow and I'm not leaving your side, not for a moment.'

Ellie called for the flight attendant and told him that they were ready to go now. The idling engines increased to a roar, as the jet taxied to a runway and soared into the air. Once airborne, Jack unlocked the cuffs and Ellie massaged her wrist. They hadn't been too tight but her arm ached from being in one position too long. It would only take about an hour to the airport, then a short hop to the chateau. Ellie settled back and relaxed, idly flicking through a few of the onboard magazines. Jack stared out of the window and stretched out on the leather seat, playing with the recline settings till he was comfortable. A small meal appeared and they enjoyed the haute cuisine, instead of the staple diet they'd had at the farmhouse.

They landed at a small airstrip and transferred to another helicopter, the ride allowing them to view the French countryside, which was devoid of snow. The terrain was listless and damp, in the aftermath of more torrential rain. They landed on the front lawn of the chateau in the gathering dusk and the great doors opened, flooding them with light.

Alistair was waiting in the hall and greeted Ellie as if she had just been out on a long shopping trip. He made no allusions to her escape, and greeted Jack as if he was one of her staff. They were ushered into the library, where a side table was laid for tea. Ellie sat by the fire and Jack hovered uncertainly, as if he didn't know what to do, or where to sit.

As she sat, Ellie said, 'Alistair, I want it to be made very clear from the outset that I'm here because I want to be, not because you were going to kidnap me again. We are going to sort this out once and for all, and you are going to stop messing up my life again and again. Jack is with me as my friend, and he will be accorded all the privileges of being a guest in your house. He is not a servant and I won't have him treated as one.'

Alistair clapped his hands softly together. 'Well said, sister. I apologize to Jack unreservedly.' He stood and showed Jack to a chair that included him in the circle. Ellie noted that there were only two cups and she looked at them pointedly. 'I'll ring for another cup straight away. I have to hand it to you, Ellie, you are a very determined woman and have cost me a lot. Our brother met his end, and you destroyed a helicopter. Need I go on?'

'Max was trying to kill me, and he told me that himself. He would have no doubt succeeded at some point, because he thought I was going to take his place by your side. I am not, I repeat, not, going to take any place at your side, now or ever—and although I regret his death, I'm sure he would have killed me if he'd had a chance.'

Alistair and Jack both looked at her as if she'd sprouted horns and although Ellie was quaking inside, she thought she'd better just get on with it and tell it how it was.

She continued, 'I am not your prisoner and I will go where I want, when I want and with whom I want. Jack will have an adjoining suite to mine and the staff will treat him with due respect. Believe me, Alistair, you need me a lot more than I need you and I don't care a toss about your feelings, or how you appear to the outside world, so be warned—I'm not going to roll over and do as you wish. Remember I'm here because I choose to be.'

Ellie didn't think anyone had ever spoken to him that way before, but she had gone past the point of no return, and felt her fear turn to anger at the way he had treated her. She wasn't going to take any more of it. To his credit, he looked as if he'd taken what she'd said on board and the ball was now firmly in his court. Ellie sat and waited for a response. The door opened at that point and a footman came in, with more food and the third cup and saucer. He placed them carefully on the table and retreated quickly, almost as if he could sense the palpable tension in the room.

Ellie began to pour the tea and handed the cups round. Jack and Ellie helped themselves to the food as she sat and waited for Alistair's response. Eventually, it came.

'I understand that you are outraged at the way I've treated you in the past. I did it because when I found you, I couldn't risk you leaving, and you know that. Perhaps the leash was too tight and with more freedom, you may have wanted to stay.'

'No, Alistair, that was never going to happen. You have stolen innumerable art works of national importance; you have killed innocent people and terrorized others. You have made my life absolute hell and jeopardised my relationship with my fiancé. I cannot and will not be part of any of that, in any way, shape or form. I don't think you're going to change in an instant, so as long as I'm well away from all your unsavoury dealings, I'll stay till we've worked out a deal.'

Ellie was most emphatic and felt she had to spell out every little nuance in great detail, so there would be no misconstruction on his part at all. She began to feel calmer and even more in command than before, and thought it was probably a good place to stop. She rose and thanked Alistair for the tea, and requested a footman to take them to their rooms. Ellie also asked for some clothes for Jack, as they hadn't had time to pack before leaving England. On that sarcastic note, Ellie beckoned Jack and did her best to sweep out of the room, not looking back at Alistair at all.

Upstairs, Jack and Ellie sat in her room while his was prepared.

'You don't think I went too far, do you?' Ellie asked Jack uncertainly. 'It came over me all of a sudden. I realized I've been dealt a different hand of cards, and I can play them how I want. He may be my twin but he's still only a mortal man, so I'm not scared of him anymore. We're going to have to play along for a while, until we can get to some sort of arrangement, 'cos I'm not having my life mucked about by him any longer.'

Jack replied that he didn't think she'd gone too far, but had been very clear and concise about what she wanted, and that probably wasn't a bad thing where Alistair was concerned. He added that he doubted anyone had ever spoken to him like that and no one else living would ever dare. In that sense, she had an ace in her hand and had played it well. He added that she should be careful as Alistair could have some latent streak of madness, and may not be rational all of the time.

'I hope not, as I'm his twin, so that could be the same for me,' Ellie said horrified at the thought. 'Do you really think so, that he could be crackers?'

'Not really, but I'd still be careful if I was you. You don't know how he'll jump now you've turned up again.'

'I think that he's been used to so much power for so long that it's literally gone to his head, and maybe he thinks he's some sort of God. Well, he isn't and I'm going to bring him back down to earth and he's going to realize what he's done, and still continues to do, is wrong… or I'll die trying.' Ellie added darkly.

They sat and talked round the issues again and again and tried out different scenarios and imagined outcomes till there was a discreet tap on the door. They were informed that Mr Jack's room was ready, and dinner would be at eight in the dining room. Ellie told Jack to dress in black tie for dinner, and hoped some clothes had turned up for him. Ellie would stay in her room till Jack called her and they should be ready for 7.30, as drinks would be served in the drawing room beforehand.

Ellie mentally girded her loins for the evening ahead and chose a very discreet outfit and sensible shoes, as you could never be sure with Alistair if she would have to run. She'd been caught out with that before and had learned her lesson the very hard way. Jack duly arrived and looked very handsome in his black tie. Ellie complimented him and to her surprise, he blushed. They went down, and the drawing room was resplendent with candlelight and a huge Christmas tree stood in the corner. Ellie walked over to admire it, with her favourite cocktail in her hand, as Alistair came in.

'I hope you approve of the tree, Ellie, as it is Christmas Eve today and we all seem to have forgotten it. What say we have a cessation of hostilities over the Christmas period, and enjoy ourselves a little? See, there are even presents for you and Jack under the tree.'

'I won't be so ungracious as to not accept the presents, but

I might just remind you that I would have preferred to spend Christmas with Rory, to have done my own Christmas shopping rather than being holed up in a farmhouse in the back of beyond because of you. That said, I do like the tree very much, and it was thoughtful of you to put it up. I get the feeling you wouldn't have bothered if I wasn't here.' Ellie let that hang as a question.

'How well you know me already. See, Ellie, there's no denying you can read my mind.'

'No just a lucky guess, so don't start that togetherness thing again or else I'll have dinner in my room.' Ellie looked him straight in the eye, and saw again the uncanny reflection of herself. Alistair held up his hands in mock surrender, and accepted tonic water with a twist from the footman. Jack was wandering about the room, looking at the works of art and sculptures, more than likely making a mental inventory to check what was stolen at a later date.

Dinner wasn't as uncomfortable as she had feared, as Alistair could be a charming host when he wanted to be. He even swallowed his distaste and included Jack in the conversation, enquiring politely about his hobbies and various likes and dislikes.

Jack ate his way through each and every course like a starving man, but Ellie gave up after four incredibly tasty creations. She bade Carter, the butler, to convey her compliments to the chef, who had surpassed himself for the Christmas Eve meal. Alistair raised an eyebrow at this but made no comment.

'So what's happening tomorrow?' Ellie asked. 'Is it one of those things where we serve the staff their Christmas dinner, like in big houses in England?'

'Good God, no!' Alistair looked horrified at the thought, and Ellie could barely suppress a smile.

'You know you'd love it really,' Ellie teased him. He saw the look in her eye and finally realized she was only joking and relaxed, smiling.

'I had planned to have a shoot on Boxing Day, but I think we'll give that a miss as I can't trust you with a shotgun yet, can I?'

'Not really, Alistair. Perhaps not such a good idea considering the mood I'm in at the moment. I would like to see some of the grounds though, if you could get someone to show me round.'

'I know,' he replied, as if having a revelation, 'I'll show you myself on horseback. We have a choice in the stables and we'll find a nice ladies' hack for you. You do ride?'

'No, Alistair, I don't. I've never had the privileges you have and I've never had chance to learn—' Ellie thought for a moment, '—but that doesn't mean I wouldn't like to.'

'Good, then that's settled. We'll have a ride round the grounds tomorrow if it isn't raining. Jack can come as well, if he likes.' Alistair looked at Jack questioningly.

'I suppose so, but I'm in the same boat as Ellie. I've never sat on a horse at all.'

Ellie suddenly sensed what trick Alistair might pull and said, 'Now don't put Jack on some great big beast called Hades, or anything that's going to kill him. If I don't like the look of his animal, I'll call it off, understand?'

'OK, you win. I promise I won't try to make Jack have an unfortunate accident, or cause him any harm. Is that good enough?'

Jack at this point was looking slightly sick.

'Yes, I accept your word, and I hope you stick to it Alistair, for your sake.' Ellie leaned forward to emphasize her words, and pointed a stray knife at him.

'Let's go back to the drawing room and have coffee in there,' said Alistair, rising. They all followed and Jack grabbed Ellie's arm and whispered, 'You don't think he'll really pull anything like that do you?'

'Not really, but I was just making sure. You're doing well, keep it up. Just be there for me, a bit of moral support.'

Everyone entered the drawing room and settled down in the overstuffed chairs, which Ellie found comfortable and warm. Jack was still tense and restless, and chose a book from a bookcase and began to leaf through it. She carried on her conversation with Alistair and asked him about his childhood, hoping to glean some facts about her own adoption. Jack tried to appear relaxed, but was listening intently.

'I suppose I know as much as you, Ellie.' He paused for a sip of coffee. 'Father became entangled with some woman and she got pregnant. I think her family created a big fuss about it, but she went away or was sent away, I'm not sure—and she eventually gave birth to us. As far as I know, she died in childbirth; then I was claimed back and lived with him, and nothing more was heard of you. You must have gone for adoption at that point. I didn't even know I had a twin until a few months ago. I always knew there was someone else though, as I've told you, ad nauseam.

Jack sat up and said, 'Maybe I can throw a bit of light on that. When we were in London, we actually traced the birth records for you both, and you were there, Alistair, but Ellie's name had been scratched out. More than that; it had been obliterated completely, but by Alistair's name was a small number 1. They only do that if there were twins, to show who was first born. Looks like you were the chosen one after all,' he added.

Alistair and Ellie looked at each other, then at Jack. She broke the silence, 'So it's true; more proof, besides the DNA. I wonder what went on and why he only wanted one of us, when he certainly had enough money to look after us both. So you never knew our mother, Alistair? There's not even a picture of her to look at? Did Father have the same eyes as us?'

'No he didn't, so those must be from our mother, and our hair colour is nothing like his at all, as he was very dark. I suppose we'll never know.'

'Were they ever married?' Ellie asked this, and it was like she had dropped a grenade.

Alistair sat up straight and almost dropped his coffee cup. 'I never gave that a thought. If they weren't, then we have no rightful claim to any of this. It could all go to some second cousin or something.' He was mortified at the thought.

Ellie smiled. 'Just teasing again Alistair. You've really got to get a grip on this mind meld stuff. It's all rightfully yours, as there must have been a will or something when he died, else you can be sure a second cousin would have popped out of the woodwork before now and claimed your millions.'

The sigh from Alistair was almost audible, as he sank back into his chair. 'Please stop doing that to me Ellie; you'll give me a heart attack.'

'Now there's a thought. Actually, I enjoy it.' Ellie sat back, and thought that as she got to know Alistair better, she was beginning to know which buttons to press to get responses. It was becoming fun.

CHAPTER SEVENTEEN

Against all her expectations, Ellie had slept well and awoke refreshed. It was Christmas Day, and she picked the phone up by her bed and listened to the dial tone. A voice enquired what she needed. Ellie replied that she needed an outside line for an English mobile number. The disembodied voice suggested she hold. This was obviously so they could check with Alistair if it was all right.

'You can get me my fiancée on the line now, and I insist you don't monitor the call. Is that perfectly clear?' Ellie said imperiously. There was a moments silence then came, 'Oui', and she got a ringing tone.

'Rory, hi, it's me from France. Happy Christmas,' Ellie said, as soon as it was picked up.

'Well I don't think it's very happy at all. You're over there and I'm here, still in this bloody farmhouse with John,' he said grumpily.

'They must have patched this call through to the sat phone. I thought you would have been home by now?'

'Our government doesn't run to fancy helicopters when ordinary people want to go home.'

Ellie paused, not knowing quite how to answer him. He had got the thin end of the wedge and was stuck up there in several feet of snow, with no way of knowing when he was getting home, and she was in the lap of luxury at a chateau in France. Ellie decided not to tell him about the planned horse ride, or the way things were progressing, as the conversation would disintegrate into a slanging match.

'I rang to tell you I'm okay, and to stop you worrying. Alistair is beginning to understand how things are, I think, and a few more days should see me home,' Ellie said brightly. 'I hope to be home by New Year, and that all the threats hanging over us will be gone, and we can start to pick up where we left off.'

'You think, but you're not sure, are you? You don't really know at all. You know, Ellie, I'm sick of this to my back teeth, and I'm not sure any more where I stand with you. I'm always out of the loop with you. You went swanning off to France to try and save the day with Jack, not me. I'm supposed to be the one looking after you, not him.'

It was pure vitriol. All the anger and frustrations of the last few weeks came flooding out, and Ellie squeezed her eyelids together as a tear found its way to freedom, and rolled down her cheek.

'Rory, please don't, you know I love you to bits,' Ellie begged him.

'Do you? Do you really love me, Ellie? 'Cos, I don't think you do. Answer me this, what means more to you—me, or saving him?'

Ellie couldn't answer, as she knew she needed to be at the Chateau to try and sort the situation out, or they would never be free of Alistair—but in her heart of hearts, she knew she actually liked this life, with servants, and every whim catered for. Ellie was sobbing openly now and she tried to speak, but nothing came out. The phone went to dial tone as Rory hung up on her. The phone fell from her fingers as she hugged her pillow, and she sobbed as her heart broke.

Ellie must have lay there for half an hour and cried herself out. Her sobs subsided to sniffles, and a discreet tap on the door made her reach for the corner of the sheet, and she wiped her face as the maid came in with her morning tea. Ellie sniffed for effect and told her she seemed to be coming down with a cold, and she would be a little late for breakfast.

Jack tapped at her door about half an hour later, and she was still in the bathroom, trying to repair the damage her crying had wrought. Ellie's eyes were still puffy, although she had splashed copious amounts of cold water over them, and decided to keep up the pretence of having a cold. She met him, clutching a tissue and blowing her nose, and talked as if her nose was bunged up.

'I'm not hungry this morning, but I'll come down as its Christmas morning. Oh, happy Christmas, by the way,' and when she said that, she nearly burst into tears again. What a Christmas she was having, it couldn't be worse.

Ellie walked listlessly into the dining room, and Alistair was already there. There was a parcel by her set place. It was obviously a Christmas present, tied up with a bright red bow. It seemed incongruous today, as Ellie felt like her world had ended. She didn't know how she could make it right with Rory, if she ever could. Ellie just hoped she could build some bridges when this was all over, if it ever was. She looked at the present, and there was a smaller parcel at the side of Jack's place.

'Happy Christmas, Ellie,' Alistair said, as Ellie slid into her place, I do hope you like it. A spur of the moment thing I'm afraid and I couldn't get it properly gift wrapped for you so I did it myself.' He beamed at her. 'Jack also has a small gift, just to show there's no animosity.'

Ellie felt uncomfortable, as she'd never afforded the present giving a thought—and Jack looked at her, waiting for her to take the lead.

Ellie sniffled and picked up the present. 'I'm sure it's wonderful Alistair, as you have impeccable taste, but we haven't had time to do any Christmas shopping.'

Jack turned his present round in his hands, 'It won't go off when I open it, will it?' He looked at Alistair.

'No, no, please take it in the spirit that it is intended. This is the first time I've had my sister for Christmas and I'm not so stupid as to believe it could be the first of many; so let us enjoy the moment for what it is.'

Jack looked bemused as Ellie pulled the bow; it revealed a padded leather box. She opened the box, and lying there, in all its splendour, was the necklace she had worn to the auction. It was a beautiful piece of jewellery. The diamonds and sapphires were formed into flowers and stars, which glittered in the pale morning sun. Ellie gasped.

'It has been in the family for a long time and it should be yours, Ellie, as you are family, like it or not,' said Alistair. 'Maybe it's not the best time to wear it, but you could put it on, if you want to?'

'I don't think so Alistair, as this is hardly breakfast in Hollywood—but seriously, are you sure? I mean, this is probably worth millions, and you're giving it to me? Really, for keeps?'

'Yes, for keeps. Whatever happens in the future, it's yours. It always should have belonged to you, and you should wear it, as my sister.'

'I don't know what to say, except thank you. I can only hope that our mother wore it, at sometime in her life, and I'll keep it as a link with her.'

Jack had begun tentatively pulling the bow on his present. It revealed a book, which was leather bound and had an ornate clasp. He gently opened it and pages of wonderful drawings were revealed.

'Before you say anything, Jack, no; it wasn't stolen, or misappropriated by any other means. I bought it sometime ago and I hope you like the drawings. I'm told they are quite unique.'

Jack opened his mouth as if to say he couldn't possibly accept such a gift, but Ellie shot him a look and he mumbled something, then subsided into silence. She noticed he kept looking at the book all through breakfast, and reverently turned the pages.

'I'm glad you liked your presents and I'm sorry to see you seem to have come down with a cold, Ellie—' she sniffed at that point, '—but fresh air is good for colds and I'm sure you would still like to go for your first horse ride. Before you ask, I haven't requested any animal that will do Jack a mortal injury, and I suggest we go out in about an hour, to get the best of the day. You will find clothes suitable for riding laid out for you. See you later.'

After he had left Jack said, 'Well, he's a chirpy little soul today, although I must say I didn't expect to have this.' He touched the book again.

'Alistair can be very charming and really good fun but never underestimate him; he usually has some sort of hidden agenda,' Ellie said, warning Jack not to get sucked into the persona Alistair was building at the moment.

'Well, let's go and give this horse riding a try out. It can't be that hard!' said Jack, stretching.

How wrong he was. Alistair had been as good as his word and no fire breathing monsters awaited them; instead, there were rather laid back, comfortable-looking hacks. They even submitted to all the undignified scrambling to get on with a patient air. Ellie was amazed how different the world looked from on top of a horse, and as they began clopping sedately down a track, the small wild animals and birds didn't hide or take flight. Alistair was charm personified, and pointed out landmarks and the farms owned by the estate, highlighted by the cold clear air.

They progressed eventually to an ambling trot, and Ellie managed to get the up and down movement in time with the horse to make it comfortable, but Jack struggled and was being bounced around until he could take no more.

'We're going to have to walk or go back,' he shouted in desperation, 'everything's beginning to hurt a lot,' and everyone slowed back to walk.

'Perhaps that is enough for the first time,' said Alistair, 'You seem to be doing well, Ellie, maybe you would like to try again tomorrow?' he said, as he looked at her face, which was wreathed in smiles.

'It's fantastic, I'd really like another go, if the weather holds out tomorrow,' Ellie said excitedly. Being on the horse was like coming home, and the feeling of being one with an animal was like nothing she had experienced before. This was something she didn't want to give up.

Everyone plodded gently back to the stable yard, which was hidden behind the main house and was a confection of turrets and ornate stonework. It was as grand as the chateau itself, and well-staffed with grooms, who scurried forwards to take the bridles. Getting off was easier, and Ellie swung her leg over and slid to the ground. Jack sort of hung round the horse's neck until he felt safe to let go, and his knees buckled as he hit the floor. She could barely suppress a laugh and had to look away, lest his feelings were hurt. Ellie felt invigorated, but Jack was obviously stiff and in pain as he walked to the house. 'I'm going to give that a miss in future,' was all he could manage.

Alistair remarked that Ellie looked like she was born to ride and should pick it up easily, and they would soon be cantering down the tracks. Ellie, flattered, was swept up in the moment, and said she would certainly try again as she had enjoyed it immensely.

It was Christmas Day and Ellie loved every minute of it; even Rory had receded into a bad dream. Everyone gathered in the dining room that evening for a sumptuous meal, and she wore the jewels from Alistair and couldn't believe her luck. Jack was very stiff and sore and vowed he would never get on a horse again, but thanked Alistair for the opportunity to try. It was a magical meal and Ellie was very happy. She wondered how she could possibly go back to her flat in grey London after this. She couldn't think of one good reason to go back, after experiencing life at the chateau.

That evening after dinner, they gathered in the library, and the painting of Edward was still propped on the easel in the corner. Ellie showed Jack the painting, and pointed out all the signs and symbols that made them think he had been part of some sort of cult. Everyone pored again over the map and Ellie described how she'd thought that the key could open the box in the tower, and how it had led them to the secret room.

Alistair showed the books he'd had brought up from the cave, and they looked at the secret books, full of spells and incantations. Jack was amazed at the script and quality of the illustrations.

Ellie wandered to the big desk in the corner and saw the grimoire lying open, at a page with the heading, "vincio". She asked Alistair, as he had some classical education, what "vincio" meant. He just shrugged and said he didn't know. Jack said he'd seen a Latin dictionary somewhere, and as the word sounded Latin, he'd look it up. Jack eventually found the book and told them the word meant 'to bind' or 'to fetter'. Ellie laid her hand on the open page, and felt a tingling like static running through her fingertips.

'I still don't like this particular book, Alistair. You should get rid of it, and you've got plenty of others.'

'No, that's actually my personal favourite of all of them. I think it's a very powerful book and I like to have a go at reading it, brushing up on the Latin, if I can.'

'You know very well that you have one of those memories that are phenomenal, and you never forget anything.' Suddenly she didn't believe Alistair any longer, and pieces fell into place.

'You don't read this to 'brush up' on your Latin, do you? You've been reading it to have a go at the spells. You've been using it to keep me here, that's why my real life with Rory has sort of faded from me. The word "vincio" says it all. You've used this book to keep me here, to bind me to you and the chateau. Tell me, and look me straight in the eye when you do it—have you used this book to try and keep me here?' Ellie stared at Alistair and almost willed the truth out of him. The atmosphere was electric and the surroundings went misty as they locked eyes.

Ellie was forcing her will onto his, and she wanted the truth so badly, it almost hurt. He dropped his eyes and she mentally pounced. 'The truth—have you used the book to keep me here?'

'Yes,' it came out as a vaguely audible hiss, and he turned away and shut the book with a bang.

'So now you've gone over to the dark side even more. Not content with using guns and force to get what you want—you are now dabbling with the occult. What is it with you, Alistair, why do you need to do this?' Ellie threw up her hands in despair.

Jack was still standing exactly as he was, holding the dictionary and staring at them both, bemused at what he had just witnessed.

'We're not getting anywhere in trying to find a solution to my problem of you messing up my life, are we? You've now decided to mess with my mind as well. It won't work Alistair, it really won't. I don't believe in all this claptrap of spirits and goblins, so what say we all go down to the secret room? You can try and invoke whatever you like and if you succeed, so be it. If you don't then I call the shots… forever! Is it a deal, yes or no?'

Ellie stood with her hands on her hips, and faced him. She was challenging him to a make or break deal, and she was not in the mood to back down. 'Come on then, put your money where your mouth is, whistle up a ghostie and I'll stay here. If not, you lose.'

Alistair looked at her and suddenly seemed afraid of what had happened. He hadn't intended events to go down this path, and he just wanted Ellie to like the chateau and his company so much that she would make the choice to stay on her own. But she had thrown down the challenge, and by not picking up the gauntlet he would lose anyway—and he knew Ellie would burn the grimoire there and then without question.

'Okay, if that's what you really want, then we'll go down to the secret room.'

'No, Alistair, it's what you want. Do it now, or I'll win.'

Alistair took a deep breath and picked up the grimoire, and it seemed to quiver in his hands. He wasn't sure he could control the entities in the book. Whenever he had used them before, they had left him mentally and physically drained, so much so they had seemed to take the very life force from him—but he knew without the grimoire, he wouldn't win the challenge.

It was a subdued trio that went upstairs to the bedchamber, and through the secret passage to the room. Jack hung back with Ellie, and asked if she knew what she was doing.

'All I know Jack, is that Alistair, in some way, has made me believe I want to stay here. He found us in the farmhouse when there was no way he could have guessed where we were. Whatever is happening, he really believes in it, and it's all connected with that damned book. I've got to prove him wrong. Just be there for me whatever happens, will you?'

His hand found hers and gave it a reassuring squeeze. 'I've been tangled up in this since the beginning, and I'll try not to let you down.'

They got into the room and Jack let out an exclamation when he saw the size of it, all the draperies decorated with their signs and symbols. It was a very ornate and sumptuous room, but also there was a presence that made the hairs at the back of Ellie's neck stand up. It was disquieting and made her uneasy, and she wished she could get out of there quickly. If Ellie had her way, the tunnel and steps would be filled in, and the room blocked off altogether.

Alistair went and stood in the middle of the pentacle etched into the stone floor. 'I think we have to do other things, like put salt and holy water round the outside of this, to make it work.'

'OK, let's do it; you're the expert,' Ellie said witheringly.

They hunted about and followed Alistair's instructions, placing salt, water and candles strategically round the pentacle. A dish of salt was put at each point of the star and each candle was lit.

'You know this is all rubbish, Alistair. Why don't you just concede and we can all go home?'

He ignored her and instructed them all to stand in the pentacle and join hands. Ellie had to put her hand on his arm as he held the grimoire open and began to chant the word "invoco", over and over again. His eyes were shut and he began to sway slightly, and the word seemed to blur into one long dirge. She involuntarily began to mouth the word and she noticed Jack was doing the same. The sound seemed to resonate against the walls, and it filled the room till the stones seemed to vibrate. An electric quality filled the air, like ozone after a thunderstorm, and she could actually smell it and taste it at the back of her tongue. It began to change subtly, and Ellie could smell sulphur, as if feathers were burning. It got more and more acrid and she began to get scared. Ellie held onto Jack's hand tightly and felt him respond with a squeeze. She decided she'd had enough of this and wanted out, right now. Whatever spell was happening, it was going to stop. She would even tell Alistair he'd won and live out the rest of her days at the chateau—she didn't care, as Ellie was verging on being terrified. She tried to say something but her tongue just wouldn't work, and she was locked into saying "invoco" over and over again. She was a prisoner. Jack's grip had loosened and he just stood there, like he was standing at attention, his lips were moving just like hers.

There was a darkness that seemed to seep from the stones and well up from the floor. It was nothing more than a few wisps at first, but it grew to a fog that began to swirl around the pentacle. The candle flames guttered and flickered as it got faster and faster, swirling into a vortex.

The mist seemed almost solid now and began to take a shape. A huge bird formed before Ellie's eyes, and it lazily stretched its huge wings. It had both feathers and scales, and a huge hooked beak and talons. It looked like the griffins that adorned gateposts of country houses. They were carved in stone, but this one was a living, breathing version of those beasts. Its breath was acrid, and Ellie could hardly breathe for the sulphurous smell.

Alistair and Jack seemed to wake up at that point, as if the beast had willed it. Jack looked both scared and horrified at the sight of the thing, but Alistair didn't, as if it was no surprise at all.

'What in God's name is that?' Ellie said, as her tongue unstuck itself and became active again. It was the same creature that she had seen by the woodshed at the farmhouse, but it looked much bigger.

Jack said, 'But I shot it and it flew off,' as he gripped Ellie's hand tighter still.

'This is the Chateau of the Birds, and this is the bird that lives here,' said Alistair, in a monotone. 'This is the bird which helps me; this is the bird that found you. I am that bird.'

It bent its head slightly sideways, as if examining Ellie, and the candle flames were reflected in its golden iris.

The beast spoke, 'I see that those which were apart are now together. You have come for answers to riddles made before your time on earth. This day would always come. I will answer then and take what's mine.'

Ellie was trembling and said to Alistair, 'What questions are we supposed to ask it, I don't know… Please just make it go away. It's evil, can't you feel it?' She was near to tears, but almost too frightened to cry.

'I have a name; don't you want to know it? Friends share names, do they not?' The thing was almost jocular in its tone.

Ellie stood straighter, and held onto Jack's hand like a vice. 'So what's your name?' she asked, running through every prayer in her head, as if it would make it go away.

'I have many names. The real one I'm not going to say, but I have been called S'tan by your grandfather, and then your father.' It laughed and the gust of hot fetid air blew out a few of the candles.

'S'tan,' Ellie repeated and looked at Alistair. 'That was the name on that contract written in grandfather's blood.'

'Well done, Eleanor. It is a short form; as you call yourself, Ellie, so I call myself S'tan. I believe you would call me Satan, Eleanor.'

Ellie blanched. 'What do you want with me? It's Alistair that's been using you,' she said, mercilessly throwing him to the wolves.

'Alistair has summoned me, and now it's time to pay the price. He has had all the power he wants and he has used it. Remember the contract; I will have "one of the two"—that's one of the twins. One of you is mine. You were lost Eleanor, and your father took great pains to hide you from me, but now you are together again, as it should be.' The thing settled back on its haunches, as if waiting for them to decide who was going to Hell.

'Alistair,' Ellie wailed his name, 'You want to give me to that thing? I'm not going to Hell for you or anyone,' and she grabbed the grimoire from his hands and flung it at the beast. It hit the edge of the pentacle and combusted before their eyes. Smoky ash floated down and settled both inside and outside of the star. The bits of ash outside the pentacle began to form into small creatures that were an abomination of nature, too many legs and eyes; they skittered here and there trying to find a way in.

Alistair looked down at one small demon, with a grey carapace, that was feeling its way carefully round the pentacle; he reached across the star and touched it. Smoke rose from his fingers and he snatched his hand back, with a livid burn across his fingers.

It seemed to shake him awake and he looked at Ellie, 'What have I done, Ellie? I never meant for you to go to Hell with that thing. I didn't understand the contract, or what it meant.'

'Neither of us did, Alistair, but it wants one of us, and one of us has to go now.'

It was a different Alistair that addressed the creature, he sounded unsure and uncertain. 'What if you were to have everything I owned, absolutely everything—would you leave us alone?'

The beast just laughed loud and long, 'Oh a sense of humour, I like that. I already have everything you own, except your souls. That is the prize I want. First, I will have one, then the other. Ellie's particularly interests me; it is unblemished and untainted, a tasty morsel to feed my pets.'

The thought of being ripped apart and feasted on by those evil little creatures made Ellie heave, and bile filled her throat.

'Hold hands, Alistair.' Ellie offered him her hand. 'Jack take of hold his hand, now.' Jack reluctantly held out his hand to Alistair, who grabbed it as if he were a drowning man. 'Just try that mind communication thing you've always been on about, Alistair. Just try and think of something that'll be the key to stopping that thing.'

'I'm getting tired of this and my patience is wearing thin; you've had enough time to decide which one of you I get. I prefer Ellie but will be content with the boy, for the time being,' it hissed.

'Ignore it,' said Ellie, 'and concentrate, hard, this is our only chance. It would've crossed the pentacle by now if it could, and taken one of us.'

Ellie felt the blood from Alistair's fingers slick against her hand and closed her eyes, trying hard to concentrate. The only picture that came into her mind was the little box key, made of the two curly crosses.

CHAPTER EIGHTEEN

Alistair opened his eyes and looked at Ellie. She knew what he was thinking. It was amazing, but she actually knew what was in his mind.

'Have you got it with you?' she asked, sure he was aware of what she was speaking.

'Yes,' was all he said.

'What are you on about?' said Jack confused.

'Jack, just keep holding my hand. Believe me we can't say out loud what we both just thought, but it may be the answer.' He nodded and kept silent.

The beast began to pace up and down, breathing out clouds of fire and fumes.

'Go on Alistair, do it now,' Ellie urged. Alistair loosened her hand and felt in his pocket. He palmed the little key and linked his hand back into hers. She felt it warm against her palm and felt a surge of hope.

'That which were apart are now together,' Ellie said, as if seeking confirmation from the beast.

'That is so. The two are linked together again, and they are mine,' the beast affirmed.

'Well, take them,' Ellie said and turned, flinging the joined key at the beast's head. It struck it directly in the eye, and it was if a nuclear explosion had detonated in the room. The world went white hot and the beast screeched and recoiled as if struck by lightning. Feathers were consumed in the fire and the sulphur smell increased in intensity. The beast staggered and Ellie saw one side of its face was a smoking hole; out of it swarmed myriads of small demons, fleeing from the holocaust raging and consuming the whole.

'Run!' she yelled and everyone made for the door. They skipped over the pentacle and trod on the swarming things, which made crunching sounds under their feet. The door seemed a million miles away but Alistair got there first and held it open for Jack and Ellie. They squeezed through and they slammed it with a bang behind them.

The stairs rose up slick with what seemed like blood, and the malodorous slime dripped down the walls and stuck to their feet as they tried to run. Pieces of rock began to detach from the walls and rain down upon them as they slithered and slipped up the steps. Ellie heard Jack's breathing heavy behind her and Alistair held his hand out behind him as he ran, to try and help her keep up. The overhead lights flickered and went out and she cannoned into Alistair as they reached the door to the bedchamber. Jack ran into the back of Ellie and they squashed up against the door.

'Where's the lever?' Ellie shouted as Alistair felt round the door. She joined him on the top step and felt round the doorframe. Panic made her fumble and she nearly missed it. 'Here it is,' Ellie said, and pulled the lever. Nothing happened. She pulled it again, but it was dead.

'Oh God, it won't work,' she shouted, pulling the lever frantically. Jack elbowed his way past her and Ellie stepped down a step to let him through. Jack gave the door a hefty kick and it shuddered. Alistair then joined Jack and kicked the door again and again, harder and harder. It finally gave with a crash and they were in the bed chamber, but there was the glow of fire and the brimstone fumes began to coil up from below the stairs. Jack grabbed Ellie's hand and they raced out of the bedroom, and Alistair slammed the door behind them. There was a fire alarm by the door and he hit the glass with the heel of his hand as he went by, and fire alarms began to shriek.

The whole chateau began to shudder, and pictures began to fall from the walls and tables shook their ornaments onto the floor, with crashes as broken glass rained down. The staff began to run and there was a tide of people trying to get out of the doors, and the weakest were getting knocked aside in the melee. Ellie held onto the arm of a maid as she nearly fell and pulled her along with her, and Alistair stopped to help a fallen man who lay covering his head in his hands as bricks began to fall. She saw him pull him to his feet and urge him on but then lost sight of them both as everyone was swept along. They reached the front doors and Ellie almost fell down the front steps and lost the arm of the maid—but she felt Jack gather her up and she was half carried, half dragged, across the front lawn.

They reached a small rise and looked back at the Chateau of the Birds; it was aflame and all the windows were lit up by the glow. Windows exploded and the inferno burst forth, and they all retreated further from the heat. The fire had spread very swiftly, almost too quickly, to be a natural force. The whole chateau was engulfed and brickwork was falling from the turrets, and the carvings almost seemed to be melting and running down the walls. Ellie looked round and Jack was standing behind her, and then she searched the crowd for

Alistair. He wasn't there.

'Jack, where's Alistair?' Ellie asked him, and he started to scan the people.

'Can't see him,' Jack replied, still looking.

Ellie pointed at the front door of the chateau. She could see a figure dragging something down the steps, backlit by the unholy fire.

'There he is, come on,' shouted Jack, and he began racing across the front lawn. Ellie reached Alistair slightly behind Jack, who lifted the bundle Alistair was dragging as Ellie grabbed Alistair's arm, and they ran with lungs heaving away from the heat.

The bundle turned out to be the maid that Ellie had tried to save. She was alive, and lay there with her clothes still smouldering. Jack patted them out with his hands. Alistair was in worse shape and collapsed onto the grass after his run. His breath came in heaving gasps, and Ellie rolled him onto his side and prayed he would be all right. They watched as the chateau was being reduced to a derelict shell. The flames licked and consumed it as if it were a living being. The walls imploded and fell into some sort of fiery chasm that had opened up, and the tongues of flame appeared to come from Hell itself.

They were a very subdued crowd that watched the emergency services arrive, and everyone was shepherded into ambulances and police cars to go to the hospital. Ellie got separated from Jack and Alistair and ended up sitting on a hard chair in a grey corridor with a blanket round her, after having numerous scrapes and cuts attended to. She was wearing some ill-fitting scrubs as her clothes had been cut off and discarded, and she decided to have a look for the others. Eventually she met Jack in a waiting area, as he was trying to make enquiries about her in very bad French. Ellie tapped him on the shoulder, making him jump.

'Happy Christmas,' she said. 'You come here often?'

'Not as often as you seem to,' he said and hugged her, long and hard. Ellie put her head on his shoulder, and breathed in smoke and grime from his singed clothes.

'Any idea what happened to Alistair? I saw him carted off, but couldn't go with him,' Jack asked her, and Ellie shook her head.

'What happened to the maid? Was she ok? She didn't look very good lying on the grass.' Ellie didn't even know her name. That was very bad of her, and she felt terrible about what happened to all those people. 'I really got sucked into that lifestyle, didn't I?' Ellie looked into Jack's eyes, seeking forgiveness for her insensitivity.

'Don't beat yourself up Ellie. It wasn't only your fault, as you were under some kind of spell, the same as Alistair. It looks as if your great-grandfather built his empire with the help of witchcraft. I don't believe all that stuff but we either had one hell of a hallucination, or it was real. I don't know what happened, but it seems the key did the trick. What made you think of it?'

'Don't know really, but I know Alistair thought of the same thing at the same time as I did and it worked, whether it was real or not. It was the stuff nightmares are made of, and I'm glad in a way that the whole place has gone for good. I hope Alistair never rebuilds it.' A nurse came at that point and touched Ellie's arm and said her name.

'Mademoiselle Black?'

'Oui?'

'Monsieur Morgan would like to see you, follow me please.' She led the way through the hospital to a room that was obviously one of the private rooms, as it was very different to the wards Ellie had seen in other hospitals. Alistair was sitting up in bed, with an oxygen mask on his face and his hands bandaged. In spite of herself, Ellie was pleased to see he was okay, and as she walked in, he took the mask off and smiled.

'How are you feeling Alistair?

'Not too bad,' he croaked, then coughed. 'The smoke was the worst thing and they say it has scorched my throat.'

Ellie went and sat by his bed, and Jack stood by the window, looking out.

'We've been talking,' Ellie indicated Jack, 'and we can't really make any sense of what happened, but it looks as if some pact was made years ago that involved one of us. I was given away at birth to be hidden, and bought up away from the family. That way, the contract would never have been fulfilled.'

Alistair opened his mouth to speak but Ellie held up her hand to stop him.

'Put the mask back on, it'll help.' He did so. 'So if it was true then all the power and success you were given wasn't from your business expertise, it was because our souls had been sold to the Devil. I still have trouble believing that at all, but I must admit, I was enjoying the lifestyle and could see how it would become addictive. At the end of the day, Alistair, we all have choices—and you've done some pretty bad things through your own free will.' Ellie stood up to leave.

'I'm going to find a hotel for tonight and I'll come back tomorrow, and we'll maybe be able to talk a bit longer. So I suggest you have a think about what you want, and how you intend to achieve it.' With that, Ellie left with Jack, and they walked in silence to the foyer.

'We'd better just find a hotel and get some rest before we do anything,' Ellie said to Jack. 'I'm totally washed out, and I think I need some clothes.' She pulled her blanket closer round her shoulders.

Jack put his arm protectively round her, and they walked from the hospital to try and find a taxi. In the end they did find a small hotel with one twin room free, and Ellie just crashed onto the narrow single bed and went to sleep. She must have slept most of the next day and awoke as dusk was falling, and she realized she was very dirty and extremely hungry. Jack must have covered her with the duvet, and she was warm and cocooned from the outside world. Ellie heard a key in the lock, and Jack came in carrying some bags.

'I had to have a guess at your size, and there wasn't much choice on Boxing Day, so I hope these are all right.' He dumped the bags at the end of the bed. 'I'll leave you to have a shower, then we'll find something to eat, as I'm starving.'

Ellie looked at the bags and suddenly realized how much she actually owed Jack. He didn't say a lot but he had been there when she needed someone on her side, and he really was a thoughtful guy.

'Thanks for everything, Jack, I really mean that. You've been a rock through this, and without you I think I'd have gone insane before now.' Ellie climbed out of the bed and looked in the bags; everything a girl could need was in there, and they looked better to Ellie at that moment than the pricy clothes she'd had at the chateau.

'Thanks again, I don't quite know how I'm going to repay

you for all this, as I haven't got any money—but I have still got the jewels Alistair gave me. I think I'll offer them back to him,' she said, holding them out to him.

Jack took them from Ellie and examined them. 'They really are pretty spectacular. Let's just put them in the safe and think about it later.' He put them in the mini safe, and Ellie felt better they were hidden from view. The staff at the hospital must have thought they were fakes, as none of them had commented on the necklace.

'Don't worry about the money. I've been on the phone quite a bit and everyone is just glad you're safe, so it's all come out of the department budget. You'll have to pay by sitting through endless rounds of questioning with Phil and Claire; they'll have their payment, one way or another.' He smiled. 'Better have a shower now.' He wrinkled his nose.

Jack had managed to secure a table at a small bistro that was open, and they sat and talked through the recent events over and over. Some of it made sense but a lot didn't, and there were questions Ellie didn't think they could ever answer. She sipped her country wine that didn't come out of a fancy bottle and cost the earth, and enjoyed it more than she could say, as she finally felt free, and lots of the loose strings of her past life were now knitted together.

'I suppose I'll go back home soon and see if I have a job and a flat to go back to. I might still have a fiancé, but I'm not sure about that. Rory and I had a conversation on Christmas morning, and let's just say, it didn't go well. I feel terrible as he seems to have been pushed to the side. He's been through a lot, and I'm sure he really loves me.' Ellie tailed off lamely.

'Forgive me for asking, but did you, or do you, really love him?' Jack's eyes met hers over the table.

Ellie felt as if she was put right on the spot. 'To be honest, I don't know. I thought I did, but when he proposed I wasn't sure,' Ellie twisted her ring on her finger. 'We were happy together and we were set to drift through life with no major upheavals. That's all I wanted at that time, but now so much has happened to me I don't think I'm the same person anymore. I've lived more in the past few months than most people do in a lifetime, I don't know if I can go back now. I just don't know anymore.' Ellie put her hands in her lap and stared at the plate.

'I've spoilt the evening, haven't I? I'm so sorry,' Jack said, and poured the end of the bottle of wine into her glass. 'I shouldn't have asked that, it was out of order. Not any of my business, but we've been through a lot and I feel like I've known you for years. I just want you to be happy, Ellie.'

'What about you Jack, what do you want out of life? Where will you be next Christmas? What will you be doing?'

'I think, rather I hope, I'll still be with the department and be sorting out problems. Basically, still a policeman, in a different set of clothes.'

'No, I meant personally. Will you be swapping Christmas presents with a wife etc.? Sorry, I'm being nosy, but I don't really know anything about you.'

Jack fiddled with his napkin and smoothed out the creases, then said, 'Don't know about that. There's no-one on the horizon at the moment, but hey, you never know.'

Ellie was beginning to feel a bit uncomfortable about how the conversation was going and the fact they had a twin room, so she changed the subject abruptly.

'I'm going to see Alistair tomorrow again and I hope you'll come with me. I do hope he's a bit better. I was a bit sisterly with him and he's gone through a bigger change than I have—and I hope he realizes now that he isn't God Almighty and people are people, not just pawns in his games.' Ellie sighed, and continued.

'We'll just have to wait and see on that one, but he's going to have to try to put right some of the things he's done. Take all those beautiful books he stole and sold, what's happened to those? I mean a collection like that shouldn't have been broken up and he didn't need all that money, but he was driven by something to do it. Maybe he's changed, I don't know; we'll just have to wait and see I suppose.'

They walked back to the hotel in silence, each lost in their thoughts. Ellie didn't know where Jack's were, but she was actually dreading going home, and she knew she would miss all the adrenaline and the excitement as she sank back into the anonymity and obscurity of life in London. Ellie didn't really want that any more if she was honest; strangely, she knew she would miss the danger. She had enjoyed thinking herself out of sticky situations and the uncertainty of what the next day would bring. It was perverse, but looking back, she would not have swapped the experience for anything.

They got into their room and under the cover of the darkness, Ellie unburdened her thoughts to Jack, as she instinctively knew she could trust him not to tell anyone. It appeared he felt the same and wouldn't swap his job for anything, and was worried he would be back on the beat when he got back. He also had enjoyed the danger and the uncertainty, and life in a London flat held no appeal at all. They drifted off to sleep unsure, of what life would hold for them.

The next day, Ellie and Jack went, as promised, to see

Alistair—and he was holding court from his hospital bed, swiftly taking up the reins of his empire again. His voice had obviously recovered, as various PA's and secretaries scurried away as they entered.

'You're obviously better then,' Ellie said, rolling her eyes. 'What's all this about? I thought you were supposed to be resting your voice.'

'I feel able to get out of here, except for these.' He held up his bandaged hands. 'The bandages should be down to smaller dressings within a week, and then I can leave.'

'Where will you go? The chateau is a write-off and it's probably not a good idea that you go back to London right now, 'cos they'll probably clap you in irons as soon as you set foot on the ground?'

'I've got another villa in Italy that is perfectly adequate for the time being, and I'll remove myself to there until this mess is sorted out. I've already been onto the legal team in London and they are looking into all aspects of what has happened, and we'll see what can be done.'

'What do you mean "see what can be done"?' Ellie was puzzled and sat down on the chair by the bed.

'It seems that the maid I rescued, Maria, is doing all right and should be out of hospital in a few weeks. I've made arrangements for her to have a private room, much better for her. The chateau won't be rebuilt, although I could if I wanted to, but perhaps the past should remain buried.' Ellie nodded and agreed wholeheartedly. 'It seems that no one died in the blaze which was a great relief, and I've made arrangements for them to have full pay until I find somewhere suitable for a French base. Do you approve?'

'Yes, of course I do, but where's all this coming from?

Since when did you care what the maid's name was, and if she'd prefer a private room?' Ellie looked at Jack, who looked just as puzzled as she was.

'I honestly don't know Ellie, but what you said last night made me think—and you are really very important to me.' He held up his hand as she opened her mouth to dismiss any of the twin crap she knew was coming.

'Hear me out Ellie. I feel different now. I know I've got a long way to go to be a better person, but I want you to help me, if you would? I was sort of dead inside, but I didn't realize what emotions like guilt and simply caring about things felt like. All I felt was greed and envy, if someone had more or better than me. I need help with this, to work at being normal. Will you help me?'

'That's the biggest load of bull crap I've ever heard,' Ellie said, almost laughing at him. 'You're a leopard, and I've never known one to shed its spots so quickly. You sure you didn't get knocked on the head, doing your heroic rescue?'

'Please, Ellie. Please give it a try.'

'That's the first time I've ever heard you say please to anyone. You're ill, you should stay here.'

'I also have something else that may change your mind. Please open the drawer over there.' He pointed at the chest of drawers by the window. 'In there is a box; open it, if you would.' Ellie opened the box, and in it was the key made of two curly crosses. She picked it out of the box and it fell apart in her hands. It was back to two separate parts again.

'How did you get this?' Ellie asked Alistair, amazed. 'The last time I saw this, it was deep inside the brain of that bird thing.'

'I have no idea, but it was found in my hand when I was

bought in here. Take your half back and put mine back in the box.

Ellie held onto her part of the cross. 'This saved us from God knows what, and I'm not letting it go again. Our father must have known that this was the key to defeating that thing and given us both a part. He must have hoped that if we ever found each other, we could work out the puzzle of what to do with it.'

Jack was standing by the window as usual and moved forward to join in the conversation, perching on the end of the bed. 'That's totally weird, but what exactly did you have in mind, Alistair, to put things right, besides looking after the staff better?'

'To begin with,' he replied, 'I want to get all the books and manuscripts back. I think Ellie would agree with me that a collection like that shouldn't be broken up.' Alistair looked at Ellie and she nodded. 'I want to get it all back together, but some of the people I sold it to are not the nicest people in the world and it could be very dangerous to upset them. I need you Ellie, and Jack, of course, only if you want to.'

Ellie looked at Jack and remembered our conversation last night. He looked back at her and said, 'Let's do it!

CHAPTER NINETEEN

Ellie looked happily at Jack, and they high fived. Alistair looked pleased, and waved a bandaged hand in the general direction. Then Ellie asked tentatively, 'So what are we really going to do?'

Jack said, 'I've been on the phone, and it looks as if Phil and the crew are coming over. In the light of what you've just said, Alistair, I agree that it's probably better for you to be out of the country for the time being. It may be, we can broker some kind of amnesty for you eventually. Don't hold your breath, as there are some very serious crimes waiting for you to answer to in England.'

'I know I'm guilty, even though I never actually did the crimes; I just engineered the whole thing and others carried out my orders. I've been disbanding some of the departments this morning, but many of the people involved are not going to be too pleased, and it's perhaps better for my sake I disappear for a bit.' Alistair slowly shook his head. 'I can't imagine how I did some of the things I did, and it was as if I wasn't me, just some sort of machine. I have to be very careful though not to lose control of the business, as if I'm seen as a weak head, then my enemies will become vultures, and rip me and Morgan Enterprises apart.'

Ellie looked at him, and it was almost as if he was at sea in the new waves of emotion that swept over him. He couldn't cope with it all in one go, and he actually seemed lost. This was not an Alistair Ellie knew at all, and she couldn't think of anything to say to make it better. So she tried the safe route.

'Look, you've been through a lot in the past few days and things have happened that neither of us can understand, so just take things one little bit at a time. We'll help you break the problem down into bite-sized pieces and deal with it bit by bit—won't we Jack?' Ellie looked at Jack to help her, and back her up.

Jack eyeballed Alistair and said, 'I'll give it a go—but any funny business, like kidnappings and murders… then I'm still an English policeman and I'll run you in, even if I have to carry you back to England myself. Understand?' They both slowly nodded. Ellie thought the message had got across.

'So when is everybody arriving? We're going to have to find somewhere for them to stay,' Ellie said, trying to imagine where they could get at least three rooms over the Christmas holidays.

Alistair replied, 'Now that's something I can do, as I have connections with the Royal Barrière and can probably get suites for you all.'

Ellie looked sternly at Alistair, 'This isn't one of those "favours" for the local mob boss, is it? We're not going down that road. If you threaten the hotel with something awful, in exchange for a room, then we'll camp out, freezing or not.'

'No, no, I promise it's nothing like that', said Alistair hurriedly. 'I always keep a retainer on some of the rooms for when people come to visit and don't want to be seen going to the chateau—not that there's a chateau any more, anyway,' he added.

Ellie said, 'OK, you get onto that with one of your entourage, and Jack and I will wait for the others and we can all move together. Hopefully, they will be able to get here tomorrow and we can make a start.' Ellie actually wasn't keen on having another night with Jack in the small room; even though they had twin beds, it was a bit too close for comfort.

'Jack and I will take a trip back to the chateau and have a look; then we can come back and see you again tonight if you want. I'll send your PA's back in, as I can see them lurking through the window in the door,' Ellie added with a smile, as they left.

Jack and Ellie did eventually make it back to what was left of the chateau, and the devastation was horrendous. It was a dour, overcast day, and tendrils of smoke still rose from the charred ruins. The stables and garages were totally untouched, and the staff were doing a good job on clearing up all the ash and sweeping away the sooty water from the courtyards. The fire crews were still there and advised them not to go too close, but let them through the cordon when Ellie told them she was Mr. A. Morgan's sister. They wandered about, looking at the heaps of stone and charred rafters.

'I can't believe that no one died in this, it's totally gone. It looks as if the stone has melted,' Ellie said to Jack, as she kicked a chunk of masonry, which crumbled into dust. 'I didn't think stone would disintegrate like this; there's just nothing left.'

'Alistair reckons he can rebuild it, but he'd be mad to even try,' Jack said, surveying the smouldering pile. 'It wouldn't just take a few million; it would take tens of millions. He would be better off just buying another one if he's got that much cash lying around.'

'Oh, I imagine he has but it wouldn't be the same, and I think he wants to get rid of this link with the past once and for all. I hope he is true to his word as I, for one, will never set foot in this place again,' Ellie said emphatically. 'It was evil—beautiful, but evil through and through, and even just walking about here gives me the creeps. Let's go.'

She turned to go back to the car. A light rain had begun to fall and Ellie turned up the collar of her coat to stop the drips finding their way down her neck. Jack walked beside her and put his arm round her shoulders. Ellie jumped away as if stung.

'Jack, no, please no.' She turned to face him. His face looked confused, and Ellie felt so sorry for him at that moment; how could he even have any inkling how she felt?

'Jack, I'm so sorry I reacted like that, but I'm so confused right now. I like you a lot and we've been through so much just recently. You've been my rock and I never could have got through it without you, but I've got to sort out my feelings about Rory first before I can move on.' Ellie felt a lump form in her throat as she said the words, and she wanted to put her hand out and hold his so much—but instead, she shoved them deep into her pockets and walked slowly to the car.

It was a silent drive back to the hotel where they were staying, and instead of going up to the room, by tacit agreement, they decided on having coffee in the small lounge. Things were getting more awkward by the minute, and Jack was fidgeting about trying to read a newspaper and not meeting Ellie's eyes.

Eventually he said, 'I'm going to try and get another room for tonight. I think its best, don't you?' Ellie nodded and he went to find the hotelier immediately, leaving his coffee untouched on the table.

Ellie idly flicked through a magazine and thought, Oh God, why do I seem to fuck up every relationship I ever have? First, I seem to have put Rory off forever, by trying to keep him out of things and safe. Instead, I have alienated him and relegated him to the back row, away from all the action. Then there's the other thing, that if I did try and patch things up with Rory I'd be back in London, back to my old life as a librarian in my flat.

Ellie didn't know what she wanted right at that moment, and she knew she wasn't the same person she'd been a few months ago; her world had been turned upside down and suddenly things that were important then didn't seem to matter anymore. Maybe she'd been seduced by the high life and the danger, but that was where she was right now, and she would have to think long and hard about where she wanted to be in the future. So the short answer was to do nothing and see how events unfolded. Maybe the decision would be made for her by forces beyond her control, so she decided to take the easy way out and leave it all to fate.

Jack came in then and said that the hotelier had got a single free and he had moved his stuff in. Not that he had a lot anyway, and Ellie could stay where she was. Phil had phoned and they would be with them in the morning, over breakfast, and they could all decamp to the Hotel Royal Barrière together. Ellie inwardly breathed a sigh of relief, as a night with Jack in the next bed would have been very difficult and she doubted she would have slept at all. They did decide, however, to go to the same small bistro they went to the previous night after visiting Alistair as they were both hungry, and on a more mundane note, Ellie hadn't got any money.

That evening, when they got to the hospital, Alistair was out of bed and holding court again. He seemed much more like his usual self, and the bandages on his hands had reduced greatly in size. That was the good news; the bad news was that on his left hand, where he had touched the crawly thing, the last digits of his fingers had gone black and all the blood supply seemed to have been cut off. They weren't painful at all, which was a good point, but the doctors were guarded in their opinion if it would ever be restored. They were going to leave it till tomorrow, but they had warned him that he may have to have the last joints of his fingers amputated.

Ellie must have looked stricken at the news and Alistair didn't look overjoyed. 'I just thank my lucky stars that I didn't try and pick it up. It was a vile being and I can't think why I tried to stroke it in the first place.'

'You mean that when you touched it you were trying to stroke it?' Ellie asked him, aghast.

'Yes, for some reason it looked beautiful to me and I felt an overwhelming urge to stroke it. I know it burned me, but it seems it did more than that. It seems to have killed the ends of my fingers in some way. I'm just glad I can't feel them, but I'm not looking forward to tomorrow at all,' Alistair said, staring morosely at his bandaged hands.

Ellie didn't know what to say, as she couldn't think of anything that was of any comfort, but Jack managed to stick his size ten in and said, 'Just thank God you weren't a concert pianist or anything.'

Ellie looked at him, horrified that he could say such a thing, but Alistair just laughed and said, 'I'll drink to that,' and waved towards the fridge that was now in his room.

'Let's have a glass before the evening offering of what

passes for food in this place. A good thing is that Marcel, my chef, got away unscathed and is coming tomorrow to attend to my culinary needs. At least I won't need anything cut up for me… It's just so demeaning.'

The small fridge yielded a bottle of champagne and some cold glasses. Jack did the honours, as Alistair held his glass in two hands and savoured the first sip. 'Mmmmm, nectar of the Gods, this is better than all the medicine I get at the moment.'

'You're sure you should drink with all that medication washing round inside you?' Ellie asked concerned.

'Frankly, my dear, I don't give a damn,' Alistair said, quoting Clark Gable, and raising his glass in a toast to the future.

Ellie felt much better on her way to the bistro, and realized that deep down she had been worried about Alistair, and now she felt that a weight had been lifted from her mind. He seemed to have regained some of his spirits and got back some of the zip and pizzazz that made him what he was. The lost, almost frightened, man was not the man that Ellie knew, and she was glad that mentally, he had taken a first step on the road to recovery.

The meal at the Bistro wasn't as awkward as Ellie had feared, and they both kept the conversation light-hearted and mundane. The food was good and they both enjoyed the cheerful atmosphere. It was packed out, as the Christmas holiday was ending and everyone was going home the next day. Ellie did bring up the subject of her penury with Jack, and apologized that she couldn't pay her share without pawning the family jewels. Jack only laughed and said that wouldn't be necessary, as he had a credit card from the department to cover all cost of the investigation.

'What "investigation" are we talking about here?' Ellie asked intrigued.

Well, there's murders committed in England, kidnappings, helicopter crashes in France, not to mention a chunk of the Staffordshire Hoard going missing, and then there's the theft of the manuscript collection...'

'OK, I get the picture. I'd actually forgotten about the Staffs Hoard—that was down to Alistair as well. This isn't looking good for him at all, is it?'

'Not really, so it's perhaps best if he does disappear for a bit, till we can get it sorted out. Well, we'll all get together tomorrow and try and make a plan. I know that everyone has been working flat out over Christmas to sort out legalities and get the best outcome for everyone. We'll just have to hang on and see what they have to say when we all get together. So enjoy the meal, courtesy of Her Majesty's government.' Jack raised his drink and they clinked glasses in the candlelight.

The next day was the day of the big move and, on cue, everyone arrived for breakfast. They all sat round a big table and the hotelier was in his element, serving up plate after plate of hot croissants and pain au chocolat, with cups of steaming coffee and bowls of hot chocolate. It was good to see Claire again, and she looked fit after the traumas of the past week. Phil's head wound had faded to a scar that still looked red, but the swelling had gone and he was healing well. Nigel and Robert ate well but still were in a world of their own, and played on their iPads whilst everyone chatted. By agreement no-one talked about the forthcoming meeting and future plans, but caught up with the news of Alistair's recovery and Ellie's health and well-being after the fire. She was really pleased to see them all again, particularly Claire, who had literally saved her life on more than one occasion. Claire brushed it all off with, 'Anyone would have done it,' and 'You'd do the same for me.' Ellie knew that wasn't true at all, but she felt Claire had accepted her grateful thanks.

Taxis arrived and they went to the Royal Barrière, courtesy of Alistair, and wandered round the suites, a little overawed at the lavishness of it all. Ellie was with Claire and they soon made the place their own. Ellie's wardrobe space consisted of three coat hangers, as that was all she had, but she did put the jewels in the safe straight away. Claire had looked at them with amazement, as Ellie described the circumstances of the Christmas present from Alistair, and they decided she should get them valued as soon as possible. Ellie didn't have a clue what they could be worth, and to be honest, she didn't quite know what to do with them. There weren't any places she could wear them in London, and they were more of a liability than anything, but they had belonged to her mother and it was a link with her, so Ellie decided to keep them for the time being.

A conference room was set aside for the duration of their stay, and soon links with England were established and they could speak to people in Phil's department in London. The faces that popped up on the screen were men in suits, ensconced in offices that looked over the London skyline. They were obviously high up in the government, and as Jack and Ellie looked at each other, she mouthed the words 'Who are they?' and he mimed back, 'I don't know.' Phil must have caught this and explained that the team had left the police station, which was only a temporary base, and moved back to their old offices on the Embankment.

'So you're not policemen, then,' said Jack, to the room in general, 'and Gittins wasn't your boss.'

'No, Jack. Sorry we didn't have the time to fill you in on all the details, but when you signed the Official Secrets Act, you were then one of us. We like to think of ourselves as "trouble shooters", who do sometimes work a bit outside the law. We tend to get drafted in to sort out slightly bigger messes that can't be handled by local police. We look at the bigger issues that may have an impact on destabilising governments, or generally upsetting the balance of power.'

'So you can go anywhere in the world, undercover and do stuff?' Jack said the word "stuff", as if he couldn't think of a better one. 'A bit like James Bond then.'

'Not quite, but you're on the right lines,' said Phil, smiling as Jack floundered.

'So where do I fit into all this?' Ellie asked, puzzled that she was even in the room for what could be a top-secret meeting.

Phil looked directly at her and replied, 'You, Miss Ellie Black, are the lynch pin of the whole operation. You are our woman on the inside of it all. You have been our eyes and ears, and if I may give you a compliment, you have acquitted yourself admirably. This means that I will have to second you to being part of the team; that is, of course, if you wish to carry on?'

Ellie looked at Jack. 'You knew about this all the time, didn't you? You were aware this was going to happen. I suppose I'm going to have to sign the Official Secrets Act now, and get shot at and nearly fall out of helicopters, etc.'

Claire held out a pen and paper. 'Only if you want to. If not, you can catch the first flight back to England, and our paths will never cross again.' She still held the pen out to her.

Ellie held her breath. This was it, this was decision time, and it had come a lot faster than she thought. She wasn't clever like these people, and she couldn't fire a gun, or fly a helicopter. In fact, she couldn't think of any skill she had to offer right there and then. Ellie voiced her concerns and said that she didn't think she was up to the job at all, and the indecision must have been written large across her face.

'Don't worry about your skills, they will come in time, but your job now will be to stick close to Mr. Alistair Morgan and be our "watch dog" on him. We'll need to know if his supposed change of heart is real. So unless he's planning to kill you, there should be no danger at all.'

Ellie hastily jumped in at that point, 'I don't think he's planning that; in fact, I don't think he ever meant to do me any harm at all. He certainly seems to be different now after the fire, and it was his idea to try and get the manuscripts back, and if that's all the job is then, I'll accept.' Ellie took the pen and signed.

Claire said, 'Good. Now that's out of the way and settled, we can get on planning what we're going to do.' She took the paper and made sure Ellie had signed in the right place, then folded it carefully, and put it away.

'Welcome to the team,' said Phil, and everyone quickly got down to business. It was a long meeting punctuated by cups of coffee, and Ellie felt her attention drifting away after a time as the legalities were discussed. She couldn't keep up with it all, and she eventually gave up and began to think about Alistair and what was happening at the hospital. When a lunch break was called, Ellie hot footed it to a phone and called the hospital. As she was his sister she was put straight through, as if they were expecting her call. A surgeon answered her and his English was very good. It appeared he had been flown in from Paris to perform the operation to restore the blood supply to Alistair's fingers. Sadly, it had been unsuccessful, and he'd amputated the end digits from the four fingers of Alistair's left hand. There was nothing that could have been done and the surgeon said he'd never seen anything like it before, and the fingers were quite dead. The operation had been routine and Mr. Morgan was recovering nicely, and Ellie could visit this evening.

She was relieved that he was okay, and sad at the same time that the operation was an amputation, not the hoped-for, restoration. Ellie went back to the conference room and passed on the news. Phil said, 'Well that gives you even more of a good reason for sticking close to him. You can give him some moral support and help him to get over the operation.'

'If I know Alistair at all, then I don't think he'll need either, but I'll do it anyway, without any excuses or subterfuge. If I'm honest with him, then he may just be honest with me, and I'll explain it all tonight when I see him.' Ellie looked round at them all, examining their faces for dissention.

'You play it how you like, Ellie, you know what your job is—but we're here to help you if things get sticky. We're going to provide all you need in the way of communications; hot lines and panic buttons, so that you won't feel alone in this,' said Phil and the others nodded. 'So when he's ready to leave, you're going with him to Italy and we need to find out who he sold those books to, that's the first part. Never forget, Ellie, that this guy had no notion of good and bad, or right or wrong. He's still an unknown quantity, even though he's your brother.' Phil looked very serious, and Ellie nodded and took his point.

The meeting rambled on, and Ellie was amazed how they could all keep focused for such a long time, as she began to weary of the day. The men in suits on the big screens were in agreement on the initial plan, and said they would get in touch with their counterparts in Italy to put them in the picture, and give Ellie all the help they could, should she require it. All she could do was nod, as she couldn't envisage what could possibly go wrong.

That evening, Ellie went alone to see Alistair, and found him propped up in bed, still a bit woozy from the anaesthetic. He seemed pleased to see her and told her to help herself to some champagne if she wanted, but he wouldn't have any as he was a bit nauseous.

'Have you seen the surgeon yet? Have they told you how the operation went?' Ellie said, treading a bit carefully.

'Yes, they also told me you'd called and you know the full story.' He held up a heavily bandaged left hand. The other one by comparison just had a few dressings on to protect the burns, and he even managed to waggle his fingers. 'I've lost the end parts of my fingers, but I won't know how it will look till this lot comes off. I suppose I could go for world domination and wear a black leather glove. Only joking,' he added hastily, when he saw the look on Ellie's face.

'I should hope so too,' Ellie said sternly, but smiled at the same time, as there was a little flash of humour, and he wasn't as morose as before. 'Before you drop off to sleep again, I want to explain what's been going on today, now that the team is all here. They said to convey their thanks for the accommodation—very plush—and that you'll be free to leave for Italy when you feel up to it. I'm going with you to supposedly aid you with your recovery, but we're going to all work together to try and get the books back.' Ellie added, 'Do you understand?' as he yawned.

'Yes, I do—and I suppose you're there to keep me on the straight and narrow as well?'

'Yes, I am, so I'll be there reporting back to MI something or other on a daily basis. I have told them that I'm going to be completely honest with you, and I hope you'll do the same for me. This is the end game for you, Alistair, and this is the one and only chance you're going to get. Don't mess it up. Please.'

He yawned again, 'Okay, I'll try.'

'You'll do more than try, as I don't do prison visits and I promise if you do mess up, it'll be the last you will ever see or hear from me again. You have turned my life upside down big time, and this is the last chance you're going to get from me as well.'

He stretched out his hand with the white bandage glove on. 'If I could shake on it, I would; that's the best I can do right now.'

Ellie put her hand gently on top of his and said, 'It's a deal. I'll leave you in peace now and see you tomorrow.'

'Okay,' he said and yawned, and his eyelids became heavy as he went to sleep. Ellie lowered his hand back onto the bed and left.

The next few days were comprised of more meetings, and yet more meetings. Ellie gradually began to understand more of what was going on, and that in all the plans and scenarios, it was important to cover all eventualities. She got training from Robert and Nigel on all the communications paraphernalia, and also had a satellite phone, so that if she ever disappeared off the grid she could phone for help. Ellie had also a long list of numbers that she had to memorize, and was told it wasn't a good idea to put them in the phone, as if it was hijacked, the whole team could be traced very quickly.

The fitness programme was put back in place, and Ellie went to bed each night, exhausted. There were even some sessions on self-defence, which she thought were hilarious, until Claire put her on her back three times in a row, and then she got angry and paid more attention. After a few days, Ellie began to look for chinks in the assailant's armour and even managed to disable Nigel on one occasion. She let him keep the pretence that he had let her win and save face, but she knew she was getting better.

Alistair was now down to a few dressings on his left hand, and was making plans to go to his castle in Italy. Apparently, it was not far from Naples, and overlooked the picturesque Amalfi Coast. It was quite isolated and there was only one road in and out. He had made arrangements for it to be guarded day and night, and Ellie felt totally safe to be going there.

Phil and Claire had some meetings with Alistair, and apparently had laid it on the line for him. They had enough evidence to put him away for a long time, and had come to some sort of amnesty agreement. When he got to his castle with Ellie, he would begin to contact all his "friends" who had purchased the books, and let them know, through Ellie, what information he had managed to glean about their whereabouts.

The next few days passed by quickly, and Ellie looked forward to boarding the jet to Italy—and also to a bit of winter sun, away from the cold, damp drizzle in Deauville. The weather wasn't as bad as in England, as they were still in the grip of an icy blast from the east, and having the worst snowfalls in living memory. Ellie did wonder if Rory and John had made their way from the farmhouse, but she was a bit afraid to ask, as it would stir up all the feelings, she had managed to file away deep inside her.

CHAPTER TWENTY

The day came, and Alistair and Ellie were picked up and whisked away to the private jet. Ellie was glad to be away from Deauville and looked forward to a bit of down time. The last week had been hectic, and there had seemed so much to learn and information to store away that her brain cells were in melt down. She couldn't even finish a crossword without going to sleep. With all the shops open after the Christmas break, she had managed to get herself a few more things to add to her wardrobe, and felt a bit better equipped to live life at the castle. It was probably going to be a bit quiet, but Ellie knew Alistair liked to change for dinner, and there may be guests to entertain. She could never be sure what would happen and she wanted to be prepared.

The jewels travelled with Ellie in the cabin, in a box with her hand luggage, and she would keep a tight grip on them until they reached somewhere where there would be a safe. Ellie had asked Alistair what he wanted to do with them, but he had assured her that they were a present from him, and as they belonged to their mother, she was free to do anything she wanted. It was a big responsibility, and Ellie wasn't even sure she actually wanted them, but she thought she could just put them in the safe and probably forget about them.

Naples Airport was all hustle and bustle with people searching for the sun, and Ellie was glad there was a car waiting to take them to the castle. She had asked Alistair about the castle and he was suitably vague, as ever, about its history. He wasn't really bothered about things like that and after mentioning Knights Templar, Saracens and Romans, he began poring over his Financial Times. Ellie made a mental note to try and find out more, as she was interested in things like that, and she realized that it was half hers, as it was left to Alistair by their father. All this wealth hadn't really sunk in and Ellie was, inside, still the librarian living on a meagre wage, making ends meet.

The car wound its way up hairpin bends and Ellie began to feel slightly sick, as they climbed up through rocky gorges. Then the vista opened out, and a magnificent castle was perched precariously on the top of a hill. It had battlements and turrets, everything a castle should have; even a drawbridge, that rattled as they drove over.

'What's this place called Alistair?' Ellie asked, keeping the nausea under control.

'It's Castillo Uccello,' he said, 'and before you ask, I don't know what it means. That could perhaps be something to keep you occupied when I'm working. I don't really like being this far away from the business, but I don't have a choice at the moment, do I?'

'Too right, you don't have a choice, and I'm not going to be fobbed off with the "I'm working" scenario, as I'm supposed to keep tabs on you, remember? Really, Alistair, there's only a very fine line to cross and you're back to England,' Ellie said, and he didn't deign to answer her, as he knew it was true.

The huge front door of the castle was open, and staff lined the steps to greet them. Apparently, Alistair hadn't been a frequent visitor in the past, and they were keen to get a look at the lost twin. Ellie felt under scrutiny as she alighted from the car, but just kept smiling and followed Alistair as he swept into the main hall. There were flagstones in the hall, worn smooth by the passage of countless feet over the ages, and the walls were covered in ancient tapestries. Ellie's feet echoed on the floor, and she was glad it was warmer here than in France, though there was still a distinct chill in the air. Alistair beckoned her through to a small side room, with a fire of logs blazing in the grate. It was a comfortable room and there were carpets on the floor, and armchairs surrounded the fire.

She sat down and said, 'So what do we do now?

'Before you settle into your room, I suggest we have a small glass of champagne before dinner, and then we can talk about it.'

'Well… I suppose the sun has gone down over the Empire somewhere, so I'll have a very small glass and we'll leave the work till tomorrow.'

Alistair retrieved a laptop and flicked it open. 'It seems one of my friends in Morocco has been enquiring after my health, and we are invited to a party at his villa next week. Now, he was one of the people who bought a book from the auction, so it may be a good idea to visit, as we've been invited.'

A servant came in with the champagne, and the conversation stopped whilst he poured and left the bottle in a cooler. Ellie sipped her glass and said, 'Are you sure he invited me as well?'

'Don't worry about that. As word of your appearance in

my life, and the fire at the chateau, have winged their way round the world, everyone now knows who you are.'

Ellie blanched at the thought that she had been worldwide news, and wondered if she'd bitten off more than she could chew. 'So what's the plan then? Do we go and buy the book back from him?'

'Nothing so simple, I'm afraid. I have got to find out where the book actually is first, as he may not have it at the small villa in Morocco. I may be wrong, but it could be anywhere, and I don't think he'll sell it back. It's a "one off" you see; something rare and beautiful, and he won't want to let it go easily.'

'Are you suggesting we steal it?' Ellie asked, horrified.

'Depends how you look at it,' Alistair said, putting his head on one side. 'I stole it, then sold it… so if we steal it back, the circle is complete.'

'Alistair! That's a very twisted logic you're following. He's going to be out of pocket by God knows how much, and he's going to come after you.'

'Not if he doesn't know who's stolen it,' said Alistair, and Ellie fell silent. 'Don't beat yourself up as most of his money hasn't come by legitimate means, and what he will lose will be small change.'

Ellie pondered this, and couldn't imagine a life where a couple of million pounds would be "small change".

'I can see where you're coming from, but I don't like it one bit. I'm going to run that past Claire and Phil as I promised, and they're going to have to get to Morocco somehow and be there for us. That's the deal, Alistair, so you can e-mail them the times and dates and appear to be playing your part, as well as me.'

'OK, as you wish, I'll do it. But to more mundane things; we're going to be here for about four or five days, what would you like to do? I've got doctors etc. coming in to look after this—' and he waved his hand at her, '—but it should be a fairly straightforward job of changing dressings, and all that stuff. Hopefully I can have my new glove fitted soon, so it doesn't look so ghastly.'

'You mean you are going to get a black leather glove?' Ellie asked, surprised.

'No, nothing so fanciful I'm afraid; just a soft leather chamois to protect the ends of my fingers for about six months. It should even be vaguely skin toned, so it will be less noticeable'.

Ellie thought she couldn't argue with that and just nodded, as she would have done the same. 'I suppose the first thing I would like is to explore the castle. It's very grand and just oozes history, so I'll amble about and get the feel of the place. I feel like a bit of R & R anyway, as the last few weeks have drained me, mentally and physically. I meant to ask you earlier, as every place you live in seems to have everything—has it got a shooting range, as I'm supposed to practice?'

'Yes, everything a girl could want, including a rifle range.' He smiled wryly. 'There's also a swimming pool inside, so it's heated. I won't be able to join you for the time being but feel free to use it. Just let your maid know and she'll make sure it's ready.'

'I suppose there's a wardrobe full of clothes again?' Ellie asked, already knowing the answer. She still couldn't get over the fact that money was no object, and everything would just appear if she wished it so.

'Of course, all arranged. There may be some people

joining us for dinner tonight but I've kept it small, as I must admit I haven't quite got my energy back to full throttle.'

Ellie sipped the last of her champagne and stood. 'I've only got about an hour and a half to get ready for dinner, so I think I'll go and have a bath first.' She stretched her back. 'There's still some kinks in there I need to iron out, so I'll leave the high heels for another day.'

Ellie left Alistair sitting by the fire and went in search of her room. She was approached by a footman and she asked him to give her a quick tour of the main ground floor, so she knew where she was. He opened huge double doors onto a vast library and sumptuous dining room, with a drawing room leading from it. The whole place was just as fine, but the décor was totally different from Chateau of the Birds. Someone had taken a great deal of trouble to hunt out enormous pieces of furniture that didn't look dwarfed by the arches and filigree stonework that vaulted up above her. Ellie felt a sense of awe as she gazed about, taking in the tapestries on the walls and the precious carpets on the floors muffling her footsteps.

Ellie was shown to her suite and was met by Maria, the same maid she had in France. She was recovered from her ordeal, and Ellie was surprised to see her there. She bobbed a small curtsey at her entrance and Ellie held out her hand.

'Maria, it's so good to see you here, I hope you're well. It's nice to see a face I know—oh, and please forget all that bobbing up and down. It's not necessary and I don't particularly like it.'

Maria stood with her hands folded in front of her, gazing at the carpet. 'Mr. Alistair wouldn't like it if I didn't,' she mumbled.

'I don't really care what Mr. Alistair likes or doesn't like, so you can do what you want while he's around, but here, in my room, no. Okay?' She nodded. 'I've got to ask you something, Maria. Do you really want to be here, or are you here because you have to be?'

She began slowly. 'At the chateau, I had to be there, because my father and brother had done something bad against Mr. Alistair, and he said he wouldn't do anything if I worked for him. That seemed to change when we had the great fire, and after that he asked me if I wanted to come and be your maid in Italy. I agreed, as I don't think I could have found a job quickly in France. I think it was also Mr. Alistair that saved my life, and I am grateful to him.' She paused then said brightly, 'I am also very good at the hairdressing and can do nails, makeup and other beauty treatments if you want.'

Ellie smiled at her candour, and told her that she was very pleased she wanted to help her look her best, and she would take her with her everywhere. She also had to agree that if anything was bothering her at any time, she was to tell her directly and Ellie would sort it with Mr. Alistair, as she would now work for Ellie, not him. Ellie felt Maria relax, and she smiled and said Ellie would be the best looking, best dressed woman on the planet. Maria explained it was she that had chosen her clothes, and she hoped Ellie liked them.

'Without a doubt, Maria, your taste is impeccable.' She looked puzzled. 'Very good choices, I like them a lot,' Ellie amended.

'Let me show you,' Maria said enthusiastically, and they went to the walk-in closet, carefully concealed behind a tapestry that had a door cut in it. 'Tonight, maybe this one.' She held out a Versace creation, that was very elegant and cut to perfection. 'Maybe you wear your hair up, like so.' She pushed Ellie's hair into a smooth chignon.

'Perfect,' Ellie said, and held the dress in one hand and her hair in another, and twirled to look in the floor length mirror. It wasn't the Ellie Black she knew that stared back from the mirror; she looked like something from the Vogue magazine. Was Ellie Black disappearing, or was this the real person just emerging? Tonight, she didn't have a choice of who to be.

'So Maria, we'd better get started if you're going to make me a beautiful butterfly, work your magic,' and Maria hurried off to run the bath. Ellie thought, Life isn't all bad, as she relaxed, waiting for her pampering—and thoughts of Rory suddenly came into her mind.

What was she going to do about that unfinished business? She was still wearing his engagement ring, and her hand hovered over the phone on the table. She could ring him now, and try and sort it out. She could invite him to the castle—she knew that wouldn't be a problem—but would he accept the new lifestyle, and her being part of an undercover operation? Ellie didn't think so. Her hand dropped to her lap and she bit her lip with frustration; there didn't seem a way round this at the moment.

The dinner gong sounded and Ellie made her way down the grand staircase, trailing her fingers on the stone balustrade. Maria had worked her magic, and the small gathering in the hall fell silent and stared at Ellie's entrance. Alistair detached himself from a group and came and took her elbow, steering her to the first knot of people.

'Let me introduce my beautiful sister, Eleanor. This is the French Ambassador and his wife, Estelle.' Ellie smiled politely.

'Such a beautiful region of Italy. We were so sorry to hear of your chateau burning down. We hope you will be able to rebuild it, or perhaps find another comparable,' the Ambassador said, with a small bow, and kissed her hand.

Ellie replied, 'We were just thankful that no-one was seriously injured in the fire. It was quite devastating, as we were both there at the time.' She shot a meaningful look at Alistair, but his face was a mask of urbane politeness. Alistair took two drinks from a proffered tray and handed one to her. He politely excused them both and they moved on to the next group—and so it went on, until they filed into the dining room and Ellie took her place at Alistair's right hand.

The meal was a civilized affair until tongues got loosened by the wine, and people were craving information about how they had both found each other. This part of the story was something Alistair and Ellie hadn't rehearsed. She felt a bit at sea, and mutely pleaded with her eyes for him to think of something, fast.

'Ladies and gentlemen.' Alistair clinked his fork against a glass. 'I'm very pleased you could all join me for tonight's small gathering, to herald our arrival in this beautiful country. One, I am sad to say I've not had chance before now to visit often. As you can see, we survived the fire, but I sadly had to have a small operation on my hand, so please forgive me for my American style of eating tonight.' A small murmur ran round the table. 'My sister Eleanor and I met by chance, and various tests proved she is indeed my twin sister.'

'How "by chance"?' A voice piped up from the other end of the table.

'Let's just say it was due to the ministrations of my half-brother Max—sadly deceased in an unfortunate accident—that we "ran" into each other,' Alistair replied, with a look that plainly said he wouldn't do anymore explaining to anyone. 'But please everyone, enjoy the evening.' He waved his hand expansively at the fabulous surroundings and meal.

'Well done,' Ellie said, in a sibilant hiss in his ear as he finished. He smiled at her in return, and whispered back, 'I've always been a good liar.' Ellie was enjoying the evening, but that comment put her back a few months and she still wondered if she could truly trust him.

The evening ended on a high note for the guests, as one of the rooms in the castle had been converted to a casino, and as Ellie had never been to one, she found the whole experience interesting. It wasn't so much the betting, as Alistair had given instructions that no guest would lose much money, but watching the people and seeing how they reacted to the spin of the wheel or the turn of the card fascinated her. Ellie tried her hand at roulette but failed dismally, and just wandered round chatting to guests with a glass of erstwhile "champagne" in her hand. It was, in fact, soda water with a splash of apple juice, to make it look authentic. She really didn't want to get drunk and say things she shouldn't as she didn't know anyone there, and she'd learned the hard way that people aren't always what they appear to be.

The French Ambassador eventually cornered her, and Ellie tried to copy Alistair with his mundane chit-chat, but he was having none of it.

'I am enchanted to meet you, Miss Eleanor.' He bowed over her hand again.

'Likewise, Mr Ambassador. I do hope you're enjoying the evening. Your wife, Estelle; she seems to be enjoying the tables.' Ellie glanced over to where she was engrossed in the next turn of the card.

'Yes—but I actually wanted to ask you what really happened at the chateau. I have had various, let's say, 'intelligences' about the happenings of that night, but I really wanted to hear the true story. It was devastating to my country to lose such a national treasure. I hope you can throw, how do you say, some light on the matter?'

He was fishing, and Ellie knew it. He'd probably been sent by some arm of the French Secret service to gather information, and had picked on Ellie as he knew he wouldn't get anywhere with Alistair.

'Mr. Ambassador, it was a frightful experience,' Ellie said, putting a hand to her throat as if the memory was too dreadful to contemplate. She decided to play the "dumb" sister that hadn't a thought in her head besides what she was going to wear the next day.

'There were flames everywhere and we were so lucky to get out alive. The staff were magnificent and I believe Alistair personally saved my maid, Maria, who is here now with me. I hope my brother will take the time to find another chateau in your beautiful country, as I simply loved it.' Ellie gazed at him ingenuously. Luckily, Alistair detached himself from a group and, spotting her, wandered over to join them.

'I hope my sister isn't taking up too much of your time Ambassador,' he said. 'Let me refresh your glass and we can help your wife win a little more; she's quite the artful player.' He put his hand on the Ambassador's shoulder and gently steered him away. As he glanced back, Ellie mouthed, 'Thanks,' to Alistair and quickly made her way to the tables, so she couldn't be cornered again. She'd have to watch being on her own with guests in the future, as she realized she couldn't lie with aplomb and if someone really put the pressure on, she didn't know what she might let slip.

In frozen London, Karl sat at his desk and absently played with a pencil. He tapped it on the desktop with a monotonous regularity, and thought about his position at Morgan Enterprises. He had worked solely for Max, and that bitch had murdered him. Karl had worked for Max for so long that he thought of him as his own brother; in fact, he was the only pseudo family that Karl had ever cared about. After the big shake up in the company, Karl had found himself as the head of security. It was a good job and paid well, but there was no adrenaline coursing through his veins as he watched monitors. There were no little "problems" to sort out for Max, and no one to intimidate. He'd been good at his job, enjoyed it to the hilt, and he missed it.

Maybe, he mused, he should take a holiday. God only knew how much holiday he was owed, and he could take a few months off with no recriminations. Max needed payback; revenge should be taken against the bitch who had robbed him of his job. He twisted the pencil between the fingers of his left hand, and it snapped. Yes, he made his mind up, that's what he'd do; snap the bitch's neck like a pencil.

In another part of London, the team was gathering for the last meeting, to firm up the plans to meet Ellie in Morocco. There couldn't be any infiltration of the host house, but they would be staked out at various points to extract Ellie and Alistair if it all went wrong. The villa that magnate Kahlid Dehbi was using for the party wasn't his main residence, but a palatial estate nestling at the foot of the Atlas Mountains. It lay east of Marrakesh, and was surrounded by a high stone wall.

Information from the area police had told them that Mr. Dehbi was well known to them, but they preferred not to be involved with the operation. Deniability was their watchword. If anything went wrong, they would blame it on extremists, and basically look the other way.

'Phil, all this sounds like the police over there are in this Dehbi's pocket,' said Claire, shuffling through the mountain of reports strewn across the desk. 'It would have been nice to get just a bit of co-operation but we'll have to tread very carefully now, as we don't know who's in his pay and who's not.'

'Yep, I agree,' replied Phil. 'Maybe we should send them word that we're not going to get involved at all, so they won't have anything to report to Dehbi. Let's just pretend we've called the whole thing off and leave it at that. It'll make it a bit more difficult to get into the country with all the kit, but I've got an idea.'

'Go on then, what's the brilliant no-fail plan you've got up your sleeve? Dress up as Berbers and storm the place on camels?' she said sarcastically.

'Not far from the truth, actually.' Phil grinned at her.

'You're not serious!'

'Well, Jack and I can go in over the Atlas with suitable cover from the Western Sahara and Rob, Nigel and you can go to Marrakesh as tourists. We'll carry all the kit in diplomatic bags; don't know about the camels though, maybe Land Rovers. We can be doing an archaeological survey or something like that, so we can have all sorts of electronic stuff about. What do you think?'

Nigel and Robert looked at each other, and started scribbling frantically on their pads.

'Everything will have to be sand proof, and the heat even

at this time of year could be a problem,' said Nigel thoughtfully.

'Don't forget it's a bit of a drive down south if you want to avoid Morocco altogether,' said Robert.

'Best get started then,' said Phil. 'What about you, Jack, you up for it?' and all eyes turned to Jack, who was trying to make himself look inconspicuous at the end of the table.

'I'll do it, but I've never even been near a desert, so I don't really know what to expect. As Ellie seems to have come good with the information, and it is a chance to get one of the manuscripts back, I'll do it—but I still don't trust Alistair. When he said he'd steal it back I didn't like that at all, but I can't think of any other options right now; so as a plan, I suppose we've got to go with it. It's a good job they've got the invite, or else I don't know how we'd get in—but Ellie said she didn't think that was where the manuscript was, so we'll have to rely on them finding out. That's the bit I really don't like,' said Jack leaning forward to emphasize the point.

'Point taken, Jack, but I can't think of any other options at the moment, and it's too good a chance to miss. It may be, she can't get the information at all and we'll just have to try another day, but we'll still end up with more info on this Dehbi guy than we had before. So we'll give it a go, agreed?' Everyone nodded and began poring over maps and lists to get the ball rolling.

It appeared that the best place to go from was Oran in Algeria and cut down south west; then they could probably get over the border unseen. They would have to be on the trail by the next day if they were going to be there, and set up, by the time Ellie got to the villa. No one was going to get any sleep that night.

Claire, Robert and Nigel had left England straight after the meeting and landed in Marrakesh, happily playing the part of tourists. It was a lively, bustling place and it was easy to see why many millionaires had hideaways in the country. The market square was a frenetic hive of sellers and the group all sat round a big stall, eating aromatic tagine of chicken and apricots. As darkness fell the whole place got even busier, if that was possible, and street entertainers lit up flaming torches and performed to the crowds. Storytellers had the biggest audiences, and the age-old skill and craft of keeping a mass enthralled by words alone worked its magic. The stories probably had never been written down, but handed on from father to son for generations.

The next day they had booked a short tour of the Atlas Mountains, and hoped to get some idea of the actual terrain and pick up any pitfalls they couldn't have foreseen. It was all reconnaissance and they were mentally storing away information, whilst laughing and joking between themselves.

Phil and Jack were on a flight to Oran, under the guise of workers for the Archaeological Institute, to survey the eastern side of the mountains. Jack was devouring books on archaeology and hoped to sound reasonably knowledgeable if questioned. His mind was bending round "stratigraphy" and other unfamiliar terms, until his eyes shut and the drone of the plane engines sent him to sleep. Phil took Jack's book away, settled back to rest, and tried to plan each move. It was an unpredictable situation. If Ellie did manage to locate the manuscript, on the off chance that it was still in the country, getting it out would be very risky. He still didn't trust Alistair one bit, but he was the only way they had of locating the prize, so he had to go with what was given and work accordingly. He also had to try to keep Ellie and Alistair out of it at all costs, as they were the link to the next part of the puzzle and he couldn't risk blowing their cover. This recovery job would be very delicate, to say the least.

CHAPTER TWENTY-ONE

The plane landed at Es Sénia Airport with no mishaps, and Phil and Jack stepped out into the warm, humid air. The place was a hive of activity and Phil had no problem locating a taxi. He gave the address of their hotel in the district of Sidi El Hourari, on the north side of the city. They both sat back and watched the vibrant, colourful city unfold as they travelled. They were to meet a local contact, that would set them up with the Land Rover and the gear they would need for their desert trek. To Jack, who had never been out of Europe, it was a sensory overload. He could see the colours of the market stalls piled high, with anything; from clothes and carpets, to the pyramids of spices. He could smell the amazing variety of aromas from the cooking, both in the restaurants and at the roadsides. He was also battered by the noise of the incessant honking of car horns, and the seeming chaos of the throngs of people going about their daily lives. He was quite glad when they entered Sidi El Hourari and found their hotel. It was tucked away in a backstreet of the old quarter and, best of all, it was relatively quiet.

'Okay, let's make contact with the guy who's going to be our link here. He's been very useful to us in the past, but don't be fooled by his outward appearance. He's a taxi driver now and has a small business with his son, but he was also a professor at the local university until he decided to retire. Also, he knows everyone, and can get anything for a fair price, so he's the one to ask if you want anything.' Phil got out his phone and was soon chatting.

'Hi Beni, we're finally here; so meet you in about an hour, if that's okay.' Phil listened, then soon switched to Arabic, and kept nodding. He broke the call and said to Jack, 'Well, that seems to be all right. He says he's got the Land Rover and most of the kit inside, so we can start at first light, but he'll come here and have a drink and something to eat with us first. So we better get booked in and sorted.'

Jack just followed in Phil's wake, as he didn't quite know what he should do and felt a bit superfluous at that point. He was quite hot and sticky after all the travelling, and thought a shower would be good. He was also doing a mental inventory of the clothes he'd got with him, and wondered if they would be suitable for this climate. He hadn't really known what Algeria and the desert was going to be like.

The rooms were comfortable but there wasn't really any point in getting totally settled in, as they were to leave for their desert trek in the morning. Jack leaned out of his small balcony and looked across at the teeming streets to the Hassan Pasha mosque, and mentally stored up all the pictures. It suddenly struck him how lucky he was to be here, and he was excited about going into the desert and what tomorrow might bring.

Beni was waiting for them, securely ensconced in a large wicker work chair that dwarfed him. He stood as they entered. Phil performed the introductions and had his hand shaken and his back slapped many times. Beni was obviously overjoyed to see Phil again, and Jack wondered what history the two had shared in the past.

'Pleased to make your acquaintance Mr. Jack. My name is Karim Bensoussan.' Beni offered his hand and Jack shook it, and they all sat down round a small table. 'Now we are friends you may call me Beni, and I will be your guide round the beautiful city of Oran.' Beni winked at Phil. 'I've spoken to the Archaeological Institute and they have turned a blind eye to their logo being used on a vehicle, so you have a Land Rover that looks like theirs. You may wish to donate it to them when you've finished with it, perhaps as payment for their help?'

Phil nodded. 'Good idea, Beni. Let's just hope it comes back in one piece,' he said hopefully.

Beni continued with the kit list he had managed to put together, and Jack was impressed with the speed at which the guy could work. In little over a day he'd given them the perfect cover, with everything they could have asked for, and a few things they had forgotten, for the desert trip. Hidden under everything would be some guns and ammo, in case the going got tough, but they hoped that would be a last resort. He'd even thought of a phrase book, so that Jack could learn a few words and help smooth the way with the nomadic Berbers they could meet on their travels.

After a couple of hours, Beni's son turned up after his taxi shift and they all sat down to a meal. Beni ordered course after course, and each one was a revelation to Jack. The subtle spices and fruity aftertastes lingered on his palate, until were washed away with crisp wines. He did draw the line at the tobacco water pipes at the end, but the fragrant aromas of apple mixed with tobacco dulled his senses even more. He caught Phil looking at him and smiling.

'You'd better get a few hours' kip, as we're going to be

out of here before dawn and it'll be all systems go for a very long drive.'

Jack mumbled something then left the others and decided to have a short walk to clear his head, then get some real sleep.

In Marrakesh, Claire, Nigel and Robert were on the guided tour of the High Atlas Mountains. The grey peaks were in stark contrast to the verdant countryside, which stretched to the coast. The peaks were richly veined with magnetite, which threw all their compasses out of alignment. All the phones had GPS but there was nothing like a bit of "low tech" back up, should batteries fail. The rains from the Atlantic reached the mountains and stopped there, shedding the water on the western side. It ran down and fed the fruit groves and farmland, but not a drop fell on the other side into the Western Sahara Desert. They saw mansions and gardens that were beyond belief, as it was a playground for the rich and famous, and, from on high, they saw Dehbi's villa. It wasn't small by anyone's standards, and looked to be well fortified. The view was even more daunting than the overview they'd seen on Google Earth.

Robert had the binoculars. 'Lord, how are we going to get in there?' He handed them to Nigel, who scanned the terrain.

'It's worse than I thought,' Nigel grimaced.

'But don't forget we're going to have some help from the inside with Alistair and Ellie,' Claire added. 'They should be arriving in the next day or two, and will have time to recce the place and make sure the manuscript is there before we go in.'

'I certainly hope so and I hope that Alistair is on the side of the angels this time, and doesn't revert to type,' said Robert morosely.

Maria and Ellie were going through her wardrobe, trying to decide what to pack. Ellie bowed to Maria's excellent dress sense and allowed her to pick and choose. Time had slowed down for Ellie, and she had slipped into a privileged lifestyle with barely a ripple. All her worries seemed to recede, and she hadn't tried to ring Rory again since Christmas. She'd put this problem in a small box and locked it away in her brain. She still wore his ring, but was avoiding digging up the memory of the last phone conversation. She knew it would all surface eventually, and probably would be worse as she'd put it off so long—but right now she didn't want to deal with it. England was still in the grip of a record-breaking winter, and he was probably still marooned in the North; which wouldn't help his temper at all.

Ellie hadn't spoken to Maria about the plans to regain the lost manuscript when they got to Morocco. She had learned the hard way that people sometimes aren't all they appeared to be, and she wasn't sure about her new-found friend. She also treated Alistair with caution, but he was still charm personified and was working hard to strengthen his company. He was trying to turn bad press into good press, and seemed to be winning on that score. He had announced who would be travelling with them to Morocco and besides Maria and Ellie, he would be taking Karl as his new Chief of Security, as well as Carter his manservant. Ellie had blanched when she heard the news about Karl and tried to dissuade him, but he was adamant and she couldn't think of a really good reason why it shouldn't be so.

On the morning of their departure Ellie sat with Alistair at breakfast, perusing the English newspapers.

'Looks like your shares have gone up again after that slump,' said Ellie, sipping her coffee.

'Yes—and since when did you know about shares?' asked Alistair, surprised.

'Since I've heard you on the phone and made it my business to know,' said Ellie, looking over the top of her paper. 'I'm a part of this now. That's what you've always wanted, isn't it?'

'Yes, but I didn't think you'd be interested in the companies,' said Alistair, flummoxed.

'Why not, Alistair? You're the one that kept banging on about the missing piece of your life. Also, I'm supposed to keep you on the straight and narrow in your dealings. You've got a lot hanging over your head now, and I've told you this is the Last Chance Saloon. Didn't I make myself clear enough?' Ellie raised her paper again and allowed a slight smile to curl the edges of her lips.

'Okay, I get the point, but I didn't think I would be sharing boardroom battles with my sister,' Alistair replied, while he spread some toast.

'Whatever,' was all that Ellie said, signifying the subject was closed for the time being. She had made sure she was around when Alistair was working, and had gleaned a great deal of information on what he did. She had also relayed a lot of this to Claire, and whilst not wanting to destroy her twin, she was making sure he was being one of the good guys for now.

Jack and Phil were up before first light and collected the Land Rover, complete with extra jerry cans of diesel strapped on the outside and loads of tents, shovels and matting on the top roof rack. They set off down the N6 highway to Béchar province, and it was a long, dusty road stretching some three hundred miles. They hoped to do it all in a day, then rest at Béchar, before turning west to go over the High Atlas. Outside of the city, the sun came up and gently fried both of the occupants; the glare was intense. They had decided on two hourly shifts of driving, so that their concentration wouldn't lapse too much. It was a mind-numbing drive, with only the odd flock of goats being herded by a Berber child to break the monotony. Conversation soon lapsed and after a few hours, Jack was feeling fatigued. The driving was slower than they had anticipated as sand had drifted across the road, which sometimes disappeared altogether. The sense of adventure soon left Jack and he felt tired and gritty, and would have sold his soul for a shower and a cold beer. Phil was relentless, and pushed Jack when he sensed his attention wandering and the vehicle slowing down. Time was of the essence, and they had to meet up with Claire, Robert and Nigel at the rendezvous point.

After nine hours of solid driving, with only ten minutes' rest stops and food on the go, they saw the settlement of Béchar on the horizon. It was a shifting image in the heat haze, but they were both very relieved when they realized it wasn't a mirage. They were not going to stay in the desert town but camp on the outskirts, so they wouldn't be remembered by any hotelier or barman. A small grove of trees, fed by an aquifer, provided the necessary cover and they finally parked up. Jack unwound himself from the cab, and did a full body stretch to get the kinks out.

'Let's see how you are at making a camp,' said Phil. 'Make like a Boy Scout,' he laughed.

'Yeah, I suppose we'll have to do a full kit inventory as well, while we're at it', said Jack. 'So what did Beni pack for us to eat tonight? Even those goats over there look appealing right now'.

'You got it in one, Jack, but I've got no idea what he's put in there. It'll probably be half cooked by now anyway, so let's get digging through this lot and see what we've got.'

They pitched a small tent and put two sleeping bags inside. 'We're not going to need those, surely,' said Jack, as he was still sweating.

'You sure will, as it can drop to near freezing in the desert at night. The huge land mass doesn't hold the heat like big bodies of water and the temperature will drop very quickly once the sun goes down,' Phil explained. He continued to rummage through the kit, and came up with some packets of dried food, that were basically "add water" and it reconstituted itself into army type rations. 'See, Beni thought of everything, we just have to add boiling water and you've got either chicken casserole or beef stew. Which do you fancy?' He held the packets out to Jack.

'Not what I would have chosen, but food is food at the moment and I'm starving.' Jack lit the small camping stove and began to boil a pan of water.

They ate, then sat and watched the sun disappear in a red blaze over the desert horizon, and Jack soon felt the chill creep into the air. They retired to the warmth of their sleeping bags and reviewed their plans for the next day, when they would head straight over the top of the mountain range.

Ellie and Alistair boarded the jet for the short hop to Morocco. The staff had already gone before them with all the luggage, and everything would be in place when they arrived. Kahlid would be sending a car for them, and they would be at the villa mid-afternoon. In spite of herself, Ellie was quite looking forward to the gathering of international jet-setters and wondered how many famous faces she would spot. When she had said this to Alistair he had smiled, and told her that she was now one of them herself and the expurgated story of their meeting had now gone global. She was famous in her own right. This was a sobering thought, and Ellie mentally shook herself and told herself not to get carried away, but to concentrate on the task in hand. She must find the manuscript and get it back somehow. She only had two days to do it, and the clock was running.

The jet and the car met on the tarmac and Ellie and Alistair were whisked away, in air-conditioned luxury, to an enormous villa nestling in a fold of the mountains. There were lush gardens and every imaginable sub-tropical flower growing in abundance. It was like a walled paradise on earth. Ellie could only draw breath and admire the colourful vistas at every angle. She also noted the huge gates and the ten-foot-high walls topped with razor wire. There seemed to be many guards, dressed in desert fatigues, patrolling, and lots of them had dogs. This wasn't a good sign, as Kahlid seemed to take his security very seriously. Ellie wondered if the team would be able to get in here at all.

Their host, Kahlid Dehbi, was there to greet them, and he led them into a cool, shady courtyard where there were staff waiting with chilled drinks for the guests. A few people were there already strolling about and admiring the gardens.

'Miss Black—' Kahlid said, bowing low over her hand, '—we have all heard so much about you, and I'm glad this is the first engagement you have chosen to accept.' He placed a chilled glass of champagne in her hand. 'My humble home is yours for as long as you wish to stay, and please consider what is mine is also yours,' he added effusively.

Ellie could only smile as she thought, Little do you know, but she said, 'I'm sure I'll be more than comfortable in your gorgeous villa, which has surpassed any expectations I may have had.' She thought I hope I've outdone him on the complimentary scale with that one!

Kahlid turned to Alistair. 'You did not tell me your sister was so beautiful; I am honoured she is here.'

Alistair gazed down at the slightly shorter man and made a bow. 'Yes, Eleanor seems to have inherited all the good-looking genes from the family whilst I, alas, seem to be left with the poorer quality ones. She is also a bit of an antiquarian, and I know you have some wonderful pieces in your collection that do surpass my own. Perhaps someone could take an hour out of their undoubtedly busy schedules and show her some of your finer examples of manuscripts; perhaps some of the Koran writings?'

Ellie couldn't believe Alistair had actually bowed to this guy, but he was obviously playing his part to the hilt. She was now an "antiquarian" and maybe could get a look at where the manuscripts were housed. Well done, Alistair she thought, and smiled at Kahlid, in what she hoped was a winning way.

'But of course.' Kahlid waved his arms expansively. 'I'll get my head curator to do it. He'll enjoy showing you; just tell us when you want to go, and his time will be yours. But sadly, I must mingle with my other guests, as my duty of host must not be forgotten in the face of such beauty'. Kahlid bowed to them both again, and wandered to the next group.

Ellie faced Alistair. 'You laid it on a bit thick, didn't you?'

'I think he likes you,' was all Alistair said, with a smirk.

'Maybe so, but he had sweaty palms and I kept thinking he was sizing me up for his harem!'

'Could be,' said Alistair. 'Anyway, you've got what you wanted, access to his collection, so you've just got to pick your time now. Don't imagine I'm going to be anywhere close by when you do this, as I'm going to distance myself very firmly away from the action. I can't let myself be seen as any part of this, or I'll get ripped to shreds.'

'Well, thanks for that, Alistair; I knew I could rely on you,' said Ellie scathingly. 'You'll steal off innocent people, but when it comes down to your so-called smarmy friends, who are probably thieves in their own right, you won't lift a finger.'

'No, you haven't thought it through, have you? If you want to get all the manuscripts back, then we're going to have to go to a lot more house parties like this one. If word gets out I'm "stealing" from friends, then we won't get any invites from now till Doomsday. So tread very carefully, Ellie, as you can't raise any suspicions.'

Ellie was dumb after this statement. It was all true. She couldn't mess this up, as then the collection would be lost forever—and she needed Alistair to get her into the rich and famous circles she would be denied on without him.

Ellie and Alistair were shown to their respective suites, and Maria was on hand to get Ellie anything she wanted. Ellie was wrestling with the enormity of the task she had set herself, and Maria noted her pensive mood.

'What is the matter, Miss Ellie? You don't look like you're enjoying Morocco at all. It is a beautiful place and the sun is shining, the birds are singing and you look, how you say, glum.'

Ellie threw caution to the winds. 'Yes, I've got a problem and I don't know what to do.'

'Let me help you, as you helped me. Mr. Alistair saved my life and gave me good job in the end, so I'll help you.'

Ellie suddenly was wary. She signalled Maria to come into the bathroom with her and turned the bath taps on full force. She mouthed to Maria, 'They may be listening' and then said, 'No, you don't understand, Maria. I can't drag you into this; you've been through enough and I'll be truthful, I don't know if I can trust you,' Ellie said, looking Maria in the eye.

Maria took a step back. 'Miss Ellie,' she said indignantly, 'I am your friend and I will help you, as I know you are a good person. You came along and Mr. Alistair, he's changed. He's let my family go and said the debt is forgotten, he's given me good pay for doing very little so I can help my family out, and he saved my life. So I will help you in any way I can to keep you safe, as without you none of this would have happened. So what is the problem?'

'Okay Maria, you win! I'll tell you, but you can't breathe a word of this to the other maids. Also, you can't tell Karl or Carter, as I don't know what they'll do. I'm glad I haven't seen Karl yet, but he scares me, and I'm sure he doesn't like me as he was Max's man.'

'Yes, Karl scares me as well and I promise I won't breathe a word to anyone, cross my heart.' Maria solemnly made a cross on her heart and Ellie believed her.

She sat down on the edge of the bath and outlined what she was intending to do. It sounded worse when she said it out loud, and she hadn't really got a plan at the moment, but at least she had been granted access to where the rare books were stored.

Maria stood and chewed her lip, then said, 'How about if I go with you, with a camera and iPad, as if to take notes and photograph the books, for you to study at a later time? Then we could steal it!' She smiled widely at this, as if it solved everything.

Not wanting to curb her enthusiasm, Ellie smiled at her. 'That's the best plan at the moment, as I haven't got another one. So we'll go with that.' Inside Ellie was quaking, as the plan was very flimsy to say the least and she didn't know how they were going to get it out of the villa, even if they could just take the book.

'I do have some help on the outside, but I'm not going to tell you anything about that, as the less you know the better, and, if it all goes wrong, you can't tell anyone else.' Maria nodded, but Ellie knew how dangerous this was really going to be and whilst being grateful of the help, she didn't want Maria involved, and she was really, really, scared for her. 'I've got a special phone to talk to them, but I think it may be monitored, you know people listening in—so I need to get a message to them. Do you think you can do that? First of all, we have to choose a time to see the books, then let my friends know so they can be here to help. Are you okay with that?' Maria nodded and her look was serious.

'It may be better if there is a crowd of us going to see the books. If there's just me and you then, we'll be spotted on the cameras, so let's go and mingle with other guests. I can chat to them and let them know about the viewing in the conversation, and you can hover on the edge and come with me when we go in.'

Maria nodded. 'It's a good idea, when do we do it?'

'No times like the present; so, a quick slap of make-up and I'm ready to "rock and roll".

'Whatever you say, Miss Ellie. I'll find some afternoon wear for you and we'll go down.'

Ellie found herself the centre of attention when she went back down, and many more guests had arrived. She was more confident in her role and wandered about from group to group, chatting urbanely. She managed to work the viewing of the books into her conversation, and quite a few of the guests suggested they accompany her. She accepted every invitation, but wasn't really sure if they wanted to be with her or if they were really interested in the manuscripts. It didn't really matter, as she had the crowd she needed. Timing was the next issue. It was better to do it under the cover of darkness and decided that after dinner would be the best time, when everyone would be strolling about the grounds.

Calling Maria to her, she quickly explained what she was going to do and at what time. They retired back to the suite and Ellie gave Maria the sat phone. She told Maria to say to the other staff she had to get something for Ellie from the nearest town, so she wasn't missed. She was then to ring Claire and tell her the plan. Ellie drilled Maria with the number as she couldn't risk writing it down. Maria eventually got it perfectly and understood what she had to do. She also had to buy the goods, as to return with nothing would raise suspicion.

Maria would leave at once after she had put Ellie's evening clothes out for her, as if it all went wrong Ellie still had to play her part. Maria showed her that underneath her white apron, there was a large open pocket sewn into the front of her dress. That was there so that Maria could carry anything Ellie might require for the evening, unobtrusively.

'That's brilliant, Maria, I didn't know about that.' Ellie suddenly had a plan how to get the book out of the vault. 'The sat phone will fit in there, so you can get it out of the villa as well.' Maria nodded and smiled.

Ellie picked up the internal phone in the room and ordered a staff car for Maria as she needed some things from the nearest town, and was assured it would be there in ten minutes by the main gate. Maria nodded and carefully put the sat phone in her hidden pocket and went to the door, turned and gave a thumbs up sign to Ellie, who gave her a watery smile. Ellie couldn't believe what she'd done by involving Maria in all this, and she was sure that the maid couldn't possibly understand the danger she was in. She vowed she would never do it again, and she even began to think that books weren't worth it. But right now, she was committed to the plan and couldn't let everyone down by bottling it at the last fence.

Maria got in the car, went to the nearest town and asked the driver to wait for her for fifteen minutes whilst she made her purchases. She nipped into an alley and quickly dialled the number she had committed to memory.

'Hello, is that Claire?' she whispered, when the phone was answered.

'Yes, who are you?'

'I'm Maria, Miss Ellie's maid, and I have a message for you. I can't stay long as I've got out of the villa and have to be back soon. Tonight, after dinner, over the wall on the western side.'

Claire repeated the instructions and the phone went dead in Maria's hands. She realized then that her palms were sweating, and they were committed to a very dangerous plan; also, a very silly one, as they could get killed for this. Maria was under no illusions whatsoever how dangerous the friends of Mr. Alistair could be, and she just hoped that Miss Ellie knew as well.

Phil and Jack struck camp just before first light and got all their gear together in the chilly dawn. Today it was cross country, and they fired up the Land Rover and headed for the mountains. The sun rose over the peaks, and everything was bathed in golden light. The view was breath-taking; even Jack and Phil were silent in the face of the majestic sight. They made good time as the sand was firm, and besides skirting round a few dunes they kept on track. By mid-morning they began to climb, and Phil suggested a rest stop for some food and a chance to catch up with Claire on the phone. While Jack was ferreting in the back of the Land Rover, a stray goat came over to examine his leg, causing him to jump. A few more picked their way daintily over the scree, and Jack wondered where they had come from. Phil was leaning on the front of the Rover and hadn't seen them.

Suddenly a small boy appeared from nowhere, herding the small flock that gravitated towards them. He was a small urchin with a big smile, and he said, 'as-salaam alaikum' and Jack replied, quite pleased to show off a little Arabic.

In the blink of an eye, from a small side valley, a dust storm came. It was made by six horsemen, swathed in blue robes and brandishing nasty looking rifles. They quickly surrounded the Land Rover and gestured Phil and Jack to stand together with their hands up.

Phil tried to explain in Arabic who they were and what they were doing here, and Jack threw in the odd word, nodding ferociously at the same time. The horsemen just laughed.

Jack whispered to Phil, 'I didn't think there were bandits here.'

'There are bandits everywhere Jack, some drive Porches, some ride horses. I think we've just met some. Just play along, as we haven't got a choice; don't push it with them. They may just want the gear and the car, and that'll be that.'

'You really think so?' said Jack, partially relieved.

'Not really, but it's the best I can do.'

The leader dismounted his horse and walked—more like swaggered—towards Jack and Phil. He was a tall man, and very imposing in his robes.

'I speak American,' he said striking his fist on his chest. 'You have no business here, and this is our land.'

'We're on a survey,' said Phil, 'and we want to look for the land of your people a very long time ago. We are interested in the rocks and the soil, and we only want to help your people in the future.'

'Ha,' he replied, 'yes, you are interested only to see if oil and coal are here and you will make big towns and destroy the desert. I know you for what you are.'

'No, we're not geologists. We are archaeologists, and we have come here to look for the carvings in the rocks and the paintings on the walls of caves, to see what your people did when this was a grass plain full of animals,' said Phil, fishing desperately.

'We will see,' he said, and signalled to his men to begin emptying the Land Rover.

'Shit, the guns,' said Jack half turning his head.

The men had swiftly emptied the Land Rover and had found the guns, which they brandished on high.

Phil held his hand up, forestalling the chief's words.

'These guns were for our protection against bandits. Those bad men that may want to cause us harm, not the friends of the desert that would aid travellers, such as you.' He bowed low to the chief, and hoped he had invoked the tradition of the Berbers to help others on their journeys through the desert.

The chief laughed loud and long and all his men joined in. 'You are a clever man, you survey man, so we will let you go about your business, but—' he paused, '—with only your lives, as is the will of Allah, nothing more.'

The men quickly loaded the Land Rover back up, jumped in and gunned the engine. The chief mounted his horse and with a salvo of rifle fire they disappeared as quickly as they had come. The Land Rover went with them, disappearing in a cloud of dust.

CHAPTER TWENTY-TWO

Phil and Jack watched the dust settle and looked at each other. No transport, no phone, no food, nothing!

Jack broke the silence. 'So what do we do now? It's getting hotter, and we're basically stuffed.'

Phil wiped away beads of sweat that trickled into his eye. 'Well, we're still alive, so that's a plus. We've only got to get over those mountains and we're home and dry.' He looked at the peaks and raised an eyebrow at Jack. 'If the Land Rover was going to get over them, then I'm sure we can walk.'

'But all our supplies were in the car. We've got nothing.'

'So you'll lose a few pounds in weight. Best foot forward; we'll never know till we try.' Phil started to walk purposefully off up the slope.

'But how will we know which way to go?' said Jack, bemused.

'You've got a watch on, so you know the time; then we just work out the sun's angle and we've got direction, simple. Come on.' Phil strode on and Jack was left trailing in his wake, thinking of food and water in this seemingly barren terrain.

A few hours later, Jack was sweating profusely and his legs felt like jelly. Even Phil seemed to be flagging, and they collapsed under an overhang of rock. It was very steep going and the air was dry; all moisture seemed to have been sucked out and every breath was getting painful. The shade was blissful.

'We can't do this all day, as we're not going to be in any shape for anything when we get over the top,' said Jack.

'We've still got to be there by tonight, as Ellie's going to get hold of the manuscript then. It may be the other part of the team's already been "pinged" and they're on the radar so we're the ace up the sleeve. Someone they don't know about and are not expecting. It could be that everything's okay, but we have to be there to make sure,' explained Phil. He turned his head. 'So any good ideas?'

'We need a miracle that's for sure, as I don't think I can do another ten or so hours of this,' said Jack ruefully.

A shadow fell across the overhang and they both looked up, and saw the young boy who had been herding the goats. He had obviously been a decoy to attract their attention before the raiders struck.

Phil said, 'What do you want kid, come to look and have a good laugh?'

The boy stood mute, then shook his head. He waved his hand, motioning them to follow.

'What have we got to lose?' said Phil, looking at Jack, who shrugged his shoulders. They both got up and followed the boy, who led them into the next ravine. There, to their amazement, was the small herd of goats and some hobbled camels picking at scrub. The boy ran forward and grabbed the nearest camel, took off the hobbles, and shouted something, then the camel sank to its knees.

'You come, you come.' the boy gestured to them. 'We go, we go now,' he mimed, getting on the camel.

'Well, Providence certainly smiled today,' said Phil, amazed. 'I think he wants to help us, but I can't think why. Don't look a gift horse, or gift camel in the mouth, I say,' and he went forward. Jack followed and looked at the camel, which looked straight back at him with an inscrutable stare.

The boy produced some blue robes from the camel's pack and gestured them to put them on, and they were soon swathed from head to foot in the homespun concealment. Strangely enough, they felt cooler in the traditional Berber wear and their identities were totally concealed.

'We're going to have to pay him somehow, and I haven't got anything,' said Phil.

'The only thing I've got is my watch,' said Jack, quickly unbuckling it and offering it to the child. The boy reached out and took it and put it on his own arm where it hung, overlarge, on the bony wrist. He seemed well pleased and kept admiring it, and making the face glint in the sun. He made the other camels lie down and leapt on one, and gestured to them to get on quickly. Jack and Phil managed a very undignified scramble then hung on for dear life as the camels rose, back legs first, nearly pitching them over their heads. They headed up the mountain, swaying in time to the camel's dignified stride.

'We might still make it at this rate. I still can't believe it,' said Jack, to no–one in particular. 'The kid seems to be going the right way and we'll be over the mountains by nightfall— and this is a lot easier than walking.'

Phil overheard Jack and said, 'Yep, these camels can go where the Land Rover couldn't, so we'll be going a more direct route. That is, of course, if the kid is really trying to help us and not take us to his uncle, the Robber Baron of the Sahara?'

'No idea on that one, but we'll be over the mountains and that's a big plus. Can you find out his name and we can reward him properly later, as he's probably taking a big risk doing this for us?'

'Will do; good idea,' said Phil, and urged his camel forward, and began chatting to the boy in broken Arabic.

The day passed with the gentle sway of the camels, and the boy sometimes stopped and showed Jack and Phil where water was to be found. He would move a big stone and behind it would be a small dribble of water that had come up through the rocks. It was as pure and sweet as they had ever tasted, and the boy laughed at them as they cupped their hands and drank greedily. He would carefully replace the stone which guarded the life stream, and Jack and Phil were thankful to have the boy's desert survival skills at hand.

'He's worth more than a cheap watch,' said Jack as he drank again. 'Without him, we'd be severely dehydrated by now'.

'I agree,' said Phil. 'I know his name and his tribe, but it's still a bit tricky if we give him things later, as then his family will know he helped us. I'll think of something to reward him, as he's been better than a block of gold to us now. I must admit I don't know what we'd have done without his local knowledge—and the camels, of course.' He eyed his beast with a baleful eye, the camel stared back, unperturbed.

Darkness began to fall as they began their descent of the mountain. The camels still strode purposefully along, seemingly tireless. Jack felt much more at home now and sat tall on the saddle pad, and had one leg crooked under the other like a pro. The boy called a halt and pointed down the valley, to the myriad twinkling lights of civilization. He said something in Arabic to Phil, then peeled off and started back alone the way they had come. The camels made gurking noises as their companion left, but Phil and Jack urged them forwards towards the lights.

Dinner at the house party was an ordeal for Ellie. Every mouthful was sitting like lead in her stomach as she tried to make light, bright conversation to the other guests. She only sipped the fine wine, as she didn't want her senses dulled, but wanted to sink the whole glass in one to give herself some Dutch courage for the task ahead. Maria had given the message to Claire, and Ellie was thankful for that at least, but she knew it was all down to herself alone. There was no way that Claire or the others could get into the villa unseen, nor not be able to move about the grounds, so she had to get the book out to them.

Robert and Nigel had set up a listening post near the western wall, so they could monitor any conversation nearby. Claire was sitting, chewing her nails with frustration as she hadn't heard from Phil and Jack, but couldn't risk breaking the radio silence by calling them. If any person extraction was needed, they could do this over the mountains, as any search would, on balance, take place in the towns and villages. If Dehbi had the police force in his pocket, they probably wouldn't expect someone to try a get-away into the desert without specialist equipment, so that would be their element of surprise. It was like a game of poker, bluff and double bluff—but the stakes were extremely high for everyone.

Ellie had let her host know that there were now quite a few other guests that wished to admire his wonderful collection. She hoped flattery would do the trick and he seemed to fall for it. In fact, he seemed to be pleased to show off his collection and it was all arranged for after dinner. Eventually, when everyone was well wined and dined, Kahlid Dehbi stood.

'My good friends, and Eleanor in particular,' he said, bowing in her direction, 'I believe you wish to view the manuscripts. If you would all follow me.' He moved round the table and offered his arm to Ellie. She laid her hand on the crook of his elbow and allowed herself to be led towards the collection. Many of the other guests followed, and Ellie signalled Maria to follow them.

Ellie's stomach was churning and her knees had turned to jelly as she walked the few hundred yards to the vault. She had seen it before and it had a massive steel door that was usually shut tight, but now stood open, and subdued light spilled forth. Inside literally took her breath away, as there were cabinets and long tables displaying books, manuscripts and folios of unimaginable antiquity. The pages were from every country and era. She recognized Egyptian hieroglyphs, Roman tablets and many ancient Middle Eastern languages, long since forgotten. The curator of the books was hovering, and his face brightened when he saw the large party. It was probably an unusual occurrence for him to be able to show off his knowledge to so great a crowd.

Kahlid released Ellie's elbow and said to the assembly, 'I hope you enjoy the collection, and please ask any question you want of the curator, as I'm sure he will be most pleased to help.' He shot a meaningful glance at the man, who was now trying to make himself unobtrusive by pushing a few pages into line on the table. 'I'm going to leave you now and will be in the central courtyard, where the dancing will begin in half an hour.' He said this as if he expected them there without fail.

The guests had dispersed into knots of twos and threes, and were being issued with the white acid-free gloves they would need if they were to handle the manuscripts. Ellie blanched at this as she envisaged the damage that could be caused to the priceless collection, but she took her own pair and gestured to Maria to start to take some photographs. She wandered up and down the tables where she located the English scripts, and saw a book that was an illuminated jewel and she reverently turned the pages.

The curator was bobbing about between the guests, and he was obviously a very knowledgeable guy as he answered all the questions with alacrity. Ellie wondered how she was going to steal the book, when she noticed that some of the guests had picked up manuscripts from the table and weren't putting them back in the same places. They were showing their friends, and the curator looked as if he was going to have a heart attack at any moment at this desecration of his life's work. Ellie signalled Maria and subtly let her know that this was the book they wanted. She turned to the nearest group of people, and joined in their conversation about how a monk in a cell by candlelight could possibly create something as beautiful as this. She lurched suddenly as if catching a heel in the carpet and swept some of the manuscripts onto the floor.

On her knees she exclaimed, 'Oh my God, I'm so sorry,' as pages fluttered to the floor. She prayed Maria had put the diversion to good use and had pocketed the book in the hubbub. The curator fled over and began retrieving the papers and placing them reverently on the table. The other guests helped and the whole collection was effectively mixed up. With many apologies and thanks for his inestimable time, Ellie beat a hasty retreat. Maria followed and Ellie grabbed her arm, looking pointedly at her pocket.

'Yes, Miss Ellie, I have your cigarettes here if you want one now.'

Ellie wiggled her eyebrows at Maria, as if to ask her what she was on about.

'You may wish to enjoy one in the garden now before the dancing starts.'

Ellie quickly cottoned on and said, 'Thank you, perhaps that is good idea. A short stroll would be nice and we can see the gardens lit up. It looks like a fairyland from here.' They slid off from the other guests and headed for the west wall. The gardens were magnificent and were up-lit from every angle, giving an ethereal glow to the strange, exotic plants. They strolled and chatted, giving the impression that they were admiring the foliage, but hoping that someone was on the other side of the wall. How they were going to get the book over the wall was another matter.

Nigel and Robert were crouched in some scrub land not far from the garden and were listening in. Robert suddenly became alert.

'Think I've got them,' he whispered. The whole team's adrenaline shot up a notch, and Claire and Phil waited for Robert's next comment. At that point two Berbers and camels wandered into view and made their way over to the scrub land. Robert hissed, 'All we bloody needed right now, some nomad and a camel blocking the view.'

Claire laid her hand on his arm. 'I'll pretend to be lost or something, and see if I can get them to go away. Keep listening,' she admonished, and wormed her way out of the bushes and staggered drunkenly towards the Berbers, talking in Arabic.

Phil and Jack couldn't believe their eyes when they saw Claire weaving drunkenly towards them.

'Perhaps this is my lucky day,' said Phil, and signalled Jack to be quiet. The camels drew to a halt and Jack and Phil gazed down at Claire, who was pantomiming being drunk and lost like mad.

'Got a problem, lady?' drawled Phil, in a poor impression of a New York cab driver. Claire stopped dead in her tracks. 'Well, you did say we were going to storm the villa dressed as Berbers and riding camels. Anything the lady says goes with me.' Phil smirked under his disguise. Jack stifled an outright laugh, as he could see Claire's face turn to thunder.

'You bastards,' she hissed. 'Why didn't you let me know? I've been worried sick and it's all going down in the next few minutes.'

'Couldn't do that as we got robbed of everything, but we ended up with a camel each. I suppose fair exchange is no robbery, but run back and tell the others we're here and we'll argue later.'

'Ellie's got the book and she's by the wall, but we don't know how she's going to do this, so we're in position, awaiting developments.' Claire started to walk away, as if her conversation with the Berbers was a waste of time.

Ellie and Maria were strolling about, and Ellie sat down on a bench by the wall in a secluded arbour. 'So how are we going to get the book out of the grounds?' She looked at Maria in askance.

'We could throw it over the wall,' said Maria, with a

shrug.

'Throw it—are you mad? I can't throw it that high. Besides, think of the damage that could cause,' said Ellie.

'I can, but I don't think we have many options right now,' said Maria. 'It's easier than trying to get it out in the luggage. These people aren't stupid and they will put two and two together very quickly, and suspect you because of your interest in the books. I have it here, let's get rid of it quickly.'

'How can you throw it that high? It's a book, it won't fly.'

'Yes, it will,' said Maria. 'Take off one of your hold-up stockings.'

Ellie looked at Maria as if she'd gone mad. 'What!' she exclaimed.

In the scrub, Robert was willing Ellie to do what Maria had asked, as he could see what she meant to do. The two 'Berbers' were now in position, sitting aloft on their camels giving cover to Claire and the others. They were gazing at the stars and mumbling softly to themselves, trying to desperately blend in with their surroundings.

In the garden, a small group of guests had wandered into the secluded space where Ellie and Maria sat. Ellie had to get rid of them fast.

'Maria, give me a fag, quick,' said Ellie, under her breath.

Maria produced the cigarettes and lighter and handed them to Ellie.

'Sorry guys, just one of my little vices I was hoping to keep a secret,' said Ellie, brandishing the pack. She took one out and placed it between her lips, and Maria lit it. The smoke ripped its way down into Ellie's lungs and her eyes watered, but she waved the cigarette about and smiled, frantically praying she didn't have a bout of coughing to spoil the show.

As the guests wandered off, Ellie exhaled, buried her face in her dress and coughed explosively. She dropped the cigarette to the floor and ground it out, heaving a big sigh.

'We've got to work quickly. Do you think you can chuck the book over the wall?'

''Yes,' said Maria emphatically. 'We just need to keep the pages together and give it some weight. I can do it easily, as I was trained in shot put as a teenager. I was going to make national team, until my family had the problem with Mr. Alistair; then, I had to work.'

Ellie peeled off one stocking and they found a stone, and wrapped it all up together to make a parcel with a tail at one end. Maria hefted it in her hand and pronounced it good. Ellie stood and surveyed the landscape; there was no-one in sight or sound, and she nodded to Maria. Maria took a step back and swung the book and the stone a few times experimentally; then she gained momentum and the parcel arced its way gracefully over the wall.

Ellie sank down onto the bench again, 'I need another fag now, or a stiff drink. Come on, let's get back to the party. You make yourself scarce and I'll go and schmooze the other guests. See you later.' They both left, going their separate ways.

On the other side of the wall Robert said one word, 'Now,' and a small object that could have been mistaken for a night bird sailed over the wall. Phil caught it in the corner of his eye and urged his camel forward, managing to deftly catch it and quickly stow it under his robes. Robert and Nigel could only stare, wide eyed at this. Claire covered her face in her hands and muttered, 'I don't believe it,' again and again.

Claire recovered and said, 'Okay everybody out, now,'

and made a slashing movement across her throat to the two 'Berbers'. The post was quickly disbanded, and camels and Berbers went one way, and Claire, Robert and Nigel went the other.

Maria and Ellie strolled back to the party, and there seemed to be a bit of change in the atmosphere. Guests stood around, clutching drinks and talking in hushed tones. Maria signalled that she was going back to the room and melted away. Ellie went to the nearest group and asked what was amiss.

'It seems there's been a theft,' said a tall guy, who looked like a politician.

'What!' exclaimed Ellie. 'Are you sure? What's gone missing? Not someone's jewels, I hope.' She put her hand to her neck as if to check the empress's necklace was still there.

'Doesn't seem like it, but Kahlid's asked that we all stay here, as they're going to do a thorough search.'

Ellie had a glass of champagne from a footman, realised her hand was still shaking, and nearly downed it in one gulp. Alistair joined their little group a moment later, and Ellie asked him what had gone on.

'Seems like someone has stolen a piece of Kahlid's collection,' Alistair said meaningfully.

'What? The beautiful books and things I saw earlier? You can't be serious, Alistair.' Ellie looked at her twin wide-eyed. 'Who would do such a thing? Surely no-one here needs to steal, and everybody could build their own collection by fair means if they wanted to.' She waved her glass expansively round the room.

The politician said, 'Yes, I suppose they could if they wanted to. Maybe it's just a prank. I'm sure it'll all be over soon.'

'Let's hope so. I'm ready for a bit of dancing now, are you?' Ellie looked at the tall politician as her means of escape. He seemed flattered, and offered her his arm as they strolled away.

The hue and cry finally died away, and the dancing began. Ellie made sure she was seen virtually every minute, and danced with nearly any available male at the party. The adrenaline had gone; relief took its place, and she enjoyed herself tremendously. She danced with the host on two occasions and enquired solicitously about the drama that was on everyone's lips.

Ellie felt his hand slide down her back and hitched it up, with comments such as, 'Oh, Kahlid, you shouldn't,' and 'Kahlid, I've barely met you,' hoping to forestall any further advances. She also refrained from mentioning the collection again, except to thank him for the opportunity of a viewing, and to say that Alistair had a veritable library and it would take her a very long time to go through it. She hoped that would plant the idea that she wasn't anything to do with the theft.

Phil and Jack had turned their camels round and headed back into the mountains. They stopped in a rocky ravine and managed to get the beasts to lie down and managed to dismount. They then urged them back to their feet and pointed them in the right direction, giving them a slap on the rump that sent them back the way they had come. They hoped that the camels would have some sort of homing instinct and head that way. The beasts swayed off into the darkness. Phil and Jack had decided to keep their disguises on and set off back down the track to civilization.

'Do you think they'll get back to the lad?' said Jack trudging down the stony track.

'I hope so, as he didn't deserve to lose his camels,' answered Phil. 'Now it's "get out time"—and we may or may not be able to go with the others, as we haven't got passports, remember?'

'Bugger, I'd forgotten about that,' said Jack. 'So what do you plan to do?'

'We could give Beni a ring and see if his contacts spread this far, or try and make contact with Claire and see if she's got any good ideas. Other than that, it's hoof it to the nearest embassy and see if they'll help. We could spin a tale about being ambushed and having all our kit stolen. We've still got the Archaeological Institute cover, and if we keep near enough to the truth we won't get caught out,' said Phil.

'I like the idea of the embassy,' said Jack. He knew he would feel a whole lot safer on English soil.

'Okay, the embassy it is; so we'd better start walking. We'll get rid of the costumes when we get into the nearest habitation as you don't speak another language, and you'll get caught out quickly. You can only play my mute brother for so long,' Phil laughed. He had the book tucked firmly into his waistband and his shirt covered the priceless prize.

It would be a long night's walking before they reached home soil.

Ellie had gone back to her room when her feet could take no more, and Maria was there waiting for her. Ellie shook her head to forestall any conversation about their exploits and kept to the mundane. Ellie thanked Maria for all her efforts with her hair and make-up, and said she was now going to retire. Ellie and Alistair planned to leave tomorrow and Ellie asked Maria if she could just have a few breakfast things on a tray, as she wouldn't be going down in the morning. Maria bobbed a curtsey just to annoy Ellie, and swept out with a smile. Sassy maid, thought Ellie and sank into her pillows with an identical smile and let relief and satisfaction sweep over her.

Claire, Robert and Nigel were in a bar celebrating. This was down time, and they enjoyed relaxing, as a group of friends should. They played pool and Nigel won, amid many ribald comments, and Robert started showing off the bar tricks, and proved he could be something of an amateur magician with his sleight of hand. Their flight was tomorrow and they would be well away. Claire could hardly wait to get Phil and Jack cornered and hear the whole unexpurgated story, including the use of camels. She hadn't had contact from them but she knew they were all right, making their own way out somehow, and they would meet up in London soon. She still couldn't believe the catch Phil had made when the book came winging its way over the wall. She also still couldn't believe it was Phil and Jack dressed up as Berbers that had appeared right on cue. Someone was smiling on them.

The next day Claire, Nigel and Robert, clutching souvenirs, boarded their flight to Heathrow.

After a very long walk, Jack and Phil reached a British embassy and got passports and a flight home.

Alistair and Ellie were chauffeured to the jet, and made their way back to their Italian Castle.

After the dust had settled, all the pieces were back in place on the board as before, and each person had fallen back into their allotted role. Ellie received a call from Claire.

'We're all planning a visit to Italy soon, and we need to

meet up with you and Alistair to have a chat about where we go from here. Also, I've got something important to tell you, but I'll leave it till we're all together.'

Ellie's heart sank, as she had been basking in a euphoric glow after pulling off the theft, but suddenly reality struck home and she realized she'd have to do it again!

'Yes, sure, I mean okay. When and where? Wait a minute—you could all come here, as we've got lots of space and it'll be easier all round. What do you think?'

'Great, if you'll have us. We'll arrive the day after tomorrow and we'll only be there a day or so, as we'll have lots to plan and get sorted back at base.'

'I'll make the arrangements then; just let me know when you are due to arrive in Naples and I'll send a car for you.' Ellie hung up and went to tell Alistair, who took a very dim view of the whole proceedings but couldn't really argue.

The cars were duly sent to the airport on time and Phil, Claire, Robert, Nigel and Jack were deposited by the main door of the castle.

'Wow, just look at this place,' said Nigel, staring appreciatively at the soaring architecture. 'It's certainly better than my flat.'

'And mine,' re-joined Robert.

Ellie greeted them at the door and gave Claire a quick hug as she led them into the expansive hall. She took them into the smaller ante-room, where she had arranged for a log fire to be lit to give the room a welcoming feel. They all sat down and tea appeared. Ellie could hardly wait to hear the full story of the mission. Phil and Jack started with their adventures in Algeria and the ambush. Ellie sat, mesmerized, as they were both good raconteurs and the bit about the camels had them all laughing unrestrainedly. Ellie wiped her eyes, and listened as Claire took up the story of how Jack and Phil had appeared as if they were desert apparitions, at exactly the right time.

Ellie broke in at that point. 'The book—did you get it, is it all right? There wasn't any damage?' The questions came thick and fast.

Everyone looked at each other, and Robert and Nigel then stared at the tea cups they were cradling. Phil stared at the fire, as if hypnotized by the leaping flames. Jack stared out of the window at a large bird that was circling lazily, caught on an updraft.

Claire broke the silence, 'Well, you see, Ellie, it's like this.' She paused.

'It was the wrong book!'

The End.

www.ingramcontent.com/pod-product-compliance
Lightning Source LLC
Chambersburg PA
CBHW032218050726
47591CB00001B/179